UNSUSPECTING TROUBLE

UNSUSPECTING TROUBLE

THE INSCRUTABLE PARIS BEAUFONT™ BOOK 3

SARAH NOFFKE

MICHAEL ANDERLE

DISRUPTIVE IMAGINATION®

Copyright © 2021 LMBPN Publishing
Cover copyright © LMBPN Publishing
A Michael Anderle Production

LMBPN Publishing
PMB 196, 2540 South Maryland Pkwy
Las Vegas, NV 89109

First Edition, May 2021
Version 1.01, May 2021
eBook ISBN: 978-1-64971-755-9
Print ISBN: 978-1-64971-756-6

THE UNSUSPECTING TROUBLE TEAM

Thanks to the JIT Readers

Dave Hicks
Dorothy Lloyd
Diane L. Smith
Zacc Pelter
Angel LaVey
Micky Cocker
Veronica Stephan-Miller
Debi Sateren
Deb Mader
Jackey Hankard-Brodie
Jeff Goode

If I've missed anyone, please let me know!

Editor
The Skyhunter Editing Team

To Paul, for all the inspiration and keeping the Great Library organized.

— Sarah

*To Family, Friends and
Those Who Love
to Read.
May We All Enjoy Grace
to Live the Life We Are
Called.*

— Michael

CHAPTER ONE

The key to success was knowing how good people behaved under the worst circumstances in life and taking them down when they were most vulnerable. That's how the Deathly Shadow had forged his empire, taking over huge domains, stripping their resources, and killing all who got in his way. Bad men went after other bad men. The worst men went after easy targets.

Evil men responded with greed and anger and were formidable opponents to take down. The Deathly Shadow had watched as many of them destroyed each other—wasting resources, losing fortunes, being maimed as they clawed their way to the top of the proverbial mountain. Simply by watching, the Deathly Shadow had breezed past the wasted men who demolished each other as he took over the easier fortunes to win.

Good men were the ones to take down. They stood by their principles instead of guarding and defending their wealth, health, and life force. Invariably, they fell fairly easily. The reason most didn't go after the honorable of the world was because of guilt. It could burn a man's soul straight out of him if one weren't careful. The Deathly Shadow had seen that happen firsthand. Karma was real. It put a bullseye on one's back and took them down for their misdeeds, but to him, it was worth it. Karma was merely a debt, and he happily paid it in exchange for power unlike most ever held or knew existed.

Taking down bad men was permissible. However, destroying the good people of the world was marked and punished. For the Deathly Shadow, it had been worth every sacrifice. A soul was useless. Most didn't know it chained them to the defined world. It chained them to the way things were. The Deathly Shadow was something new. He was something more powerful than anything before—all he needed to utilize it was a new body.

Soon he would have that. All the wisps of smoke and clouds that currently comprised the Deathly Shadow needed were to trap a good person once again and take what they valued. The honorable always had the most valuable things, another thing that the evil men of the world didn't know as they took down their own.

The Deathly Shadow hovered outside the modeling shoot in Vancouver, Canada, waiting for his prey to exit the building. He didn't want her. She was a means to an end—the bait. She was how he'd get what he wanted. The Deathly Shadow knew that without a doubt because when someone was in danger, the good guys came to the rescue. They cared little for self-preservation or all else when the innocent were in trouble. Instead, they risked it all to save someone else and therein was their ultimate downfall.

Paris Beaufont had escaped the Deathly Shadow's grasp several times. After all this time, he'd tracked her down. Knew who she was and how to find her.

However, the halfling had friends who were helping her and protecting her. Keeping her safe as he stalked her like the wind, trying to pull the protective charms from her and taking her life force—the one thing he needed to regain his body.

At Happily Ever After College, the half-fairy, half-magician was protected. However, she couldn't stay there forever. The Deathly Shadow had considered murdering everyone Paris cared about, but that would only make her retreat. Instead, the key was to draw her out by threatening another person because the good people of the world turned into heroes when others were in danger. The key was to make Paris Beaufont come out of hiding. The way to do that was to give her a reason she couldn't resist. What better than abducting someone very much like her, someone she sympathized with? Someone she felt responsible for. Someone she knew was taken because of her. Another halfling.

The Deathly Shadow watched as one of the triplets belonging to King Rudolf Sweetwater exited the building, looking around for the limo that was supposed to be waiting for her. It wasn't there. It wouldn't be coming. The Deathly Shadow had seen to that. The only thing coming for the half-mortal, half-fae was the cloud of smoke wafting in the beautiful woman's direction. One pass from him and Captain Morgan Sweetwater would be passed out and gone for hours. Only to wake up his prisoner.

Then he'd have to wait for a hero to come after her. When Paris Beaufont learned what had happened, all because of her hiding away, she would have no choice but to rescue the girl. To do what all good people did and sacrifice themselves for another. Hers would be the Deathly Shadow's gain. It would be the beginning of the end and would unleash his true, unyielding power. A power that even the father of time couldn't stop.

CHAPTER TWO

"What's your favorite song?" Faraday the talking squirrel asked.

Paris glanced at him, pulling her gaze away from her image in the mirror. She wasn't getting ready for that day of classes at Happily Ever After College as much as studying her features, wondering how she looked like her mother or her father. Sophia Beaufont had promised to send her a picture of them soon, but currently, her phone wasn't receiving text messages inside the bubble that was fairy godmother college.

"Who wants to know and why?" she asked skeptically.

"Me, of course," he replied, messing with her phone, having promised that he could do something to make text messaging work at the college. The squirrel had successfully built a messaging device from AI magitech parts, so she hoped he might be able to although the idea that a rodent was doing it was strange.

"The question remains, why?" Paris questioned.

"Music helps me to work more efficiently." He scrolled through options on her phone that she'd never seen before.

"Usually the fear of starving in the winter makes squirrels work better," she countered.

"Again, I don't forage or hibernate or put on a winter coat," he muttered, seemingly thinking as he tinkered.

"Rock," she answered simply.

"Rock what?"

"I like rock music," Paris explained. "The harder, the better."

"I asked for a song," he mumbled. "Can you sing me something?"

"I can scream you some death metal if you like."

Faraday shook his head. "That's not what I had in mind. Do you know something more mellow?"

"Like emo rock?"

Again he shook his head, looking irritated. "I was thinking something more like Elton John or Freddy Mercury or even some Eric Clapton?"

"Who? Who? And who?" she asked, peeling away from the mirror.

Faraday sighed. "A little education in classic rock hits might do you good. It's good for the soul."

"But what will I do with all this angst?" Paris teased. "You're the one who didn't know the *Wizard of Oz*, and now you're trying to lecture me on learning music?"

He shrugged. "I like music. It calms my mind."

"Well, get in line with Wilfred, who is trying to get me to learn ballroom dancing and manners," Paris countered. "Between the two of you, I might learn how to twirl and sing a ditty."

"We have arduous tasks ahead of us," he said, almost in a whisper.

"What was that?" Paris looked back in the mirror and arched an eyebrow.

"Nothing," Faraday chirped.

"Yeah, right," she seethed, studying her image. Until recently, she had never questioned where her blonde hair came from or her blue eyes or her high cheekbones, or her tendency to rebel. It turned out that she'd been spelled never to wonder. They were all characteristics of her parents. According to the last phone conversation with Uncle John, when Paris explained how Papa Creola had let the cat out of the bag, she'd learned that Liv looked like her. Her mother...Liv... And her father, Stefan Ludwig, was rugged and tall, dark and handsome. A demon fighter with a taste for stamping out evil. Plus, both her parents could make their enemies laugh with their snark, which was usually the moment before they slaughtered them.

These two people had given up everything for Paris. Everything to protect her and keep her safe. Now they were trapped... for fifteen years. She could only hope that they were still, well, wherever they were. It would be her job to get them back. After that, she didn't know what happened. Probably a long game of catch-up and awkward silences. Uncle John had said, when allowed to speak freely for the first time, "I have so much to tell you, but only in person. Your mother deserves that I describe her in person."

So it was... Once again, Paris had to wait to hear her story. The story of her parents. To learn where she came from and the mysteries that surrounded her. She was okay with that at this point, having gotten accustomed to it after her brief time at Happily Ever After College. Well, and her lifetime of being spelled not to care about anything.

"Do you want to know what my favorite song is?" Faraday sounded perplexed as he messed with her phone.

"I think that regardless of my answer, you'll feel compelled to tell me." She pulled her gaze away from the mirror.

"I applaud you for picking up on social cues. I didn't think it would be too hard for you, despite the rumors."

She shot him a pursed expression. "What rumors?"

"Nothing," he answered quickly. "To answer your question—"

"Which I didn't ask," Paris cut in.

"My favorite song is 'Don't Stop Believing' by Journey," he stated.

"So you have or haven't heard real rock music yet?" she teased. "Sorry, but I only know the lyrics to Old MacDonald, and on his farm, he wears a squirrel hat," she joked.

Faraday shivered with disgust. "Fine. Regardless of your lack of helpfulness, I've been able to enable text messaging on your phone."

Paris rushed over, picking up her device and scrolling through the options. "What did you do? Enable nuts? Find a hack between two branches? Discover a backdoor to some burrow?"

The talking rodent rolled his eyes. "The squirrel references aren't appreciated."

"They aren't lost on you, which is the point." Paris picked up her phone and scrolled through her contacts. It was time to put Faraday's skills to the test. Despite being a four-pawed rodent, the squirrel had come through. It appeared she could send text messages. She started right away by sending one to Sophia, Clark, and Uncle John, hoping that she could meet with them to discuss in person what she'd learned from Papa Creola about her parents. That felt like the best method, although she'd briefly told her uncle what she'd learned over the phone.

Glancing up from her phone, Paris caught Faraday staring out the window to the Enchanted Grounds of Happily Ever After College. "What will you do today?"

"The same thing I do every day, Pinky," he said in a voice very uncharacteristic to his own. Turning around, he gave her a mischievous grin. "I'll try and take over the world!"

"Say what?" She lowered her phone.

He slumped. "It's a quote to Pinky and the Brain from *Animaniacs*, a cartoon from the 1990s."

"So you don't know the *Wizard of Oz*, the most famous movie probably of all time, but you do know a song by Voyage—"

"Journey," he corrected.

"Same thing," she spat.

"Not at all," Faraday countered.

"You know a weird cartoon from the nineties?" Paris asked.

"The best cartoon from the nineties," he stated. "The Brain was a mouse scientist who wanted to—"

"You lost me at mouse scientist," she interrupted. "No need to continue. I simply can't buy that a rodent could fix an electronic device, let alone take over the world."

"You don't have data," he muttered grumpily, indicating her device.

Paris lowered her phone with a frown. "I thought you said you fixed it."

"You can text, but no data." He held up his paws in surrender. "What can I say? I'm a dumb rodent."

Paris nodded. "So are you going to pick fights with Casanova the cat today? Find a girl squirrel to get twitterpated over? Maybe find a tree to burrow within?"

"I was thinking of investigating the Bewilder Forest tonight," he suggested.

Paris planted her hands on her hips. "The Bewilder Forest is off-limits at night."

"Exactly," he countered.

"What if you get hurt again or in trouble like you did in the Serenity Garden?" Paris argued.

He mirrored her stance. "What if I find something that makes it worth it?"

Paris sighed. "Fine. If you need help, don't call my mobile."

"Like I have a phone to call you, or that anything will work in the Bewilder Forest," he said with a dramatic sigh. "Have you read the interference coming off that place? No devices can work anywhere near it."

"Surprisingly, I haven't reviewed the readings or done anything to do with that place since I've been trying to track down who I am and why I'm being hunted," she joked.

He glanced back out the window. "Sounds fascinating…" Faraday didn't at all sound interested as he glared out the window in the direction of the thick and foreboding set of trees that lined the mysterious Bewilder Forest.

Paris shook her head and made for the door. "Try to stay out of trouble, will you? I don't want to have to bail your tail out of a mess again. You nearly got me kicked out of here."

"Sure thing," he sang as she opened the door. "Also, Paris…"

"Yeah?" Paris ducked back into her room.

"If anyone needs to stay out of trouble, it's the hunted girl with two parents living in alternate dimensions, so be careful," he stated. "Call me if you need me."

She chuckled. "I would if you had a phone and I had your number, and oh, you weren't a squirrel."

"All small details, I assure you."

Paris nodded. "Somehow, I doubt that, weirdo. Have a good day."

"Have a good day, crazy-o," Faraday replied as she pulled the door shut.

Paris giggled, enjoying her banter with the squirrel more than she thought she should as she set off for breakfast.

CHAPTER THREE

"Did you hear what happened to Paris?" Christine asked loudly across the breakfast table.

Paris lowered her fork and gave her friends an exasperated look. "I'm right here…"

"Well, then, you're in the best position to fill in the details," Christine said with a dry smile.

Chef Ash, Hemingway, and Penny laughed.

"My life is funny now, is it?" Paris pretended to be offended and crossed her arms over her chest.

"As if," Christine replied. "Your life is the coolest of the cool. You're born to magician parents because you're a wish from a genie, and they're stuck in another dimension because they were trying to protect you. That's, like, the coolest thing ever."

Paris lowered her chin. "Here I thought my secrets were safe with you, Christina."

"If you would ever call me by my real name, they would be." She sighed.

"Would they?" Paris asked.

Christine shook her head. "No, probably not at all. Sorry."

Everyone at the table laughed, including Paris. That's what she needed right then, amid the craziness that was her life—her friends, even if she didn't know them well. Even if she didn't trust them. They were all she had, and they were enough.

That was one of the main reasons that Paris had confided in Christine, Penny Pullman, Chef Ash, and Hemingway about the most recent developments that were her life. She was still processing it all, trying to understand if the meeting with Father Time was real or part of her imagination. The things he'd told her...well, she only truly believed them when she spoke them aloud to her friends, explaining how her parents had gotten trapped protecting her from an entity that had sought her out for her uniqueness all so he could steal her life force.

The reactions on their faces when she disclosed her story made her feel less crazy. For all Christine's usual lightness, she'd been deadly serious after learning the truth, in awe of the story that felt so strange it must belong to someone else.

Surprisingly, Penny broke the silence first. "Opening a vortex won't be easy, but it can be done," she said at once, then chewed on her lip.

"My concern would be more about the deadly darkness thing." Christine shivered. "Like, how are you going to kill that thing?"

"There has to be a way," Penny mused, continuing to look off in thought as though she was piecing something together.

Paris watched her, curious what she had to be thinking. Chef Ash pulled them both from their reverie.

"I don't know about you all, but this whole thing gives me an idea for a new ravioli." He pulled the pencil from behind his ear and sketched something on a paper napkin.

Hemingway shook his head with a sideways grin. "No, it's definitely you, mate. Hearing that Paris is in mortal danger and has to face a deadly villain to recover her parents doesn't make me think about a new pasta recipe."

Chef Ash looked up in thought, his eyes far away. "Like, it could be rainbow-colored on the outside, but when you cut into it, the filling has a spiral effect maybe..."

Paris shook her head. "I'm glad the whole thing inspires you. If you figure out how to kill a deadly nonbeing of sorts, jot that down too."

Chef Ash nodded, continuing to write notes as if he was listening to her, but she figured he was off in thought about roasted asparagus and mixed cheeses and other things he could use to fill pasta.

"You know, you're not alone in this." Hemingway slid his hand across the table in Paris' direction, stopping it a few inches from her.

She looked at him, not knowing what to say. Paris felt alone. How could she not? Her fate, whether she was planning to bring her parents back or not, was tied to that of an evil being who was no longer human. No matter what, the Deathly Shadow would come for her.

The only way to escape him was to stay inside Happily Ever After College, and that wasn't an option. That was running. Hiding. Leaving behind any semblance of a life. She'd never see Uncle John or the family that she'd never known if she did that. She'd never complete her training with the fairy godmothers. She'd never live. So there was only one option. Face an evil that sounded strong enough to swallow the world whole. That was what Paris had to do, but how? That was yet to be determined.

With uncertainty, Paris glanced around the table at her friends.

"I think the important thing to remember is that we'll help you," Christine said, sounding uncharacteristically unlike herself.

"For sure." Chef Ash surfaced from his sketch.

"Without a doubt," Penny echoed.

Hemingway simply looked at Paris, and she knew that he was in too. He was always in if it meant helping her. She knew that on a deeper level. She had friends who were sticking by her side even when she was up against the worst. That meant the world to her because unfortunately, she was up against the very worst.

CHAPTER FOUR

Holding up a hardback of *The Princess Bride*, Headmistress Willow Starr smiled at the class. "To help us better understand the art of love, you all were asked to read this novel and watch the movie version of it."

"Who hasn't watched the movie?" Becky Montgomery remarked from the back of their Art of Love class.

"Me," Paris replied at once, holding up her hand and glancing over her shoulder at the snob perched on the edge of her seat.

"What, were you raised in a hole?" Becky pursed her lips at Paris.

"Roya Lane actually," Paris retorted. "Some of us didn't bore ourselves with Disney princess movies when there were better things to be doing."

"Roya Lane is a retail area, not a place where people live," Becky commented. "And learning etiquette from a Disney princess might have done you good. Then at least you'd know that your hair is a mess."

Paris ruffled up the hair on the crown of her head, making it look more disheveled. "Oh, you don't like my 'do? I was going to offer to do your hair. Too bad."

"You don't do anything to your hair," Becky spat. "Do you even brush it?"

"No, which was why I had loads of time to both read and watch *The Princess Bride*." Paris tapped the book sitting on her desk.

"Very good," Willow said in her polite tone, trying to recapture the class's attention from the front of the room. "It's true that many of you were already familiar with the story, as it's a classic and teaches some important fundamentals when we're studying romance and love."

"It teaches us the false idea that women need to be saved by a prince," Paris grumbled, rolling her eyes.

In response, many of the women behind her broke into sudden whispers of disapproval.

"It's romantic for a man to risk his life to save a woman." Becky instantly sounded offended.

Paris spun in her seat, one arm on the back of the chair. "Is it? Is that what you need for someone to prove their love and commitment to you? Them to fight a pirate, possibly lose an eye, nearly die and maybe get some gnarly scars? Nothing says romance like a permanent wound to the face."

Becky grimaced. "A man worthy of one of our Cinderellas or me would win the fight and not get scarred."

"I hate to break it to you, princess, but even the best fighters meet their match." Paris shook her head. "There are a lot of factors when it comes to fighting, and if you pull a sword, chances are you're going to get hurt."

"I wouldn't know," Becky replied, her eyes tiny little slits. "A real lady doesn't fight."

"A real woman doesn't allow others to fight her battles for her," Paris argued, spinning back to face the headmistress. "Do we really require our Prince Charmings to save our Cinderellas as if they're some damsel in distress? That's a little outdated in this modern world, don't you think?"

Willow considered this for a moment, offering a thoughtful expression. "I'd like to believe that chivalry isn't dead and that a man standing up for a woman is still very meaningful."

"Because why? Because women can't stand up for themselves?" Paris fired back. "Are we really teaching women in this day and age to look for men who will fight their battles for them instead of creating ones who can do it themselves?"

"I think we can teach both," Willow countered. "Just because a woman can stand up for herself doesn't mean that she has to. It does show a man's commitment to her if he fights for her honor."

Paris rolled her eyes, slumping in her seat. "We're not living in the day and age when evil wizards captured princesses and locked them in a tower in a forbidden land. I thought *The Princess Bride* was funny and whimsical, but the concept isn't relatable to our modern world. Women aren't usually forced to marry an evil prince anymore. If they are, it should be their job to stand up for themselves. I mean, if I'm honest, I don't want a man who is all 'as you wish' about everything."

"No offense," Becky began. "But I don't think you're the type of woman that men who say that kind of thing fall for. Most respectable women would die to have a man willing to give them whatever they want."

Paris turned again, her wicked grin on her face. "It's cute when you say 'no offense,' and you totally mean to be offensive. And no offense to you, meaning definite offense intended, but I think it says a lot about your lack of character that you would die for a man to be your slave. I would rather a man have a backbone."

Becky narrowed her eyes, fine lines spraying around them like spider webs. "Wanting someone who will give you whatever you want doesn't reflect on character."

"Needing someone to give you what you want because you lack in yourself is exactly how character is defined," Paris countered.

Becky's gaze shot to the headmistress as if she expected her to intervene. Paris also glanced in Willow's direction, curious about her reaction to this exchange.

She smiled politely. "I think that these kinds of discussions are very helpful when we're studying the art of love. There are usually no right or wrong answers and Paris is correct that the modern world has changed some of our outdated practices. That's one reason the faculty is reviewing the curriculum and trying to make it more relevant to today's world."

"I disagree that the modern world should have any bearing on our curriculum," Becky stated. "Mother says that if Happily Ever After College starts changing things that their funding will see a serious drop, not to mention that Saint Valentine will be notified."

Paris glanced back at the woman. "That sounds like a threat there, Rebecca."

"It's the truth," Becky replied bitterly. "The headmistress is well aware that the alumni for the college are proud of the traditional curriculum and the hint of it changing amid some other more scandalous news has many unsettled."

Paris laughed. "By scandalous news, do you mean the fact that some heathen halfling is traipsing around the college?"

"Fairy godmothers are supposed to be fairies, plain and simple," Becky fired back. "There are those who don't approve of us being anything else, especially in the Montgomery family, which has a long line of fairy godmothers."

"Your family sounds like such tolerant and open-minded people," Paris joked, shaking her head at the other woman.

The class all looked at Becky as if the ball was in her court now. "Fairies understand love in a way that a magician can't. It makes zero sense for a race that is obsessed with skill and information to try to be experts in love."

All eyes darted to Paris. "Right, because adding some objectivity to matchmaking makes zero sense. Maybe it's your inability to think for yourself that's the reason you need a man to save you.

Things evolve. The world has, and with it, love has changed. If you weren't so obsessed with outdated fairytales, you'd see that the modern woman is no princess."

"Love is timeless," Becky spat, nearly yelling, her face flushing red. "The art of love has and will never change. If you knew anything about it, you'd know that."

"Love might not change since the principles should always be the same," Paris argued. "But dating practices and relationship dynamics have changed. Women aren't these little flowers who need a knight in shining armor to slay dragons for them anymore. They are educated and equals in a world where the glass ceiling has been lifted. I bet you're also going to require your date to pay for everything, is that right?"

Becky scoffed loudly. "Of course. If a man doesn't pay for a date, it's offensive."

Paris laughed. "So a man has to do 'as you wish' and risk his life to prove his love and pay for the meal to win your affection. Wow, you're a real catch. Bet you have the suckers lining up to put a ring on you."

Becky fumed, her face growing redder. "I have a fair number of suitors. All respectable men who see me as a prize."

Paris nodded. "Yep, a prize they can buy like a hook—"

"Don't you dare insinuate that I'm one of those," Becky interrupted, nearly shaking with anger.

"I don't think I was insinuating at all," Paris teased, enjoying this way too much. "If they can buy your affection with fancy meals or whatever, I think we both know what that makes you."

"Don't you dare say it," Becky seethed.

"Easy," Paris chimed. "You are quite simply easy and also totally lazy. Buy you a meal, do whatever you say, and fight your battles. That's all one has to do to win your affection. Does personality or who someone is matter to you?"

"Of course it does," Becky stated. "I only date men who have a distinguished pedigree."

Paris chuckled. "Like a dog, right? Got to find someone who comes from the right family and is well-trained. You say 'sit,' and your doggie sits. Sounds so romantic."

Becky threw her finger in Paris' direction, glaring at the head-mistress. "She's making a mockery of this class and the art of love."

Unhurried, Paris turned to see a calm expression on Willow's face. "I think that Paris brings up some interesting points and again, we need to consider if certain dating practices are outdated. As far as the Montgomery family goes, if your mother or grand-mother has a problem with the fact that we're educating a halfling here, they can take it up with me directly. Saint Valentine is well aware, but he does not run this college as that responsibility falls straight to me."

Paris wanted to see Becky's expression but decided to stay facing forward and count her wins. She was grateful that the head-mistress was supportive of her despite facing criticism for her decision to keep Paris at the school. She didn't want to push her luck and hoped that Willow didn't regret that decision—which meant that Paris had to prove her worth.

CHAPTER FIVE

Although Paris wasn't going to admit it, ballroom dancing class hadn't proven to be the torture she originally thought it would be. She still didn't understand the point regarding being a fairy godmother, but she did appreciate that it was about obtaining skills and being well-rounded.

Paris had promised Headmistress Starr that she'd maintain an open mind, even if it still seemed backward to teach women to be poised and refined to find love. She realized things couldn't change overnight at Happily Ever After College. And Paris liked learning some of the dance moves and secretly thought it might make her a better fighter.

Wilfred, the AI butler and dance instructor, clapped his white-gloved hands to gain everyone's attention at the start of class. "Some of you will work on the tango today. Others have progressed to the rhumba and cha-cha. If you haven't mastered the waltz, you'll review that fundamental dance today. We can't learn the advanced moves until we know all of the beginner steps."

Paris could have sworn that Wilfred's eyes slid to her briefly.

She knew that she hadn't mastered any of the dances, but she felt like she could keep up well enough with most of them and caught on quickly.

"Now, please partner with someone working on the same dance as you and get started," Wilfred advised, clapping his hands again and ushering students in different directions, helping them find a suitable pair.

Paris noticed Hemingway striding straight in her direction, weaving around the other groups on his way to her. He was often her partner during ballroom dancing since she was admittedly behind. It had been Wilfred who suggested that Hemingway help her since he didn't want her to learn bad habits pairing with another student.

However, to Paris' surprise, the rigid butler hurried over and stepped between Hemingway and her as he arrived. Wilfred held up a hand, halting Hemingway.

"Today, Paris isn't going to have a partner," he said firmly.

Hemingway blinked at Wilfred in confusion. "What? Why? I thought you wanted me helping her."

Wilfred pursed his lips. "I did, and you were, but now I think that you're enabling her."

Paris sighed. "Oh, man, I can't win for trying."

The butler gave her a pointed glare. "Hemingway is skilled in all our ballroom dancing and leads you well. So well, I'm afraid it doesn't force you to learn the actual moves."

"Well, do you want him to sweep my legs out from under me a time or two or something?" Paris asked.

The stuffy AI blinked at her. "I'm not sure what that would accomplish."

Hemingway nudged him in the arm. "That's one of those jokes. I don't think Paris thinks I'll sweep her legs out from under her. Besides, I don't want to sport a black eye."

"I'm not sure why you'd have a black eye for dancing poorly." Wilfred appeared confused now.

Paris laughed and shook her head at Hemingway. "I think we better stop with the jokes. They might make his head explode." She pursed her lips at Wilfred. "So I need to dance with someone who won't enable me, is that right?"

He shook his head. "You need to dance alone."

Paris glanced around the ballroom where the other students were all paired up, tripping from time to time but at least doing it with another person. "Wait, you want me ballroom dancing by myself? That seems sad even for me. Isn't that like playing dodgeball on your own?"

Wilfred tilted his chin to the side, his confused expression deepening. "I've never played dodgeball, so I can't relate although..." His expression glassed over momentarily before his eyes flickered to life again. "Dodgeball doesn't appear to be an activity conducive for our curriculum."

Paris laughed. "Yeah, there would be a lot of broken noses if you suddenly forced the students to play dodgeball, although I think it would be as effective as teaching ballroom dancing."

"How is that?" Hemingway laughed, obviously amused by this conversation.

"Well, isn't dating all about avoiding getting hit while also trying to knock out the right person?" Paris deadpanned, earning another laugh from Hemingway.

Wilfred's expression remained stone. "I'm not sure I see the similarities between courting and a game that seems violent in nature."

"You should meet my ex-boyfriend," Paris joked. "He was as dumb as a rubber ball, and all I did was try and avoid him."

"Although I see that you're trying to create a humorous metaphor, I'm not sure it works for our purposes," Wilfred said dryly. "Today, I want you to work on mastering the steps on your own."

"Ballroom dancing is a two-person activity," Paris argued.

Wilfred nodded. "Correct. But one has to know the steps on

23

their own so they don't rely too much on a partner. It truly is a two-person activity."

Paris deflated but nodded still. "Okay, fine. You want me to work on the waltz? Master that before moving on?"

Wilfred shook his head. "Unfortunately, I don't think you're ready for the waltz quite yet. Instead, I'd like you to go back to basics and master the box step."

"Box step?" Paris' face flushed red. She didn't dare look at Hemingway, suddenly embarrassed. "That's like making me do front rolls all over the ballroom when everyone else is doing cartwheels."

"The class is dancing, not tumbling, I'm afraid," Wilfred corrected.

Hemingway released a small smile, nudging the butler again. "That was another of those metaphors laced with humor."

"Oh," Wilfred said at once. "I realize the box step is basic, but it is crucial that you know that thoroughly before progressing. I fear in our attempts to help you catch up with the class that we've rushed you ahead. It would be best if you have the proper foundation."

"Fine," Paris sighed. "I'll learn how to do the box step with my eyes closed. Then maybe you'll let me step on someone else's toes again."

Wilfred straightened. "Dancing with your eyes closed isn't advisable, just as we don't encourage stepping on other people's toes."

"Wilfred," Hemingway began with a laugh. "That was a...never mind."

"Don't worry," Paris said to the groundskeeper and jack of all trades for the college. "One way or another, I will get Wilfred to laugh at one of my jokes."

"If anyone can, it will be you," Hemingway said, backing away. "Good luck."

"Thanks." Paris waved and put her back to the class. She might have to dance by herself, but she didn't have to stare at everyone or allow them to see how humiliating it was for her.

CHAPTER SIX

Without a valid reason to skip Astrology, Paris reluctantly found herself in the observatory and seated in the lecture hall, impatiently waiting for the session to begin. Having to dance on her own during the last class had put her in a sour mood, but she didn't know why. It wasn't like Wilfred had done it to be mean, but rather to help Paris learn the steps instead of relying on Hemingway. No one seemed to pay her the slightest bit of attention as she practiced on her own. For some reason, it felt like she had something taken away from her, and she couldn't figure out why.

"Having experienced the Spring Equinox," Professor Joyce Beacon began, striding onto the stage at the front of the auditorium, "I thought it would be appropriate for us to discuss the significance of the Summer Solstice."

Paris slumped in her seat, wishing she'd tried harder to find an excuse to get out of Astrology. She had promised to keep an open mind about some of the more outdated and archaic curricula at Happily Ever After College. However, that was much easier to do when she avoided certain classes and Astrology was one that really threatened to make her speak out.

Paris hadn't forgotten that Mae Ling had encouraged her to be herself no matter what since she arrived at the college. However, doing so seemed to make her a rebel on every level. There couldn't be more things in one place that she disagreed with and basing romance on some shoddy idea of astrology was definitely at the top of the list. Paris consoled herself with the thought that maybe this astrology lesson wouldn't be as ridiculous as the last one.

"One of the reasons the Summer Solstice is so important for our purposes as fairy godmothers is that it's the ideal time to balance masculine and feminine energies," Professor Joyce Beacon began in her usual airy tone.

Paris slid down farther in her seat. *So much for any hope this lesson wouldn't be cloaked in superstition and backed up by zero science,* Paris thought. If she chewed on her nails, maybe she could busy her mouth and refrain from arguing with the astrology professor.

Joyce Beacon wore the blue gown, the same as everyone in the room, making her long, thick dreadlocks a bluish-gray like a grandmother. The woman's dark skin was a beautiful contrast to her hair and robe, and her gray eyes were a nice complement that made her appear wise and somewhat witch-like.

"There is little denying that men and women speak different languages," Professor Joyce Beacon continued, giving Paris a pointed look.

It was as if she had read her thoughts and was challenging her to argue with her.

Fine, Paris thought. *I can't dispute that. Men and women do seem to communicate differently.*

"During the Summer Solstice when nature has reached full maturity," the fairy godmother went on, "it's the time for us to connect to the Earth to balance the masculine and feminine energies to ensure that our matches have every opportunity via the cosmos to find true love."

Here's where it's all going to fall apart for me, Paris thought, biting her nail. Maybe things wouldn't go too farfetched. She hoped. She could get behind the idea of balancing out masculine and feminine energies from a symbolic standpoint as long as it made practical sense.

"It is through rituals that we connect to the Summer Solstice, ensuring that the goddess of the Earth lavishes our matches with good fortune," Professor Beacon stated.

All the hope that Paris had banked on immediately evaporated.

The fairy godmother glanced around the room with a patient expression on her face. She definitely wasn't reading Paris' thoughts right then.

"Some ritual ideas," Professor Beacon began, "that harness the solstice's explosive positive energy would be creating bonfires, altars of lights, sun pinatas, sun wheels, sun mandalas, solstice sun tea, solstice flower essence, and flower wreaths."

"Why are we doing this?" Paris stuck her fingers more into her mouth, trying to cover her reaction. Despite her efforts, her cynical remark popped out of her lips.

The fairy godmother glanced in Paris' direction. "Well, one of the most important reasons is to ensure we make fertile matches."

"Wait, you're telling me that we have to burn lavender and Saint John's Wort or something to create 'fertile matches?'" Paris put air quotes on the last two words. "What research do we have to support this?"

Behind her, Paris heard several students groan, probably having expected her to challenge the logic but possibly disappointed that she couldn't stop herself from speaking out.

Professor Beacon also appeared immediately flustered by the question. "In many cultures, throughout history, civilizations have performed rituals at the Summer Solstice. The Pagans ran around the totem pole."

Paris nodded. "Oh, good. I was afraid you were going to

support the claim with a weird population of people who weren't hippies."

Thankfully the groans at Paris' back turned to giggles. She couldn't help but release a small smile too.

Professor Beacon didn't seem amused though. "I'll have you know that the Egyptians had a two-week festival to celebrate the Summer Solstice. The Greeks had virgins drink from special wells hoping to have visions of their future spouses. In Eastern Europe, men search for magical ferns in the forest at night and women make flower wreaths that suitors risk their life to recover as they sail down the river."

Paris nodded. "Here I was worried that your examples would make all these rituals sound weird."

Professor Beacon sighed in frustration. "Showing respect to cultures and history is important."

"And I do respect cultures," Paris argued. "I think all the ones you mentioned are fascinating. However, I would argue that as fairy godmothers we don't need to continue these ancient traditions, thinking that's how we'll solidify successful matches. That's shortsighted. The Egyptians celebrated the solstice because of fear of something happening to the Nile. Similarly, other cultures were afraid of what would happen to crops or that the gods would be angry with them and not gift them with children. We know more now and therefore shouldn't waste our time running around a totem pole when those mating rituals will do as much good as worshipping a tree."

"Actually," Professor Beacon said smugly. "In India, if two lovers are born under the influence of Mars, there's a risk their marriage won't be successful. Therefore one is required to marry a banana tree. This satisfies Mars' wrath, and the bad marriage will happen between the spouse and the tree, making the second marriage a successful one."

"Although that's fascinating, I really don't want to believe the fate of a marriage is based on when someone is born," Paris stated firmly. "If two people aren't destined to be together it's because they aren't compatible or one is a runner, or one a cheater or whatever the inherent problem is but not because of Mars. I feel like if we subscribe to these notions, we lose the power to help people find true love. Instead, we'll stay tied to rituals that aren't fact-based instead of helping lovers to connect."

Paris braced herself for the professor's reactions, which she figured would involve a fair bit of yelling. To her surprise, Professor Beacon nodded. "You make some relevant points. I'm not saying that we should dismiss the study of astrology, but maybe we need to start taking it with a grain of salt. I'll consider what you've said, but in the meantime, maybe you can indulge me by at least learning the customs around the Summer Solstice? You don't have to practice them, but knowing about them could always lead to an idea for you when matchmaking."

Paris was momentarily so shocked that she was speechless. Finally, she coughed out a reply. "Yeah, I think that sounds fair."

Professor Beacon released a small smile. "Good. I'm glad we could have a civil discussion on the matter."

Paris was glad too and hoped that other similar disagreements went the same way. However, she didn't think all she opposed would be as reasonable as Professor Beacon, although one could hope.

CHAPTER SEVEN

It was still difficult for Paris to consider that she was working on a mission with the headmistress, Mae Ling, and others at the college. That was unheard of for first-years at Happily Ever After College, but it was her rebellious thinking, which Mae Ling had encouraged, that landed her this opportunity. It didn't escape her that one behavior that had landed her at the college ended up granting her extra privileges.

Paris knew that she was subjective on the matter. Still, she did think that fixing the Amelia Rose and Grayson McGregor situation would take thinking outside the box and doing things differently than how the fairy godmothers had before. She and Christine had already done things untraditionally, sneaking into Rose Industries and McGregor Technologies to learn covert information. Now it was time to put that information to use, bring the two lovers together, and hopefully extinguish the flames of the war they kept fanning.

Taking her lunch in the headmistress' office at Willow's request, Paris sat nervously on the edge of one of the oversized armchairs. She merely eyed the neat platter of sandwiches on the desk in front of her and the others, not at all hungry.

"Thanks for joining me," Willow Starr began, smiling at the others. "This is a small task force I've put together to hopefully fix this situation with Amelia Rose and Grayson McGregor. Unfortunately, the longer they stay apart, the more the love meter goes down. Whoever thought that one match couldn't have such far-reaching effects really underestimated how much two people can do—or in this case, how much harm they can cause."

Standing stoically between Paris and Christine was Wilfred, who had his hands behind his back and chin high. Also sitting to the side of the headmistress' desk were Mae Ling and Chef Ash. All would have pivotal roles based on the plan that Paris had set out. It involved treachery, lying, and a lot of deception. If it worked, Amelia Rose and Grayson McGregor would be together, and they'd create love instead of sabotaging it.

Paris glanced at the love meter on the wall and sighed. It was still very low, the dial around fifteen percent. It was pretty incredible, in the worst way, that two people had impacted the love meter so much. Still, these were two powerful people who had far-reaching effects. What they encouraged, spread. The key was to inspire them to love, then that's what they would spread.

"So, what's the next phase?" Christine asked, sliding her hands together eagerly. It was also her first case, but she wasn't a first-year.

However, because Paris was working on the mission and didn't work well with others, she'd been chosen. Christine was smart and worked well under pressure, which some of the other, more well-behaved, rule-following fairy godmothers in training had trouble with. Breaking the rules was one reason the headmistress chose Paris after all. She didn't flinch when she lied. Paris wasn't sure that was a good thing, but in this instance, it did her favors. Before, it got her in jail. Life was ironic like that.

Mae Ling opened the folder with the plan that Paris had

outlined, which she didn't think anyone would go for. She glanced up over the folder and raised an eyebrow at Paris, almost as though prompting her.

Chef Ash, Wilfred, and the headmistress all glanced at her too.

Paris straightened, cleared her throat, and sucked in a breath.

"Okay, the next step is pretty simple," she stated, trying to inject confidence into her voice.

Christine laughed loudly. "Simple? Like calculus?"

Willow shot her a disapproving look before glancing back at Paris. "I appreciate that you think that it's simple. Maybe you can boil it down for us." She glanced at the others for support. "I think for some of us, that it might need some simplifying since it's a bit unorthodox."

This was where Paris' strange expertise came in handy. It was weird because mostly it wasn't a skill she ever thought would be necessary.

"Right." Paris puffed out her chest. "It's pretty easy. We have to sabotage and destroy two very lucrative and powerful companies. Then Step One of our plan is complete."

Christine laughed again. "Easy-peasy. I love every part of this plan. Especially Step One."

CHAPTER EIGHT

An uncomfortable cough escaped Willow's mouth. "It's that whole sabotage thing that gets me. Is there a way we can avoid it?"

Paris glanced at the report she created and shook her head. "I don't think so. It's about taking away options. We have to reduce these two to nothing…"

Willow gulped. "Really? Nothing? Like, maybe we could at least set up an emergency fund for them. Some way to help them out if things get dire."

It was thankfully Christine who cut in for Paris, keeping her from having to sound like the heartless devil. "No, I've heard about something related to this. If a person has a backup plan or a Plan B or a safety net, well, they don't pull out all the stops. Rose and McGregor have to think the entire bottom has been pulled out from under them. Only then will they believe they have no options and get desperate."

"And by desperate, you mean?" Chef Ash pulled the pencil from behind his ear and eyed her.

"I mean, they drop the ego act and start using their hearts," Christine said victoriously.

Paris was grateful that her friend was on this mission with her. Christine's rebellious spirit was exactly what they needed. It would ensure they were closer to success because it was about breaking down the walls around one's heart, and unfortunately, the ego created the toughest barriers.

"It's true," Paris affirmed. "So we have to destroy their companies. Then they'll fall into each other's arms...hopefully."

"They will." Christine injected confidence into her words.

"So how do we destroy their companies?" Mae Ling asked while reading through the report.

"That was my question too," Chef Ash mused. "Do we blow them up? Or bomb them somehow? The whole endeavor, I'm sorry to sound conservative, sounds very deceptive and mean."

Paris nodded. "It is. Although that's not my specialty, it is something I think I can manage. But no explosives if we do it right. I think a few well-placed pieces of information is all we need. In this day and age, you don't need to throw rocks to hurt people. Only information." She turned and grinned at the butler. "That's where you come in, Wilfred."

CHAPTER NINE

"I'm not aware of how I can aid in this part of the plan." Wilfred's gaze fell to one of the reports on the desk. "Actually, I'm not certain how I can aid in any of it."

"You're the master of information," Paris argued. "If anyone knows something, it's you."

"Although I'm in total agreement, that's because I'm connected to all public domains globally," Wilfred stated.

"Exactly," Paris agreed triumphantly. "I think that if you can access these databases to get information, it's simply a matter of reverse engineering to have you plant information."

Christine's mouth popped open. "No way. You're not thinking?"

Paris nodded and pulled out the instructions Faraday had sketched for her that morning before fixing the messaging on her phone.

The headmistress glanced between Christine and Paris, confusion heavy on her face. "I'm not following you. What is it you're not thinking? Or rather, are thinking?"

"I asked my friend who has experience with magitech AIs about this," Paris began, giving Willow and Mae Ling knowing looks.

Both nodded, apparently inferring that she was referring to Faraday, the talking squirrel they rescued from the Serenity Garden.

She smoothed out the piece of paper, which the squirrel had filled with equations and diagrams. "Apparently, it is very possible for Wilfred to be able to hack into various news sources and plant seemingly legitimate stories."

"Did you say 'hack'?" Willow swayed as if she might suddenly pass out.

"Think of it more as using a back door," Christine offered, giddy with excitement.

"Is this door locked?" Willow questioned.

Paris handed the instructions to Wilfred, returning her focus to Willow. "It's firmly shut. How about that?"

"I know that being open to new strategies is important," Willow began. "And this situation is more complex than one of our normal cases, but I'm starting to reconsider this approach."

"Change is difficult, and Paris definitely is challenging us in that regard," Mae Ling argued. "It was her idea to gather the covert information used to craft this plan. Sneaking into corporations and sabotaging them isn't something a fairy godmother does—"

"Ever," Wilfred interrupted tersely.

"I understand that," Mae Ling said flatly. "But also, it was a fairy godmother who got us in this situation, and she was relying on old ways that obviously didn't work. Although the idea of hacking and bringing down companies feels wrong, it is a means to an end that will bring about more love worldwide. We must ask ourselves if it's permissible to destroy one or two things to build something better in its place. I think the answer has to be yes."

"Okay, so back to the strategy." Willow let out a long breath. "These news stories…"

Paris nodded. "We would be leaking the information Christine and I learned about when under cover. For Rose Industries, we'd reveal they have inhumane working conditions and have failed to comply with strict standards in the factory."

"Is that true?" Willow asked, her eyes widening.

"Well, it's a rumor," Paris stated. "What we do know is that Rose Industries did sprout up overnight and Amelia is very new as a leader. It wouldn't be hard to believe that some special considerations to working conditions were overlooked on the path to take over the industry from Grayson."

Willow shook off the uncomfortable look brewing under the surface. "Very well. And this claim?"

"Well, if planted on legitimate news sources, it would effectively ruin Rose Industries," Paris stated.

"Not only from a reputation perspective," Chef Ash began. "There would be an investigation, and that could close things down for a while. If found in violation, the company's doors would be closed. Even if not, it would still tarnish public perception."

"Yes, unfortunately, rarely is a verdict remembered but rather the allegations," Mae Ling added.

"And for McGregor Technologies?" Willow asked, sounding heavy still, the guilt already weighing on her.

"That one is more of a leak and less of a supposed allegation," Paris stated. "When we were undercover, we learned that McGregor Technologies has some products with faulty wiring that have been linked to fires."

"So we have to expose this information," Chef Ash said victoriously. "Then the company would be tied up in so many legal battles that it would take forever for it to recover."

"The hope is that both CEOs decide to throw in the towel and start over," Paris stated.

"But together," Christine offered.

"Well, that will take more planning, but first we start with taking down the two companies," Paris imparted. "That's Phase One."

The headmistress gave the butler a look of hesitation. "Wilfred? Is it possible for you to…" She swallowed, appearing very uncomfortable. "Is it possible to hack into new sources and plant this information?"

The AI blinked at the crinkled piece of paper and then glanced at Paris. "Your friend…the one…he gave you this?"

Paris nodded, keeping her gaze away from the others. Although Willow and Mae Ling knew about Faraday and Hemingway did too, Chef Ash and Christine didn't. Paris didn't think that broadcasting the information would be very good. She felt that she was already taking advantage of the headmistress' good nature by having the squirrel there on the grounds of Happily Ever After College.

"He appears to understand my inner workings," Wilfred stated.

"Who is this character?" Christine asked. "He sounds smart. Is he cute?"

"A-freaking-dorable," Paris joked, laughing.

"I think that using these instructions, I could hack into major news sources," Wilfred stated at once. "If you all can supply me with the stories you want planted there."

"I've already written them up." Paris retrieved another two pieces of folded paper from her leather jacket.

"Do you ever sleep, woman?" Christine asked in surprise.

Paris shook her head. "Not really. Not anymore." She passed them across the desk to the headmistress.

Willow scanned the first page before glancing at the second one. "This is well written and will leave most scrutinizing both organizations heavily."

She handed them to Wilfred, who didn't read them, but rather folded them up and slid them into his jacket pocket.

"I don't see any reason the source of the articles will come under scrutiny," Mae Ling stated. "Especially if we use a bit of spell work to keep people from asking."

"Does that mean you're volunteering for that job?" Willow asked hopefully.

"Of course," the other fairy godmother answered.

"And my job in all this?" Chef Ash inquired.

"I figured we could put your construction skills to work." Paris indicated the back of the report. "Do you think you'd be up for something like that?"

Chef Ash flipped to the back page of the report, and his eyes widened with delight. "Up for it? This is like a dream come true. When can I start?"

"Well, we're not there yet," Paris stated. "The first step is to bring down the companies."

Christine flipped through the report. "Then we have to break Amelia and Grayson up with their fiancés."

Mae Ling nodded, smiling slightly. "*Then* we put them together and let love take over."

Willow sighed with relief. "I think this could work. It isn't something that makes me feel comfortable as a whole, but I like that it has the potential not just to bring love but also a better future for many. When two people who are supposed to be together find each other, I believe they become better versions of themselves. Then they make the world better."

"Sadly, when they aren't with each other, they have the opposite impact." Mae Ling glanced at the love meter.

Paris needed this plan to work. Not only because it was her plan and so many were relying on her unorthodox and rebellious approach. But because the lower the love meter got, the more difficult it would be to recover. For some reason, she instinctively knew that.

CHAPTER TEN

The Enchanted Grounds were unsurprisingly the perfect spring temperature with a gentle breeze that carried notes of lilac and vanilla. Paris held her chin up and sucked in a full breath, grateful to finally be able to get outside after the long morning.

For a girl who grew up on a cobbled lane in the middle of London, she didn't realize how much nature made her feel better. Being around trees and flowers that grew in the ground instead of in pots gave her a peacefulness she'd never known.

At the greenhouse where Hemingway usually taught the Magical Plants class, Paris found the building empty and a note on the door. It read,

We're meeting at the stables today. Find your way down there, but try to be quiet. – Hemingway

Going down to the stables filled Paris with sudden dread, taking over from the euphoric feelings she'd had moments prior. The last time she'd seen a horse at Happily Ever After College was on her first day when one tried to trample her, and she climbed her first tree. She enjoyed the climbing part but could have done without the whole nearly run over one. Since then, horses hadn't been a part of any of her interests at the college.

It wasn't until the second or third year that the students were apparently required to take equestrian studies. The idea that it was mandatory was further perplexing to Paris. However, she didn't understand most of the curriculum so this was another point of confusion that she'd no doubt argue against.

The class was gathered around the red barn when Paris made it down to the area behind the Serenity Garden. That area was still off-limits and under construction after Faraday's adventures there. Mirror Lake sat on the other side of the stables and lived up to its name nicely, reflecting the puffy clouds overhead and as placid as an actual mirror.

When Paris poked her head into the crowd, Hemingway cleared his throat softly and murmured, "Today we're studying magical creatures and their importance in the eco-culture of our grounds as well as outside the bubble that's Happily Ever After College."

Paris searched the grounds, expecting to see one of the neat hummingbird hawk moths that she and Hemingway had spied recently. They were rare, and like the deadly nightshade, their appearance had been a surprise. For whatever reason, new things had been popping up at the college and Paris had the creeping feeling it had something to do with her. Hemingway had said as much.

"I had you all meet me at the stables," Hemingway began, "because it's a safe distance from the lake and I plan to bait a creature who lives there. She is fascinating and devilishly helpful in maintaining the health and balance of Mirror Lake. However, she's also very dangerous."

At this, many of the girls broke into tense whispers and glanced toward the water.

Hemingway held up his hands to pause them. "Do not worry. I know many of you boat and swim in the lake, which is fine. My little friend who lives at the bottom doesn't desire to nibble on you as long as I keep her fed. She spends most of her time asleep. To be honest, she doesn't prefer to feast on fairies. They are apparently too sweet. Give her a magician though, and she might change her mind." Hemingway's gaze connected with Paris'. "So it probably goes without saying that someone in particular should stick to swimming in the pools and not the lake."

Noted, Paris thought, a shiver running down her back. She hadn't spent any time swimming anywhere since arriving at Happily Ever After College, and there was a very specific reason—she didn't know how.

Unsurprisingly, growing up on Roya Lane offered zero opportunities for swimming. However, she had played with the idea of putting her feet in Mirror Lake a time or two and was glad that she'd abandoned it, not wanting to unlace her combat boots. Most things were about practicality for Paris. The notion there was something—a female—in the lake that might want to take a bite of her because she was a magician was perplexing.

"Why magicians?" Paris whispered, needing to know.

Hemingway grinned at her. "My friend says that magicians are nice and salty. That's a staple to her diet as she prefers to feast on kelp and other types of seaweed when not eating meat."

That produced a lot of excited chatter. Hemingway held up his hand. "Let's try and keep it down. My friend won't show up if it's loud, which is another reason why she usually would leave you all alone. I'm not sure any of you ladies stop talking for a moment when near the lake or anywhere else."

This earned a few giggles.

"Now, as some of you know," Hemingway continued. "Mirror Lake is actually a saltwater pond, and the reason is that it gives us access to many special magical species. My friend—Moira—is one of them."

47

Hemingway reached down into a bucket that was beside him and retrieved a bloody piece of red meat. "Thanks to Chef Ash, we have a nice raw rump roast, which should be a nice treat for Moira, although she gets most of her nutrition eating fish and sea vegetation. Without her, the biggest predator in Mirror Lake, it would be overrun with small fish, disrupting the balance. So, as you can see, you need a big fish in a little pond. Now let's meet this fish."

Hemingway tossed the slab of meat through the air, and it landed in the water with a splash, creating ripples in the once placid water. The blood from the beef seeped out immediately, creating a weird sight.

Everyone watched silently, most seeming to hold their breath before they laid their eyes on Moira—the mysterious sea creature. Paris couldn't fathom what fish could communicate, lived in salt-water, and preferred magicians over fairies to eat.

When the head of what appeared to be a hideous woman popped out of the water, it all made sense.

Of course, Paris thought. *Moira was a mermaid.*

There were several gasps from the crowd as the mermaid grabbed the hunk of meat and sank her razor-sharp, pointy teeth into it. She rolled over on her back, most of her midsection in water still as her emerald green fin splashed on the surface. As though ravenously hungry, the half-woman, half-fish, tore into the meat as she continued to float on her back.

Mermaids weren't the pretty little picture that Disney had painted for young girls. They appeared hungry and violent and ugly. Moira had green hair that draped over her face like she was wearing a mop of seaweed on the top of her head. Her eyes were large slits and mostly black. The mermaid had sharp, high cheek-bones and pale skin, and she had apparently skipped Cotillion classes since she ate the meat like a hungry dog.

"By now, you've guessed that Moira is a mermaid," Hemingway said in a low voice. "They're known for being very territorial, the downfall to most sailors on the open seas and blood-hungry. However, they also have a venom that can be used in powerful potions with varying useful purposes." He held up his arm to show a rather gruesome wound. "Although their bite is quite painful and can be deadly if not treated quickly."

"She bit you?" a girl asked.

"I thought you said they wouldn't harm us," another student said, sounding fearful.

"I have no reason to believe that Moira is the least bit interested in you," Hemingway stated. "I got too close during feeding. All is forgiven now. Like I said, she does an excellent job of keeping Mirror Lake tidy. Also, she's very helpful at retrieving things for us from the bottom of the lake. That was our agreement if we didn't dive to get it ourselves. We stay out of her home and she gets us things we need. Remember, mermaids are territorial, and the bottom of Mirror Lake is strictly her domain." Hemingway laughed and winked. "So don't go down there unless you want her raving mad at you. Moira has a temper that would make a mino-taur look like a puppy dog."

The class laughed.

Hemingway picked up a book lying in the grass beside him. "By now you all should have a copy of *Magical Creatures*, the most complete guide on these types of animals, written by Bermuda Laurens. She is the premier expert on magical creatures and constantly updates the book as she furthers her research. This is a valuable resource, and as the famous Hemingway said, 'There is no friend as loyal as a book.'"

Many of the students pulled out the hardback books from their robes. Paris had hers, along with *Magical Plants*, pressed to her chest. The rustling made Moira glance over in their direction. As though she finally realized she was in the company of others, she plunged under the water, taking the rump roast with her.

"For today's lesson," Hemingway continued. "I want you to review the section on Happily Ever After College in *Magical Crea-*

tures. It is quite small, but Bermuda was allowed entrance to the Enchanted Grounds to catalog a few of our rare and exotic species. Feel free to take a leisurely walk around the grounds and through the Bewilder Forest, searching for some of the animals listed in this section. I'd like a full written report on the animals you discover by our next class."

With the mermaid gone and the new assignment given, the students broke out into excited chatter.

"Oh, and feel free to go near the lake," Hemingway offered. "Moira has gotten her meat and won't be hungry for a day or so, although I think she'd have to be starving to bite one of you fairies."

Many giggled before moving off, having taken the hint from Hemingway that the assignment portion of the class was to begin.

Paris was about to stride in the direction of the Bewilder Forest. Most weren't making a beeline for it, probably due to its sinister appearance even during the day.

"Oh, Paris," Hemingway said behind her, making her pause.

She turned to face him with a questioning look.

"Would you mind lending me a moment of your time?" he asked sincerely. "There's something related to today's subject that I'd like to discuss with you."

CHAPTER ELEVEN

"When were you going to tell me that Moira would fancy eating me?" Paris asked, pretending to be offended.

Hemingway hazarded a smile at her. "If I'd ever seen you venture down to Mirror Lake, I would have, but honestly, she's pretty tame and probably wouldn't want a halfling. I'm guessing you're still too sweet for her."

Paris pointed at the bite on his arm. "Seems like she's as tame as a wild lion, biting you, fairy."

His eyes darted to the ground. "Yeah, well, it's a risk that goes with the job. Anyway, I hoped you'd read some of the book I gave you, *Magical Creatures*."

"In all my spare time," Paris joked.

"Yeah, I heard you're working a mission." He looked impressed. "That's pretty unheard of for a first-year...or a second-year, even."

"I fell into the whole thing by sticking my nose into things and making bold suggestions when the headmistress was desperate," Paris remarked.

Hemingway laughed. "That seems like your style. Anyway, I hoped that you'd read a certain chapter."

"Oh," Paris said with surprise, cracking open the book to look for the table of contents. "Is there one on halflings? I didn't think to look."

"No, and I think that's probably because there's little known about you," Hemingway answered. "I bet that Bermuda Laurens would love to talk to you for research purposes."

Paris did a poor job of hiding her groan. "Like a lab rat?"

He shook his head. "Like someone who is unique and extraordinary."

She instantly felt bad for her remark. "Yeah, well…"

"I'm sure it's not easy being the topic of so many people's interest," he consoled. "Anyway, I hoped that you'd read the chapter on animals that can talk."

"Oh. No, I haven't." Paris scanned the table of contents, looking for it.

He shrugged. "Well, there isn't much to it. Mostly Bermuda states that they're a rarity and usually a result of unique circumstances. However, I wanted to point it out since I learned about your little friend."

"Faraday is rare and not only because he can talk," Paris stated. "He fixed my phone this morning and drafted plans for hacking into a news site."

Hemingway's eyes widened. "Wow, I heard he had done some pretty impressive stuff during his adventure in the Serenity Garden, but I had no idea he was quite that tech-savvy. That affirms what I thought."

"Which is?"

"Well, I understand that he's your friend, but it might be worth learning more about him. Has he explained why he can talk?"

"He said it was a part of a spell. Apparently, he was a smart squirrel that followed professors at the university around," Paris stated. "He's always been curious about things."

Hemingway raised an eyebrow at this. "A spell shouldn't be able to do that. I've known a lot of animals, and even the most intelligent can't master talking."

Paris pointed at the lake. "It sounds like Moira can talk."

"She's not a rodent." He gave her a sympathetic look. "I don't mean to sound skeptical, but talking animals are a cause for question. Maybe the way that Faraday achieved the ability is innocent, but he also could be a result of strange magic."

"Headmistress Starr and Mae Ling didn't seem concerned," Paris argued, suddenly feeling very defensive.

"The headmistress tends to be very open about things and doesn't usually consider the negative aspects related to things." He shrugged. "She's wonderful in many ways but a bit naïve when it comes to real-world perspectives. I think it's a result of only studying love. Fairies tend to see only the good in things."

Paris laughed. "Which is why I'm considered the Negative Nancy at this place."

"I wouldn't say that since your thinking landed a mission in your first year," Hemingway pointed out. "Anyway, I thought that investigating why Faraday can talk and his background wouldn't be such a bad idea."

"Wait, why are you paranoid, fairy?" Paris challenged with a grin.

He shrugged. "My experience with animals and on the grounds of Happily Ever After College gives me a different perspective. Again, I'm not saying there's anything wrong with Faraday, but a talking squirrel is a very curious thing. I think looking into things could be worth your efforts."

"Well, I'm not sure what he'll tell me that he hasn't already."

Hemingway nodded. "I don't think he'll offer any more information. From the little Bermuda Laurens wrote on the subject, she stated that talking animals are usually very mysterious and tend to be secretive."

"I wonder why," Paris mused.

"I've never met one or had the opportunity to figure that out.

My guess would be that illegal magic, or something very powerful made them the way they are, and they don't want the wrath of the House of Fourteen coming after them. Still, that's only a guess."

"Well, since we've both concluded that Faraday probably isn't going to indulge me with his life story, any other ideas for how I'll figure out something about the talking squirrel?" Paris asked.

Hemingway pointed at the book still open in her hands. "I'm in favor of going straight to the source to get information."

Paris glanced down at the book. "You mean the author of *Magical Creatures*? Bermuda Laurens?"

He nodded with a grin. "She's an expert on magical creatures so if anyone has insights, it will be her."

"How do you propose I get this famous author and expert to talk to me? Do you think she has a website?"

Hemingway shook his head. "I thought about that, and it doesn't appear as though she does. I've studied her book extensively but not until I thought that you should contact her did I comb through the entire contents."

"You discovered her home phone number then?" Paris joked.

He grinned. "No, I remembered that a covert way of learning about an author is to read the acknowledgments in their book. It tells you personal details that can help you track them down."

"Wow, you're a regular Sherlock Holmes," Paris remarked.

"I don't know about that, but when I read Bermuda Laurens' acknowledgments page, I found something of interest pertaining to you." Hemingway pointed at the book in her hands. "Check it out."

Paris flipped to the back, thinking that was most likely where she'd find it. Her eyes scanned down the long list of names Bermuda Laurens had mentioned, thanking various people for discoveries or help.

Her eyes landed on a name, and her heart leapt. It read, "Thank you to Liv Beaufont, who despite being a magician and a total thorn in my side, has somehow managed to aid my research with her investigations as a Warrior for the House of Fourteen."

Paris glanced up in surprise.

"Keep reading," Hemingway encouraged.

She continued to scan the rest of the page, her eyes finding another familiar name. It read, "Thank you to Sophia Beaufont, who is singularly responsible for stopping the extinction of dragons. Without you, the section on the new generation of dragons in this book would be empty."

Again, Paris jerked her head up. "My aunt! Sophia has to know Bermuda Laurens. You think she'll introduce me," she guessed.

He nodded victoriously. "I don't see why not. It's worth a shot."

"You think Bermuda will help me with information about Faraday?" Paris asked.

"With a name like Bermuda, how could she not be helpful?"

"Okay, well, I was planning to see Sophia tonight, so I can ask her about Bermuda then," Paris stated. "Maybe Bermuda Laurens can make you and I both more at ease about this Faraday situation, although I think even if his background isn't sketchy, that doesn't mean he'll stay out of trouble."

Hemingway laughed. "Yeah, breaking into the Serenity Garden on a Tuesday was pretty bold. He's a curious little guy."

"Yeah and he's probably going to get himself into trouble again tonight."

Hemingway arched a curious eyebrow at her. "Oh? What's he got planned?"

"Well, if something is off-limits, he has to know why."

Hemingway's eyes widened suddenly. "He's not thinking of going into the Bewilder Forest, is he?"

"Yeah, he is," Paris stated. "Why? Can you tell me why it's off-limits at night? If so, I can pass along the information and keep him from getting his tail chomped off by the Sasquatch you're hiding in there or whatever it is."

Hemingway's expression stayed serious. "I can't tell you. You have to stop him. No good can come of anyone going into the Bewilder Forest at night. There's a reason that it's off-limits then."

"So you do know, but you're not going to tell me?"

"I can't," he urged. "Faraday. You have to stop him. He can't go into the forest tonight or any other night."

Paris' heartbeat suddenly thumped. "I don't know where he is or how to stop him. Usually, I only see him at night and in the morning."

"Hmmm," Hemingway mused, obviously flustered. "I'll see if Casanova knows his whereabouts."

"Funny how you're all concerned about my talking squirrel so you're going to ask the talking tattle cat about it," Paris joked.

Hemingway shook his head. "Casanova can't talk freely. He can only relate information if someone is doing something wrong. Since Faraday isn't technically supposed to be here at the college, the cat can tattle on him."

"So Casanova doesn't go on about his favorite music then?" Paris joked.

Hemingway flashed her an amused look. "Faraday does? Seriously, that's not even remotely normal for a squirrel. You find the strangest friends."

"I'm not sure you should be surprised by that at this point," Paris offered.

Hemingway winked at her with a playful look in his blue eyes. "Honestly, I suspect you'll continue to surprise me for a long time to come."

CHAPTER TWELVE

Paris kept running her eyes over her mother's name in Bermuda's book. For some reason, it made Liv Beaufont feel closer, like if she was mentioned in an acknowledgment that she had just been in her dimension.

Paris' mother sounded like a pain in the ass. Maybe that's what everyone meant when they said that she was a lot like Liv Beaufont. Paris was self-aware enough to know she was a royal annoyance to most she came in contact with. Usually, she prided herself on that since she mostly annoyed bullies who deserved her wrath.

Flipping through *Magical Creatures* instantly enthralled Paris with all of the information. The book was relatively compact but seemed to go on and on. Paris suspected that a spell was on the pages to make all the details fit in such a small space.

Randomly she paused on a page about mermaids, reading much of the information that Hemingway had told them that afternoon. Continuing flipping, she found the section on talking animals, but again Hemingway had already summarized its contents.

Paris halted at the sight of a picture of one of the strangest creatures she'd laid eyes on. It was a lion with a goat's head on its back and a snake for a tail. For a moment, Paris thought that this section had to be about mythical creatures but the first line she read informed her otherwise:

"The chimera has long roamed the planet but is rarely seen. Incredibly powerful, these magical animals can take the form of any animal they choose. They're known to shrink their incredible size to fit in a very tiny space. The reason for this is that they've long been protectors of special beings, but it's believed they do their best job protecting when unnoticed by a potential threat."

That was fascinating, although she didn't know why. She continued to flip through the book, finding the section on fairies, which described them as "having their head in the clouds most of the time" and "ignoring logic and critical thinking since emotions ruled them."

That seemed about right to Paris. She instantly wondered if the section on magicians said the opposite. No sooner did she have that thought than she immediately turned to the chapter on magicians.

Not only did the book have a compacting spell on it, but it appeared to know what Paris was looking for and delivered it.

"Should I be offended that you're studying for another class when in mine?" Chef Ash asked, striding over to her workstation in the demo kitchen.

Paris closed the book and blushed. "I'm sorry. That's rude of me. I was fascinated by some new information I've learned on magical creatures."

"I can completely understand," he said good-naturedly. "I've always been ruled by too many interests. I think that's a good thing. You're curious, and your passion for learning is refreshing."

Paris glanced around at the class where most were working on dosing their dishes with cannabis. That was today's lesson, which Paris hadn't completely understood and was afraid she'd get high and miss her meeting that night.

"Refreshing?" Paris asked. "Do fairies not like to learn?"

"They do," he replied. "But there's less of a hunger for it. Fairies learn for the purpose of manifesting love and romance usually. It's a means to an end. Magicians, I've learned, want knowledge because they crave it. In that way, it is the end for them."

"I bet this section was about to tell me that." Paris indicated the page she'd paused upon about magicians.

"Probably." Chef Ash tapped on the other book beside Paris. "Now, maybe your interests will lead you over to *Magical Cooking and Baking.* I hear there's some fascinating information in there too."

Paris smiled. "I'm sorry, but I don't understand today's lesson. Why are we cooking with cannabis? Does getting high promote romance for two people?"

"Hopefully, if the love is real, the romance makes two people high," Chef Ash answered. "Honestly, my lessons aren't always about creating matches. I think food nurtures our body, mind, and soul. It has so many different ways that it can heal or make people feel different states of being. Getting high on food can have its purposes, and that's why I've found that a chapter on proper dosing is important. You can make a man euphoric with the right amount of cannabis, and you can also make him crazy. So it's important to practice it."

Paris looked around the room, noticing many of the students giggling as they took bites of their creations. Some looked ready to fall asleep in their chowders or prepared to eat all of the potatoes laced with saffron-scented cannabis oil.

"Yeah, I guess that makes sense, but can I have someone else sample my dish?" Paris asked. "I have an important meeting tonight and need my wits about me. I didn't want to have a family reunion and finally learn about my parents while thinking my face was melting or a salt shaker told the best jokes."

Chef Ash laughed. "Yeah, I can understand that. Most of these students will probably be frolicking around the Enchanted

Grounds or lying on the floor in the conservatory after today's lesson."

Paris sighed. "Oh, to have such luxuries. Alas, I have genealogy lessons."

He shook his head at her. "We both know you wouldn't do well with free time."

"You know me well already," Paris said.

Chef Ash patted her on the arm. "Don't worry about today's lesson. You can learn about cannabis dosing another time. Or never. Honestly, this is a throwaway lesson, but I taught it to give me extra time to come up with the construction plans you have for me for the Amelia and Grayson mission."

Paris beamed. "I'm so glad you're working hard on it. That's wonderful."

"What's wonderful is to be using my talents for something that I think can bring love to others." Chef Ash sighed. "I love what we do here at Happily Ever After College, but if I'm honest, it's been a long time since we've brought love to others."

CHAPTER THIRTEEN

Paris hurried back to her room after her last class but didn't find Faraday. She worried like crazy about him going into Bewilder Forest after Hemingway's warning, but she didn't know how to prevent it.

Knowing that she had a meeting at the Rogue Riders Mansion in Beverly Hills, Paris scribbled a quick note for the talking squirrel, hoping he found it and heeded her warning.

Glancing back over her shoulder at the spot on her dresser where she left the note, she hoped that Faraday returned after dinner, anticipating that Paris had left him a cheese sandwich before his adventures. Then he would get the warning and not go on another venture that would nearly end him and possibly many others.

Paris wanted to stay but had already set the wheels in motion for the meeting that night. It was one that she hadn't known she'd wanted so badly, but she did. More than anything.

The Rogue Riders Mansion appeared bigger than the last time that Paris had been there. She reasoned that it was because she'd ridden up the drive in a car instead of walking up with a new protective charm fastened around her neck. Apparently, Mae Ling had left the new amulet on her dresser that afternoon. Paris had found it when she set the note out for Faraday.

Paris knew that it was unlikely that she could hold onto the protective charm if the Deathly Shadow wanted it. That was the point about a protective talisman. They protected but were easy to take off someone. Life was stupidly ironic.

Paris stood frozen in front of the enormous stone mansion for a solid minute. She knew that seeing Uncle John would be healing for her. Reuniting with Clark would be interesting. Being with Sophia would be fun. Still, the bigger implications were intimidating.

They'd all been spelled not to talk to her about anything. Now, that spell—along with a lot of others—was broken. Her family could speak. They could tell her secrets. They could tell her about her parents. That was exciting and terrifying to Paris all at the same time.

She had heard so many amazing stories about her parents and what awesome warriors they were. About her mother's sassiness. Her father's bravery. How much they loved each other. But....

What if they weren't amazing?

What if things didn't measure up and Paris wished she hadn't learned the truth? Ignorance might be bliss. Maybe not knowing the truth was better?

Paris didn't like the idea. It felt foreign and wrong to her, but she worried about learning about two people who had a stellar reputation in her eyes and lost it. She wasn't sure if she'd rather sit in the Hall of Ignorance and Bliss than enter the Kingdom of Truth and Reality. One seemed right and real, and the other was merely comfortable. Strangely, Paris wasn't sure which was which at this point.

She stood at the entrance to the Rogue Riders Mansion for a solid minute, wondering if she should proceed or wait until the actual minute she'd told Sophia that she'd be arriving. Then she caught sight of a figure striding down the driveway where she'd come from.

As her eyes adjusted, Paris' eyes homed in on the familiar image of none other than Uncle John.

CHAPTER FOURTEEN

It felt like too long since she'd seen him.

When Paris ran into his arms, it felt like too long since Uncle John had wrapped his hands around her. It had never been often, but enough that she knew how he gripped her tightly and made her feel like he never wanted to let her go. She currently felt the same way. This was her happy place.

When she finally peeled away from him, he wore a concerned smile. His white hair swept to the side as usual, and a twinkle showed in his blue eyes. "You okay, Pare?"

"Okay?" she laughed. "Thinking back, I haven't been okay in a long time, but yeah, I'm here because I'm more okay and trying to make things even more okay."

He chuckled. "Spoken like you in your true style."

"What's that mean?" she challenged.

"It seems a Paris thing to say," he replied with a smile in his eyes.

Paris glanced at the house in the distance, thinking they should take off for it, but paused for a moment.

"I know something about you," she said in a coy tone.

"I have a feeling, after your conversation with Father Time, that you know a lot about me and more," he stated matter-of-factly.

The real question that Paris had been rehearsing for diplomacy and sensitivity reasons tumbled out of her mouth without warning and with none of the thoughtfulness she'd practiced. "You gave up your girlfriend for me."

Uncle John glanced at her, utterly dumbfounded. "I-I-I...I didn't..."

"Papa Creola told me," Paris argued.

He sighed, looking heavy. "It's not all so easy as everyone makes it."

"So you didn't allow your girlfriend, Alicia, to marry my Uncle Clark so the Beaufonts could stay in power in the House of Fourteen without losing their spots?" Paris challenged.

"Well, I did, but it's not like I had a choice," he answered.

"You didn't become a fairy of sorts and give up your place in the House of Fourteen as a Mortal Seven for me?" she continued.

He pointed directly at her. "To that, I can say a firm no. I didn't. I didn't give up my position with the House of Fourteen as a Mortal Seven. That would be absurd..."

"But you did become a fairy, didn't you?"

"Technically, in a way." He squinted in the afternoon sun streaming through the trees.

"Uncle John, will you level with me?"

He pointed at a stone bench. "Always, Pare. I think we're overdue for a long conversation. Why don't you join me before the festive gathering?"

She nodded, sat, and waited for him to join her moments later. When he did, they were quiet for a while. Finally, Paris looked at him, sincere sadness welling up in her. "You changed everything in your life for me."

Uncle John looked at her with complete sincerity. "No, Pare. I did everything to save this world, your mom, and your dad. Then also to save you, the person I had no idea would become my favorite in the entire world."

She didn't know what to say for a long moment. He'd spoken with such sincerity. She knew it to be true. Still, it was hard to realize so much had been done on her behalf.

"You are mortal...." she said, awe in her voice as this set in for the first time as she looked him over.

He nodded, shame on his face. "I'm afraid so. I'm just glamour and magitech and all and nothing special. I can do magic with objects, or rather they can do magic for me, but not real well. Nothing like a real fairy but it's been enough to fool those who matter."

"Uncle John, you're the most special person I know," Paris stated. "I'd love you as a fairy or a mortal or whatever. I mean, I'm not perfect. I'm a halfling..."

"You're better than perfect," he said right away.

"You've always loved me the way I was even when I was starting trouble," she replied.

He thought for a moment, his face suddenly looking so much older than usual. The wrinkles made him not look like himself. Finally, Uncle John said, "Pare, you have to understand that when your parents disappeared, we made decisions to keep you safe, to keep them protected, and to protect everything they represented. Your parents weren't like two regular people when they went missing. It was like a hole got cut out of the universe and the rest of us had to fill it in."

"With yourselves," Paris guessed.

He nodded. "That's what you do when two important people leave and give you the most important person to watch."

Paris didn't agree with that at all. It felt wrong and so intimidating and scary. *But what if it was right,* she wondered. "Uncle John, you gave up your girlfriend," Paris repeated.

He smiled like he did when he let her beat him in an arcade

game. "Alicia took on a job she didn't like so much and did much more too."

"Like marry my other uncle?" Paris decided to be bold. What was the point in not being so?

"Pare, you have to understand that we did a lot of untraditional things, thinking that Liv and Stefan would be back in a matter of days, then weeks an…"

As his sentence trailed away, it set in for Paris. She'd made this about her, but it wasn't. It was about her parents and the ones who loved them and more. All of the people in their lives did so much to ensure they got back or that things weren't too different when they did. She was trying to figure things out, but she had no idea what all was sacrificed in the interim of her parents being gone—or more importantly, the fact that many didn't suppose it would be so long.

"You thought…my mom…my dad…my parents, were going to be back any day right after they left," Paris guessed, drawing out the words. "It has to have broken your heart every day that they haven't."

"I won't lie to you," Uncle John said at once. "It hasn't been easy. Raising you, well, it was unexpected. It was a blessing I never expected and embraced, never knowing when it would be over. But yes, every day that your parents have been gone has broken my heart. I'm not alone there. Your parents' absence has made the world what we know. Illegal magical activity has been on the rise and in turn so much more. The demon population is at an all-time high. I bet you see a result of all of this at that school, Happily Ever After."

"Love on the decline, you mean? That's because of my parents?" Paris asked.

Uncle John nodded solemnly. "I think if things were operating normally in the magical world, other things wouldn't be so out of balance."

"How do you know they're out of balance?" Paris asked.

"I feel it," he answered. "I think we all do."

Paris nodded solemnly. What could she say? The magic meter was out of whack. The world was constantly under threat due to the Deathly Shadow. She felt so much more pulling for her attention, but that would need her help later...once this was all resolved...hopefully.

"Back to what we were discussing. You changed everything in your life for one reason or another," she stated.

"Pare," he began heavily. "If I didn't give up Alicia—if I didn't take a break from the Mortal Seven, or Clark didn't do one thing or another, if Alicia didn't, if a lot of other people didn't—quite simply this world would have quit spinning on its axis. But we did, and it didn't, and things have a chance." He blinked at the sky in the distance morphing into blues and pinks. "I hope it does have a chance, you know."

"That's why I'm here, and that's why we're here," Paris stated with conviction. "We have a chance."

CHAPTER FIFTEEN

As they walked up to the mansion, Uncle John explained that although the truth was out about Paris, he and Alicia couldn't be together still. She was a Warrior for the House of Fourteen in the hope that she'd reserve Liv's position for her. If she suddenly went back to John, everyone would know the marriage to Clark had been a hoax. They'd have to handle things very carefully when the time was right.

"Plus, who knows if she wants to be with me." Uncle John shrugged. "It's been fifteen years since I've seen her. We simply couldn't be around one another. None of us were allowed to see each other except for Clark, Alicia, and Sophia since they worked together."

"Alicia asked about you," Paris stated. "Of course she wants you back. How could she not? I can't even fathom giving up the person you love for all this."

Remorse covered his face for a moment before he recovered with a fake smile. "I love a lot of people, your mother included. Father Time knew you couldn't remain in the mortal world and be safe. Liv had left you with me. When it was decided I'd take on the role as a detective for the Fairy Law Enforcement Agency, I didn't question it."

"And you thought it might only be for a day or a week," Paris murmured, still having trouble processing all that so many did for her and her parents. "Do you think you'll stay as a detective now that you don't have to? I mean, I realize Alicia can't be with you because then she'd lose the position with the House of Fourteen, but you don't have to be a detective anymore since I know the truth and I'm not living on Roya Lane."

Uncle John thought for a moment as they paused beside the front door. "I've thought about that. I like my job more than I thought I would, but I miss the electronic repair store. However, going back there, well, it might bring back too many memories of your mom. She worked there with me for so many years. In a way, I had it easier than Clark and Sophia because Father Time gave me a new life with you on Roya Lane. I didn't remain in the same house that Liv had lived in, like Clark. I wasn't in Los Angeles like Sophia, always reminded of her sister." He pressed his lips together and smiled. "But I got you, and you've reminded me of Liv every single day in all the best ways. I feel bad that the others didn't get to see you grow up, but so no, I have no regrets. We all gave something up to protect you from the Deathly Shadow, but I was given the best reward in return."

Paris threw her arms around Uncle John's shoulders, hugging him tightly. He seemed surprised for a moment but then pressed her tight, choking out a laugh.

"Hey, you two shouldn't go in through the front door," a voice said, interrupting the pair hugging.

Uncle John released Paris, and they both glanced up to find the large blue dragon blinking at them from the side of the house.

"Lunis?" Uncle John said with surprise. "Is that you?"

"I go by Sir Lunis-Awesome-A-Lot now, but yeah. I've grown, huh?"

Uncle John chuckled, and Paris noticed there was a tear in his eyes. "I couldn't say. You've always been large to me since the moment you hatched."

"Hey, Lunis." Paris waved. "Why shouldn't we go through the front door? Is something wrong?"

The majestic dragon shook his head. "Unfortunately, no. I keep childproofing the house, but the other riders keep getting in."

Paris and Uncle John both laughed loudly.

"The reason you should follow me around to the back is that Sophia set up dinner on the veranda, as she likes to call it," Lunis explained. "It's a slab of concrete, but she likes to sound fancy."

"Well, that will be nice." Uncle John smiled.

"It's because I don't want to be left out and every time I go inside the Rogue Riders Mansion, Sophia yells at me."

Uncle John pursed his lips. "That doesn't sound like my little Sophia."

"Oh, well, she's different now," Lunis explained. "I break one priceless magical antique vase given to her by Cleopatra when we time-traveled to Egypt, and she throws a fit, and I never hear the end of it. I mean really, I told her I'd get her a new vase at Pier One that was pretty much identical, but no, she'd rather be mad."

Uncle John laughed and shook his head. "Lunis, you haven't changed a bit, have you?"

The blue dragon shot him a look of offense. "Of course I have. I'm way funnier."

CHAPTER SIXTEEN

When Paris rounded the corner to the large mansion, she saw a blur of blonde hair rushing in their direction. It took her a moment to realize it was Sophia, running at Uncle John. The dragonrider moved unlike any other and was so fast. Within a second, she had thrown her arms around Uncle John's neck and hugged him in tightly.

"It has been way too long!" Sophia exclaimed, her chin pressed into his shoulder.

He wrapped his arms around her, and when he hauled her off her feet, Sophia looked small although there was nothing small about the dragonrider. She felt larger than life to Paris.

Standing back a foot, Uncle John looked Sophia over, his eyes watering. "You look the same. How is that possible?"

Sophia beamed. "I have the chi of the dragon to thank for that."

"You are welcome," Lunis chimed in from beside them.

Sophia nodded in the dragon's direction. "Although this one tries to take years off my life with bad jokes, it hasn't worked."

"My jokes keep you young," Lunis argued.

"They remind me how immature you are." Sophia winked at Uncle John. "You look great too. You don't seem to have aged at all."

Uncle John grinned. "Well, I can thank Paris for that. She's kept me young at heart." He turned, offering her a thoughtful look.

"I'm sure that Pickles helps." Clark strode forward and offered a hearty handshake to Uncle John.

He wrung his hand with a broad smile on his face. "Yes, he definitely helps. Good to see you, my friend."

"Who is Pickles?" Paris had never heard the odd name.

Everyone fell silent. Uncle John's eyes slid to the side. "He's… like a protector to the Mortal Seven. Specifically to the Caraways."

"Who are the Caraways?" Paris asked.

The hesitation deepened on his face. "My real name was John Caraway before Father Time had it changed to John Nicholson."

"As a Mortal Seven, you have a protector?" The questions streamed through Paris' brain faster than she could ask them.

"Well, yes, all Mortal Seven have one," Clark answered.

"Yours is Pickles?" Paris questioned. "Where is he? Why have I never met him?"

"Well," John drew out the word, obviously nervous. "I haven't needed him around since I'm not active as a Mortal Seven member. I still have my role and represent the balance needed in the House of Fourteen."

"The Mortal Seven are more about symbolism in modern times," Clark explained. "They're sometimes called on to advise on issues in the House of Fourteen or to vote, but for the most part, they're more about keeping the balance between the magical and mortal world. They have a huge amount of energy that helps to govern magic even if they aren't actively doing anything."

"So Pickles keeps you young?" Paris asked. "But he's not around, right? So how does that work?"

"He's around in spirit," Uncle John explained, still not looking directly at her. "If I ever need him, he will be here."

Paris scratched her head, feeling like she was missing something. "So all this time, you've had this protector named Pickles, but he only shows up when you need him?"

Uncle John sighed. "I couldn't be recognized as a Mortal Seven to keep my new identity and keep you safe, and although chimera are good at disguising themselves as any animal—"

"Pickles is a chimera?" Paris interrupted, nearly yelling, thinking of the passage she'd read in *Magical Creatures* on the strange animals. What had it said, she wondered.

The words from Bermuda Laurens' book instantly came back to her:

"The chimera has long roamed the planet but is rarely seen. Incredibly powerful, these magical animals can take the form of any animal they choose. They're known to shrink their incredible size to fit in a very tiny space. The reason for this is that they've long been protectors of special beings, but it's believed they do their best job protecting when unnoticed by a potential threat."

Uncle John nodded. "Yes, you've heard of them then."

"You probably realize that having one in any form around John would be a giveaway," Sophia explained. "So Pickles has been hiding."

"Hiding where?" Paris looked around as if the chimera might pop out of a bush and say, "Surprise!"

Uncle John waved her off. "That's not important right now. It's reunion time." He smiled at Sophia and Clark. "It's wonderful to see you two. How have you been?"

To hear that her Uncle John was this mysterious Mortal Seven and had a chimera protecting him was almost too much for Paris to handle, but she should be used to surprises at this point—although she wasn't.

"I'm great," Lunis answered. "You know, the rotation of the earth makes my day."

Sophia groaned, but Uncle John laughed.

"Things are pretty much the same," Clark answered.

To make things even stranger, Paris realized that Clark was married to Uncle John's girlfriend, but the two were very happy to see each other still. All parts of this were weird.

"Sorry to be rude," Clark began, looking at Paris. "I didn't mean not to greet you. I was so surprised to see John after all this time."

"Of course," Paris stated at once.

"What's your excuse for ignoring my presence at every one of our meetings?" Lunis swished his tail back and forth.

"I told my brother that if he ignores you, it's hoped that you'll not talk as much," Sophia joked.

Lunis huffed, smoke issuing out of his nostrils. "Fat chance of that."

Sophia strode over and hugged Paris, holding her tightly. "It is so nice to see you again. I hoped to get to the college soon to visit you, but you arranged this first."

"That would be so nice," Paris said when they parted. "I have so many things to show you. Like, I have a talking squirrel named Faraday. Actually—"

"Did you say, Faraday?" Clark interrupted.

Paris arched an eyebrow. "Yes, why?"

"That's the name of a famous scientist who studied electromagnetism," Clark stated, his eyes to the side like he was thinking.

"Oh, well, Aunt Sophia, I wanted to ask your help with that," Paris began. "I hoped that you could introduce or set up a meeting for me with Bermuda Laurens. I understand you know the magical creatures expert."

"I do." Sophia also looked unnerved by the mention of Faraday. "I'm sure I can arrange that. Why do you want to meet her?"

"Well, I have a friend at the college who thinks that animals shouldn't be able to talk," Paris explained, turning to Lunis. "But you can, and that's not weird."

"I'm not an animal in the same way that your squirrel friend is," Lunis stated, looking rather grumpy. "But thanks for likening me to a rodent." The dragon looked around. "Anyone else starving? I'm craving fairy."

Sophia shook her head. "It's an honest mistake. Paris, animals usually don't talk. It's very rare and strange magic that would make a squirrel be able to communicate like that, but Bermuda would be a good source to ask if you're curious."

"Right," Paris drew out the word.

"Don't worry for now," Sophia said with a forced smile. "We're all reunited, and I hoped we could celebrate. I'm sure you have lots of questions, so let's sit down and dine."

"Sounds good." Paris looked around the veranda in the distance, which was empty. She didn't know where they were planning to do this dining since the expansive grounds were mostly empty.

"I hope you're hungry because I cooked," Sophia stated.

"By that, she means she ordered out," Lunis corrected.

"Exactly." Sophia smiled.

Again Paris didn't know where this dinner was so she simply offered a small smile.

Sophia looked around as if confused. "Now, where did I set us up? Oh, that's right. Over there." She pointed to a corner of the veranda. "The table is over there."

Paris blinked, wondering if she was missing something. From where she stood on the grass, the entire concrete slab appeared empty. "I'm sorry, but what table?"

"Oh, you can't see it yet," Clark explained. "It won't appear until you step foot on the veranda."

Sophia nodded. "I decided it was best for us to dine under an invisibility tent so we could have privacy. For one, I know we'll be discussing private information, and also, there's our guest who I know didn't want anyone to know she's here. The Rogue Riders can be so nosy."

"I don't mind anyone knowing I'm here," Paris argued.

Sophia shook her head. "I don't mean you. I'm referring to Mama Jamba."

"Mama who?" Paris asked.

Sophia threaded her arm through Paris' and led her forward. "Mama Jamba. You'll meet her, although I know for a fact she's already met you. You're in for quite the treat."

CHAPTER SEVENTEEN

When Paris stepped across the threshold to the veranda, her mouth fell open. What had appeared to be an empty concrete area was covered in dazzling lights that draped over a long dining table. It was covered in flowers and filled with dishes in an array of colors. The smell of roasted vegetables and fresh bread was instantly tantalizing to Paris' tastebuds.

Sitting at the far end of the table was a small woman wearing a pink velour tracksuit and a cunning smile. She had a head full of short bluish-gray curls, reminding Paris of the hair the fairy godmothers wore. However, this woman was old, not merely supposed to look that way. She wasn't sure how she knew that, but it seemed true as she stared at the woman with periwinkle blue eyes.

In front of the old woman was a plate of pancakes, and she gave Paris a calm expression as she sat.

"It's nice to see you again, Guinevere Paris Beaufont," the woman said in a southern twang.

Paris blinked at her in surprise. "You're Mama Jamba? We've met? I'm sorry, I don't remember."

"No one ever does." The woman picked up a fork and shook her head. "Yes, we've met many times, but you would remember it differently than me."

Uncle John bowed low to Mama Jamba before sitting next to Paris.

"Jonathon Caraway, please don't do anything to your back that I'll have to fix with all those pleasantries." Mama Jamba put a heaping bite into her mouth and chewed with delight.

"Of course." He looked around at the many delicious options on the table. "Everything looks great."

"Like I said," Sophia stated proudly. "I cooked."

"She puts on an apron to order food and calls it cooking." Lunis laid down next to the table, a huge tray of meat in front of him.

"My name," Paris began, the mention of her real name bringing a question to the forefront of her mind. "Why was I named Guinevere?"

Clark and Sophia looked at each other across the table, a brief moment of hesitation passing between them.

"You haven't heard yet," Clark muttered as he pulled a fluffy roll from a covered basket.

"No, she asked because it's part of your quiz session," Lunis stated sarcastically. "Hurry, first one to answer gets ten points. Buzz in with the right answer."

Sophia shook her head, ignoring her dragon. "Again, I knew you'd have many questions about so many things. I'm so happy you asked for this meeting. It's a delight and so nice to know we can speak freely without that silencing spell. There are so many things to tell you that I can't figure out where to begin."

Mama Jamba pointed a fork in Paris' direction. "I believe you can start with telling her about her namesake. That's what she asked about."

"Yes, I was wondering why my locket's initials changed after I learned the truth." Paris retrieved the golden heart-shaped locket from the pocket of her leather jacket, holding it up for all to see the initials "GB" on one side. On the other, never having changed was the famous phrase she couldn't figure out by the famous poet Rumi: "You have to keep breaking your heart until it opens."

Uncle John almost spat out his drink of water. Clark's mouth popped open. Sophia smiled.

"There it is," Sophia said with satisfaction. "You did give it to her."

"Of course I did," Uncle John stated at once.

"Give me this?" Paris asked, pulling the locket back to her. "I thought you said you found it in an evidence locker, Uncle John."

A look of shame covered his face. "Obviously, I had to lie a few times over the years, Pare. You know I never wanted to. The silencing spell prevented me from saying much, but when I could, well, they had to be things I might have to tailor."

"So if the locket didn't come from an evidence locker, where did it come from?" Paris asked.

"From me," Sophia answered to Paris' surprise.

"You?" Paris asked.

She nodded. "Yes, for some reason, I was told to give it to you. At first, I didn't know why, but later the reasons seemed clear."

"Because of the identity spell?" Paris remembered what Wilfred and Faraday had told her about the locket and why the initials had changed after she learned the truth about who she was.

"You know about that then." Clark looked around the table with trepidation as if the food options made him nervous.

"Well, yes," she replied. "I mean, it used to say 'PW,' and now it says 'GB.'"

"You're named for our mother, Guinevere Beaufont," Sophia supplied. "I didn't know her since she died when I was very young, but Liv loved her dearly."

"There wasn't anything not to love about our mother," Clark added. "She was the fiercest Warrior the House of Fourteen had ever known until Liv came along. Mom paved the way for much of the progress we've known. She and Father, who was a very skilled Councilor for the House."

Paris glanced at her uncle. "So you gave me the locket to help seal my identity?"

He nodded, looking ready to choke on the bread he was chewing. "Yes, among other reasons. I'm glad you keep it with you."

"What are the other reasons?" Paris questioned at once.

"You should keep it with you at all times," Mama Jamba cut in before taking a bite of pancakes.

Paris gave her a questioning look. "Why is that?"

The old woman chewed and then smiled. "It matches your eyes."

"Mama, you're always so complimentary." Lunis chewed on a bone.

"I love my children. What can I say?" The old woman took another bite.

"I wish I could say the same," Lunis offered. "You know today my son asked me—"

"You don't have a son," Sophia interrupted.

"Thanks for ruining the setup to my joke, Soph," the dragon grumbled.

"Continue," she encouraged.

"Well, today, my son asked, 'Can I have a bookmark?'" Lunis began, a laugh in his voice. "I then burst into tears. I couldn't believe it. My son was ten years old, and he still didn't know my name was Lunis."

"Wow," Sophia said over all the laughter. "That was bad."

"It wasn't his best," Mama Jamba added. "But I understand. Most of my children don't know my name."

"You have many children?" Paris asked, interested.

The gray-haired woman gave her a pointed look. "I'd say. Roughly seven-point-nine-billion children. That's not counting the animals, insects, and whatnot."

"W-Wh-What?" Paris shook her head, thinking that she might

have escaped from a mental hospital. "How do you have so many children?"

"Oh, because I'm the mother of all," Mama Jamba explained, having cleaned her plate and pushing it away. "Didn't they tell you? I'm Mother Nature. I created everything on this planet—including the planet."

CHAPTER EIGHTEEN

"Y-Y-You're Mother Nature?" Paris asked, the glass of water in her hands nearly slipping out. Her hand shook as she set it back down.

Mama Jamba smiled wide, her pink lips turning up at the corners. "Not what you expected, am I? I get that all the time."

"Most probably expect you to have vines in your hair and bark skin," Sophia related, spooning potatoes au gratin onto Paris' plate without her asking. It was probably for the best because she was too overwhelmed to do it herself.

"I tried that look for a few centuries, but it got old fast." Mama Jamba rubbed her arms over her velour tracksuit. "I prefer comfort and big Dallas hair currently. Maybe in a century or two, I'll go back to the punk rock look. I quite liked wearing fishnet stockings."

"You're really Mother Nature?" Paris nearly stuttered again.

"It takes some getting used to because she's so down to Earth," Lunis remarked with a laugh.

Sophia shook her head and slid a few pieces of roast beef onto

Paris' plate. "What will it take to get you to stop with the bad puns?"

"I thought you'd know by now that you can't stop me," Lunis replied.

Uncle John chuckled on the other side of Paris and handed Sophia the green beans. She was standing at Paris' back and had nearly filled her plate for her in a very motherly way.

"You met Father Time," Uncle John thoughtfully said to her. "He's pretty normal-looking too."

"He could use a haircut," Mama Jamba stated.

"His assistant didn't seem to like me," Paris offered.

"Subner doesn't like anything or anyone," Sophia stated, taking a seat, having served Paris. "And he especially wasn't fond of Liv."

"Why was that?" Paris asked.

"Jealousy," Clark answered. "Subner doesn't like that Papa Creola likes Liv."

"Yeah, he seemed to be fond of her when we spoke," Paris offered.

"Everyone pretty much was," Sophia said. "Well, except the criminals she put away."

"Yes, and whereas I'm a ray of sunshine, Papa is about as grumpy as a volcano," Mama Jamba stated. "He doesn't usually like anyone."

"So you created everything on this planet?" Paris had to ask, totally overwhelmed by the idea that she was having dinner with Mother Nature.

"I sure did," she replied. "Well, not mosquitos or flies. I don't know where those buggers came from. Probably some joke from one of the gods in another realm. They can never leave me alone. Never have."

"There are other gods in other realms?" Paris asked.

"Well, of course," Mama Jamba answered. "I mean, who do you think takes care of the dimension where your parents are? We of course don't know where exactly they are, which is why we can't willy-nilly open a portal and get them back, but there are Mamas and Papas all over this universe doing their thing. Well, not as good as here on planet Earth, but they try."

"I hear there's a planet where time moves in reverse," Lunis offered.

Sophia nodded. "And their planet is flat."

Mama Jamba shook her head. "Isn't that the most ridiculous thing you've ever heard of? I mean, really. As gods, we were supposed to create planets and mind time. Some of us took our jobs seriously, and some seemed to make a mockery of the whole thing. You all should be glad you got my planet."

"Wow, so there are gods, and you're one of them, and there are other dimensions and planets." Paris said all this mostly to herself while staring at her food.

Uncle John patted her on the shoulder. "It's a lot to take in. I felt the same way when I learned about all this."

"I do have so many questions," Paris said, attempting to pick up her fork. "Like the solar system. Is that your construction? Our galaxy? Or is it only our planet?"

"Don't try to understand too much at once," Mama Jamba answered. "But yes, the solar system is all my construction. I might have messed up with the other planets, but I got Earth right, which was all that mattered."

"Jupiter couldn't be stupider." Lunis continued to gnaw on a bone, having eaten all the meat from it.

Mama Jamba nodded. "Don't even get me started on Saturn. But you got to burn a few matches before you light a candle sometimes."

"Incidentally, I searched for a lighter on Amazon," Lunis imparted, appearing quite serious. "However, all I could find was a hundred twenty-six matches."

A laugh popped out of Paris' mouth. "That one was clever."

Sophia shook her head. "Don't encourage him. He's showing off for you."

"Speaking of the moon," Lunis began.

"We weren't," Sophia interrupted.

The dragon gave her a pointed expression. She held up her hands as if in surrender. "Go on then."

"Well, did you hear about the restaurant on the moon?" Lunis asked the table.

"I haven't." Uncle John grinned.

"Great food, but absolutely no atmosphere," the dragon replied.

Many around the table laughed. Mama Jamba pointed at her empty plate and glanced at Sophia. "What does a woman have to do to get seconds?"

Sophia snapped her fingers, and a short stack of fluffy pancakes appeared on the once empty plate. "I cooked up extra, knowing that you'd want more."

"By cooked up, she means she ordered extra," Lunis corrected.

"Is leading the Rogue Riders and the Dragon Elite not enough?" Sophia asked. "Do I also need to cook too?"

"It wouldn't hurt," the blue dragon answered. "I do both and work at comedy clubs at night."

"Don't quit your day job, dear," Mama Jamba stated.

"Although I'm sure that Paris has many questions," Clark began. "I hoped that we could take this time to discuss something of supreme importance."

"Is this about the cheese factory in France that exploded?" Lunis asked, seriously.

Clark shook his head. "No, I hadn't heard about that."

"Oh, well, da brie is everywhere," Lunis said, rolling over on his back and laughing loudly.

Most around the table joined him. When they'd quieted down, Clark leaned forward. "No, this is about what we've all been waiting for. Paris knows who she is. She's coming into her powers.

We're finally to the point where we can face the Deathly Shadow..."

Paris gulped.

Uncle John slid back from the table, looking tense.

Sophia smiled. "That means we're one step closer to getting Liv and Stefan back."

CHAPTER NINETEEN

"Oh dear, you haven't eaten a thing," Mama Jamba said to Paris when she pushed her untouched plate away.

"I'm sorry." She glanced at Sophia. "I'm not hungry at the moment."

"I call dibs on her roast beef," Lunis chimed in.

Sophia shook her head at the dragon. "You have plenty of food and aren't taking my niece's." Returning her gaze to Paris, she said, "Don't worry. We're all in this together. You're not alone."

"Although, I'm afraid you're the one who has to face the Deathly Shadow," Clark imparted, earning a scolding look from his sister.

"I'm trying to make her feel better, Clark. Do you have to be all—"

"Yourself," Lunis interrupted.

"I'm simply honest," Clark said, defending himself.

Sophia patted the table between her and Paris. "My brother's strong suit isn't diplomacy. He says things as they are instead of sugar-coating them."

"We can help you," Clark said, his tone softer than before. "I've been researching the Deathly Shadow since you were born and the prophecy made. I can offer you everything that I know."

"Lunis and I can be your muscle," Sophia offered.

"I'm great with magitech," Uncle John stated.

"You're going to need all of that, darling," Mama Jamba said matter-of-factly. "But Clark is right. It has to be you to face down the Deathly Shadow, and only he can open the right vortex, with your insistence, that is. It all has to be carefully done with precision."

"Can you offer me more specifics?" Paris asked Mother Nature, who seemed to know more than she was letting on.

Mama Jamba smiled and cut a bite of her fluffy pancakes. "I can, but I won't."

Lunis gave Paris a commiserating expression. "That's hers and Papa Creola's way. They know a bunch, but they don't like to give us spoilers."

"What I like is to empower my children to fight their battles on their own," Mama Jamba corrected in a dignified manner. "It does you few favors for me to tell you how to do things. Honestly, just because I know most things doesn't mean that I'm right."

"There's a conundrum," Lunis observed.

Mama Jamba glanced at the blue dragon. "Information is an ever-changing thing. Merely talking about it can change it. I can tell you how to do things, and simply by relating that to you, I can change the way it's supposed to happen. Ask Papa Creola, time is a finicky thing, and the more you know about the future, the worse off you are."

Clark nodded. "This is true. Knowing the prophecy didn't help us to avoid it or protect you from the Deathly Shadow."

"Who is this soulless entity?" Paris asked.

"For that," Sophia began. "Clark is definitely the right person to ask. He's been studying him since the beginning."

"Nerd," Lunis muttered.

Clark ignored this. "He was once a man, but he's more like a bundle of energy now. Extremely powerful energy."

Paris nodded. "Yeah, Papa Creola said if he got a body that he'd be more powerful than ever and could overpower him."

"That's not speculation," Clark stated. "I think that's the cold, hard fact. The Deathly Shadow sacrificed his soul for power. Over time he lost his body, but the strength he'd taken trading his soul made him immortal. If he absorbed your power, giving him back a body that was stronger than ever, there would be no stopping him. Papa Creola would be his first target. Mama Jamba probably second. He'd eliminate anyone who posed a threat to him."

"Why, though?" Paris asked. "Why did he give away his soul and why does he want so much power?"

"Because sometimes people are born bad, my dear," Mama Jamba said. "Like Pluto, sometimes I burnt some when I made them."

"Unfortunately, no amount of holy water can fix the Deathly Shadow," Uncle John stated.

"Incidentally," Lunis began. "Do you know how you make holy water?" When no one replied, he continued, "You boil the hell out of it."

"Anyway," Sophia drew out the word. "Those who are motivated by power often become corrupt. It's a drug to them, and they don't care who they hurt or if it's themselves on their path to total power."

"I was once addicted to the hokey-pokey." Lunis pretended to be serious. "But then I turned myself around."

"He never stops," Paris observed, impressed how the blue dragon had joke after joke that loosely connected to the subject matter.

"Never, ever." Sophia groaned.

"Although I've enjoyed this reunion," Mama Jamba interjected, having polished off the second plate of pancakes, "Paris must leave."

"I should?" she questioned. "Did I do something wrong?"

"No, dear." Mama Jamba smiled. "But it's time you get back to the college."

"I love it when she does this," Lunis said, still chewing on the large bone.

"Does what?" Paris was confused.

"Tells you that you have to leave because she knows something," the dragon replied.

"Oh, like what?" Paris looked at Mother Nature.

Mama Jamba offered her a sensitive expression as she wiped the corners of her mouth. "That if you don't get back to Happily Ever After College and into the Bewilder Forest right away, your little friend is going to be in so much trouble, there will be no saving him."

CHAPTER TWENTY

Paris nearly stumbled through the portal into Happily Ever After College, her heart beating fast after Mama Jamba's warning. She had hoped that Faraday had seen her message. That he hadn't gone into the Bewilder Forest at night based on Hemingway's warning. However, it appeared that the talking squirrel had and would soon be in trouble.

Not knowing the time difference between Los Angeles and the college, Paris was surprised to find it was pitch black on the Enchanted Grounds. She didn't know what time zone the college was in, or if it was in one, or if like its weather, it was in a bubble.

One thing was certain, it was nighttime, and everything at Happily Ever After College was quiet. At Paris' back, the large mansion stood with many of its windows twinkling with lights. In the distance, Mirror Lake sat placid reflecting the stars and crescent moon overhead. Between the two was the dark Bewilder Forest, appearing as it always did, spooky and foreboding—that appearance only deepening at night.

Paris had hoped that she'd catch sight of the overly curious squirrel when she stepped through the portal to the Enchanted

Grounds, but there was no such luck. The large live oak trees of the Bewilder Forest were swaying in the wind making creaking noises. An owl hooted in the thick woods, not at all filling Paris with confidence. She didn't want to find out what else called the Bewilder Forest home or why it was off-limits at night.

The Serenity Garden had a good reason for being closed on Tuesday if maybe a bit shortsighted on the fairy godmother's parts. Paris could only guess what dangers lurked inside the Bewilder Forest, which its very name didn't fill her with confidence.

She shook her head and set off for the woods. "Faraday, if you get me into more trouble, I'm making you into buttermilk fried squirrel in magical cooking class."

"I don't think Chef Ash will approve of such ingredients," a familiar voice said when Paris passed one of the large weeping willows on the Enchanted Grounds. She spun to find Mae Ling leaning casually against it.

"Hi," Paris squeaked, surprised and also relieved to see the fairy godmother there. "I think that my talking squirrel went into the Bewilder Forest."

"No one is supposed to go in there at night," Mae Ling stated.

"I know," Paris said in a rush. "I've told him that, but he's overly curious about things and wants to know why."

"I don't think that anyone can be overly curious," Mae Ling said, not at all sounding upset about this disobedience.

"But everyone told us not to go in there, and I tried to tell Faraday not to, but he apparently didn't get the message," Paris said, hardly breathing to talk. "And I was having dinner with Mama Jamba, you know, Mother Nature."

Mae Ling nodded. "She's my boss. Well, she's everyone's boss, but specifically, she created fairy godmothers. Well, technically she created everything and everyone. However, fairy godmothers were a project of hers since love keeps the Earth spinning around."

"Right," Paris chirped, feeling her adrenaline coursing through her. "Anyway, Mama Jamba sent me back and said I needed to help my friend who was going into there." She pointed to the dark woods.

"So it seems you should probably go into the Bewilder Forest and help Faraday," Mae Ling observed.

"Am I in trouble?"

"Not with me. But I assume that your friend will find trouble in there."

"Can you go with me?" Paris asked. "I don't know what I'm facing."

"Rarely do we know what we'll encounter when entering dangerous situations," Mae Ling stated. "No, I can't accompany you, but I think you'll be in good hands." She glanced around the Enchanted Grounds, but Paris didn't know at what.

"Well, if you mean Faraday's hands, I doubt that. He only has like four or five toes on each paw," Paris joked, hoping it would make the tension in her chest lessen.

"I think you'll be okay, but Faraday will definitely need your help."

"Can you at least tell me what I'll find in the Bewilder Forest?"

"I think it's better if you learn that on your own," Mae Ling answered.

"So let me get this straight. You want me to go into the place that the headmistress told us is forbidden after dark?"

"I want you to help Faraday," Mae Ling corrected. "Yes, I think in doing so, you'll also learn other things that might be of use to you. There is no doubt that you'll be in danger in the forest at night. I can't guarantee your safety. I can't tell you what you'll encounter. I will tell you to be wary of the Lady of the Lake."

Paris glanced at Mirror Lake in the distance. She was about to ask who that was, but when she glanced back at where Mae Ling had been, the tricky fairy godmother had vanished.

CHAPTER TWENTY-ONE

"Why is it that I have a habit of people in my life giving me barely enough information to set me on a mysterious quest?" Paris muttered, looking around the Enchanted Grounds, ensuring that Mae Ling hadn't simply snuck behind the willow tree. She hadn't. Somehow the fairy godmother had disappeared without a trace.

Paris shook her head, wondering why Mae Ling wanted her to break the rules and enter the Bewilder Forest at night. That was consistent for Mae Ling, constantly encouraging Paris' rebellious tendencies. Still, she was allowing her to walk into a dangerous situation and seemingly with no help. What was it that she'd learn that could help her? Who was the Lady of the Lake?

Knowing that she was stalling, Paris faced the dark forest. Somehow it appeared more sinister than a few minutes ago. Looking around, Paris searched for a stick or something she could use as a weapon. The neatly manicured grounds ensured there were no stray branches. Suddenly Paris wished that she had a sword or something, although she liked to think her fists were pretty deadly weapons. However, not knowing what she was facing made her doubt whether punches would work against this mysterious danger.

"Faraday," Paris quietly called to the Bewilder Forest, hoping that maybe the talking squirrel was hanging out on the outskirts of the woods and would rush out when called. He didn't.

Shaking her head, Paris strode forward, her back straight and shoulders pressed down, her chin high. If she was willingly entering a dangerous situation, she was doing it with confidence— or at least pretending that she had it. *Fake it until you feel it,* she thought, stepping into the Bewilder Forest.

CHAPTER TWENTY-TWO

Hemingway Noble watched from the edge of Mirror Lake, unseen in the shadows as Paris entered the Bewilder Forest. He had hoped that Mae Ling would stop Paris from going into the woods at night. Although he hadn't heard what the fairy godmother said to Paris, it didn't seem like it wasn't to go in the Bewilder Forest. If she had, the halfling was disobeying.

Hemingway gritted his teeth and ran his hands through his hair. He'd hoped that Faraday wouldn't go into the forest at night. That's why Hemingway had stationed himself by the lake the entire night. When he caught sight of the curious creature running into the woods, it was already too late to stop him. The little squirrel was fast and had disappeared into the trees before Hemingway could get to him.

It was possible that Faraday could have gone into the woods and not disturbed what was in there. He was an animal, after all. However, then the squirrel would know what came out at night, and that would lead to more questions once he told Paris.

Once she entered the Bewilder Forest, Hemingway knew it

would reveal all his secrets. Worse was that he would have to go into the woods and intervene. The squirrel might not be in danger from what lived in the Bewilder Forest, but she would definitely come after Paris. That's why Hemingway hurried for the trees after the halfling. He couldn't let anything happen to her.

CHAPTER TWENTY-THREE

The darkness of the Bewilder Forest instantly covered Paris like a cloak. She squinted, willing her eyes to adjust. She thought about using an illuminating spell to see but thought that would be an unwise move. That would be a sure-fire way to alert whatever danger was lurking in the forest of her presence. She might as well put a large neon sign over her head that read, "Dumb Halfling Looking to be Eaten Over Here."

Still, Paris needed to see. Otherwise, she ran the risk of running straight into whatever danger was in the forest. Twice in a few steps, she tripped over thick roots from the enormous live oak trees. At this rate, the biggest danger for Paris was falling on her face or twisting an ankle.

Almost as if cued by her thoughts, little lights flickered on throughout the forest, starting at her feet and rippling out as far as she could see through the thick woods. Paris tensed, wondering if she'd set off an alarm of sorts. However, after a moment, she realized the lights were from tiny bulbs on little flowers scattered across the forest floor.

They were beautiful plants and made it so that Paris could see the path through the woods. The timing of them illuminating was perfect too, because Paris was about to run into a low branch that probably would have knocked her out. The live oak trees had twisted branches that stretched out wide, draping low and reaching back up toward the sky as if they couldn't figure out where to go. Thick green moss covered the trees' bark, and the smell of the forest was refreshing.

It was strange to think that something dangerous could reside in such a peaceful place. Paris had never been in the Bewilder Forest, its sinister appearance even intimidating during the day. However, she instantly loved it and wanted to return often—if she survived that night. One thing was certain. Faraday might not survive and not because of whatever danger lurked in the forest. Paris was going to find him. Then she was going to strangle the little squirrel.

CHAPTER TWENTY-FOUR

The twinkling flowers had illuminated as soon as Paris entered the main part of the forest, Hemingway realized from a distance, seeing the lights sparkling. That would call attention to her presence, but without them, it would have been impossible for Paris to see anything.

He considered hurrying up to catch her and stop Paris from going any further. However, he had already run through that conversation in his head. She'd refuse to leave the Bewilder Forest without her friend. That was the kind of person Paris was, Hemingway knew instinctively. She was the type of person others would want to have as a friend. Paris had lit up his world since she arrived at Happily Ever After College like the flowers lit up the Bewilder Forest.

The good news was, the sparkling flowers now lit up the entire hundred acres of the woods. That meant the Lady of the Lake would know a human was there, in her domain, but she wouldn't necessarily know where. Hopefully, she was on the far side of the Bewilder Forest.

Hemingway also hoped that Paris found Faraday right away,

and he could grab them both and get them out of there. Maybe Paris wouldn't learn his secrets that night. It wasn't that Hemingway was worried that she'd look at him differently if she knew the truth. He knew she would. The groundskeeper wasn't who he said he was. He was an imposter. He had to be because he couldn't fathom the alternative.

Hemingway knew that if someone exposed his past, it would lead to questions. The result would be obvious. If his secrets came out, he'd risk losing the only thing he'd ever had in his life—Happily Ever After College.

Worse, Paris would know that he was a coward.

CHAPTER TWENTY-FIVE

"Faraday," Paris whispered, searching all around for the mischievous squirrel. Oddly enough, she didn't spy any animals, but she figured that most would be sleeping then. Hopefully, whatever the potential monster was, it was hibernating.

Paris didn't expect to see birds in the trees, but she thought she'd hear crickets chirping or some bugs making their presence known. Instead, Paris made the only sounds in the Bewilder Forest as twigs *crunched* under her boots and she called for Faraday.

She had no idea how large the Bewilder Forest was or how long it would take to search it. The helpful little flowers illuminating the path seemed to go on for miles, but it was hard to tell since the thick woods obstructed much of her view ahead.

After a long while of not finding anything, Paris turned and gulped. She could no longer see Happily Ever After College in the distance. She was deep into the Bewilder Forest. Even scarier was she didn't know if she could find her way back—not easily, that was certain.

The padded trails through the Bewilder Forest had snaked around the live oak trees and split several times. With no indication of which direction to choose, Paris had randomly chosen which way to go when the path forked.

"Faraday," Paris said again in a hushed voice, wondering how she could find him when she already felt lost herself.

Then the thought occurred to her that she should think like the crafty little squirrel. He'd be trying to find the reason the Bewilder Forest was off-limits at night. He'd probably be using some scientific theory to guide his observations. None of that helped her to figure out where he could be. However, there was something she knew with confidence about her friend. He'd be hungry.

Holding out her hand, Paris summoned the cheese sandwich she'd left in her room for Faraday that evening. Its appearance confirmed that the squirrel hadn't gone back to Paris' room and therefore hadn't gotten her note. The sandwich rested in her palm on the floral napkin she'd wrapped it in. Thankfully, that evening's sandwich was smoked gouda on a toasted croissant—Faraday's favorite.

Paris didn't care that this was the squirrel's favorite. She was going to toss it over her shoulder once she found Faraday, grab him by the tail, and haul him out of the Bewilder Forest. However, thankfully Faraday's favorite cheese and bread also happened to be very aromatic. As soon as she unwrapped it from the napkin, the smell of smoked gouda and the buttery croissant hit her nose. Waving her hand, Paris encouraged the scent to waft through the air. It hopefully wouldn't be long until she baited the hungry squirrel.

After several more minutes, Paris started to worry that the sandwich idea wasn't going to work. She considered using a tracking spell or maybe a locator one, but she hadn't practiced those and didn't know if it would help her to find Faraday or whatever the danger was. Paris was starting to get the impression that nothing lived in the Bewilder Forest—or at least the animals who did knew not to come out at night.

"Wish a certain squirrel knew that," Paris said aloud, conscious she was muttering to herself. She often did when she was nervous or stressed or alone—which had all been often.

"Knew what?" a squeaky voice said from up high.

Paris nearly bit her tongue, the sudden response startling her although she recognized the voice. She let out a breath, finally feeling her first victory since entering the forest.

She squinted up to find none other than her reason for entering the Bewilder Forest staring down at her.

CHAPTER TWENTY-SIX

"Oh, good, there you are." Relief flooded Paris.

"You were looking for me?" Faraday flicked his tail behind him.

"No, I always stroll through the Bewilder Forest carrying a cheese sandwich," she muttered.

"I didn't know that about you," he said quite seriously.

Paris sighed. "No, dimwit. I came in here to fetch you. Then once we're out of the Bewilder Forest, I'm going to kill you."

"That seems counterintuitive." He didn't at all look threatened. "It might be more cost-effective to kill me here. Or maybe you'll consider not killing me at all."

"I'll consider it," she mumbled, looking around the forest for the potential danger. "It depends on if we get out of here unscathed."

"So if we do, you won't kill me? But if we don't, then you'll kill me. Not sure I understand the reasoning, but I'm in favor of not being killed."

"Well, let's get out of here." Paris waved the squirrel to come down the tree.

"I haven't discovered why the Bewilder Forest is off-limits at night," Faraday argued, flicking his tail again, this time seeming annoyed.

"Well, Mother Nature told me I needed to retrieve you before you were in so much trouble no one could save you," Paris said in a terse whisper. "So I say that we heed her warning and get out of here."

"The real Mother Nature?" Faraday was suddenly in awe. "Oh, wow. I'd have so many questions for her."

"Yes, and she's not what you think," Paris commented. "But I'm certain she's the real deal. Then Mae Ling reiterated that there's a danger here in the forest and you'd need my help."

"Well, as you can see, I'm totally fine," Faraday argued, holding out his front paws.

"You do seem fine and are acting more normal than ever before hanging out in a tree."

He glanced down and grimaced. "I only climbed up here to get a view."

"Well, climb down and let's get out of here," Paris ordered. "If I don't have to die today, I'd prefer not to."

"Strangely enough, I have the same thoughts, but my death is still on the table." Faraday pointed at the sandwich in her hands. "Did you bring that for me?"

"I brought it to bait you but have zero intention of giving it to you."

To this, Faraday gave her an annoyed expression, his nose wiggling.

"Fine, you can have it when we leave the Bewilder Forest," Paris acquiesced.

"Again, I haven't found the reason why the fairy godmothers have deemed this place off-limits at night," he argued. "As far as I can tell, it's a very peaceful place."

"Well, according to sources I trust more than you, it's danger-ous. Mae Ling said to be wary of the Lady of the Lake."

Faraday's ears perked up. "Lady of the Lake, you say?"

"Yep, mystery solved," Paris answered. "Let's get out of here, and I'll think about introducing you to Mother Nature."

"You're a master at negotiations," Faraday chirped. "You have yourself a deal." Very nimbly, he climbed down the large trunk of the tree, front feet first.

"Wise choice." Paris glanced over her shoulder, back the way they'd come, swearing that she heard something in the distance. "Let's get out of here before our luck runs out."

CHAPTER TWENTY-SEVEN

Hemingway let out a breath of relief, having heard that Faraday and Paris were leaving the Bewilder Forest. Maybe he'd avoided all the drama. The Lady of the Lake wasn't going to come out, and they wouldn't see her, which meant he wouldn't have to step in and there wouldn't be more questions. Somehow he'd avoided his worst-case scenario.

He watched from behind the tree where he'd stationed himself as Paris and the squirrel strode back the way she'd come. Hemingway decided that since they were leaving, there was no reason to intervene and escort them to safety. He hoped that Paris found her way out of the forest, but he'd stay close by just in case. There was a good reason that it was called the Bewilder Forest. One of those was that it was easy for anyone to get lost within the woods. Well, not Hemingway but he'd grown up running through these trees.

The area was also named Bewilder Forest because too much time in the woods led to confusion and disorientation. Again, this didn't affect Hemingway because he'd built up his tolerance. Still, anyone was susceptible to the forest's magical powers, especially those new to it, so he stayed close, moving between trees as Paris and Faraday progressed down the path.

Many times, Paris glanced back in his direction. She knew something was there, following her. Thankfully, each time she spun he'd managed to slide out of view behind a large oak tree. Now he hoped that Paris and her talking friend picked the right path out of the woods. The sooner, the better.

He glanced over his shoulder at the sound of the haunting howling. The Lady of the Lake was close.

CHAPTER TWENTY-EIGHT

Paris whipped around as a whistling sound ripped through the forest, bringing with it a gust of wind. She'd never felt anything like that at Happily Ever After College since the weather was always the same with a gentle breeze. The strong wind reminded her of the Deathly Shadow when it had come after her, and she reflexively grabbed for her protective charm, ensuring it was still around her neck.

Paris reminded herself that she was at fairy godmother college and safe from the Deathly Shadow. Whatever had caused the howling wind wasn't the soulless monster, but the mystery of it was what bothered Paris the most. She didn't see anything behind her, but that didn't make her feel much better.

Turning, she ushered Faraday down the path. "Let's get out of here. I think we're close to wearing out our welcome."

"The Lady of the Lake doesn't sound so bad," Faraday mused from the ground, scurrying beside her. "That's who's supposed to reside inside the Bewilder Forest."

"I guess." Paris hurried forward but constantly checked over her shoulder. "Mae Ling specifically told me to be wary of the

Lady of the Lake, not that she wasn't so bad or I should ask her to friend me on Facebook or ask for swimming lessons."

"Well, I know a few myths that involve someone called the Lady of the Lake, if that helps," Faraday offered as they paused where the path split.

Paris wasn't sure if she'd come from the one to the right or the left. "Do tell. I can't wait to hear…"

"I sense that you can wait," Faraday said, thinking rather than studying the path options like Paris. "Anyway, the oldest legend involves a fairy who in British literature helped King Arthur, raised Lancelot, and got rid of Merlin."

"Fascinating," Paris muttered, deciding to take the path to the right.

"It really is," the squirrel said excitedly, not picking up on the fact that Paris didn't at all find it fascinating. "Interestingly enough, in many of those tales, the Lady of the Lake is seen as a fairy godmother-type figure. Lancelot is often called Prince Charming. Oh! And often in stories of the Lady of the Lake, we see Guinevere, which is your name. Isn't that intriguing?"

"Simply captivating," Paris said dryly.

"Well, I think it is." Faraday crossed his tiny arms over his chest and didn't follow Paris.

She paused, turned to the squirrel, and snapped, "Keep up, troublemaker. I'm trying to keep you alive."

"From discovery?" he questioned. "I might want to meet this Lady of the Lake."

Right on cue, a screeching scream filled the air, followed by an icy wind that blew back Paris' hair and made her eyes instantly water. "Really?" She looked down at the squirrel. "You want to meet whoever made that screaming noise?"

"Well, maybe more like study them from a safe distance." He scurried after her, finally looking as though he had the motivation to move faster.

Paris picked up the pace, not pausing the next time she came to a split in the path.

"There's another story that involves a Lady of the Lake," Faraday continued as he ran to keep up with her. "The story involves a couple who were at White Rock Lake in Dallas, Texas."

"Thanks for all the details," Paris muttered. "Will this be on the test?"

He shook his head. "There won't be a test."

Paris ran faster as the screaming grew louder.

"Anyway, the couple spied a young woman who came out of the lake wearing a white dress and dripping wet." Faraday talked fast as he sped after Paris, who was zig-zagging down the path and looking over her shoulder often. "The woman told them that she fell out of her boat and needed a ride home."

"Not weird at all," Paris said.

"So the couple agreed, and she got into the back seat after giving them her address," he continued.

"You're not supposed to pick up hitchhikers," Paris mumbled, pausing when the screaming stopped, replaced by what sounded like chanting. She craned her head to the side, trying to make out the words, but Faraday was intent on telling his story instead.

"The car was about to arrive at the woman's home when the driver turned to ask her a question and discovered that no one was in the backseat, only a puddle of water."

"How very inconsiderate," Paris stated, the chanting faint and drowned out by a rustling sound.

"Well, the couple decided to continue to the address that the wet woman gave them," Faraday went on. "They found a man at the house and told him about the lady from the lake. He was stunned and said that they were the third couple that week to come there with the same story of a woman who disappeared from their backseat after leaving a puddle."

"So the Lady of the Lake peed in their car?" Paris narrowed her eyes as shadows moved on the trail from where they'd come.

Faraday shook his head. "No, the man then said that the woman's description matched that of his daughter who had drowned after falling out of a boat at White Rock Lake."

"Wow, what are the odds," Paris murmured, wondering if they should run and possibly get more lost or face whatever approached behind them.

The squirrel didn't appear amused by her lack of interest and dry responses. "The Lady of the Lake was a ghost, Paris. Don't you get it?"

Paris shook her head. "No, will you draw me a picture? Now seems like the perfect opportunity as I try and get us to safety after you trespassed into the Bewilder Forest at night when we were specifically told not to."

He stuck his paws on his hips defiantly. "Coming from you, that's ironic since you never do as told."

"Mama Jamba and Mae Ling told me to rescue your ass, and I did that!" Paris exclaimed, throwing her arms wide. "That story is stupid. Ghosts aren't real, and I'd think that someone as logical and scientific as you would know that."

"There's no proof that ghosts are real," he replied. "That doesn't mean they aren't."

"Oh, you're ridiculous." Paris spun and strode for what she hoped was the way out of the Bewilder Forest. "You should stay here and make a home. Then you can make friends with the Lady of the Lake, and I can have my sock drawer back."

The howling wind had thankfully died down. The screaming too. And the rustling. The Bewilder Forest was silent. Also suddenly freezing, as if they'd found a spot where the temperature had dropped sharply. But it was always the same temperature all over the grounds, no matter what…

"P-P-Paris," Faraday said from a good distance behind her. He hadn't followed as she sped off.

"Catch up, squirrel." Paris held up the sandwich still clutched in her hand. "If you want your dinner, don't hold me up."

"A-A-About ghosts…"

Paris, having had enough of Faraday's stories, whipped around then froze. The air that escaped her mouth in gasps was visible in the sudden freezing temperatures as she stared face-to-face with a ghost.

CHAPTER TWENTY-NINE

The image in front of Paris was chilling—and the temperature around them was painfully cold as though they'd suddenly stepped into a walk-in freezer.

Hovering over the path was a woman who, as in the story, was dripping wet as if she'd just walked out of Mirror Lake. However, the droplets of water that fell off her didn't puddle on the dirt below her. Instead, they disappeared. Also like the story, the woman wore a white gown. In addition, like a ghost, she was all white and see-through.

Her dark hair blew in a wind that Paris didn't feel. All she noticed was the freezing temperature that made her teeth chatter. However, she wasn't sure if she shivered from the cold or the fear as she looked at the woman who had black sockets for eyes and hollow cheeks. She was a ghost...

"Paris..." Faraday's voice vibrated.

"Yeah?" She stood frozen and stared at the hovering ghost who didn't give her a welcoming feeling.

"I think we should get out of here," Faraday said from the corner of his mouth.

Paris considered swiftly kicking the squirrel at the ghost and making a run for it, but she would never do that even if she were angry at him for getting her into this situation.

"I agree," she said through her chattering teeth. "On the count of three, I'm going to pick you up and run like hell."

"Sounds good," he agreed.

"One...two..."

The Lady of the Lake opened her mouth wide, and a scream that felt as though it could shatter glass hit the pair straight on, carrying a sharp wind with it. The gust pushed Paris back and made Faraday tumble onto his back.

Snapping down to the forest floor, Paris picked up the squirrel who was shaking with fear. She was going to make a run for it, but the ghost shot forward, barreling down on them.

An invisible force sent Paris to the ground, Faraday in her arms. The ghost was inches from her face with a wicked look on her face.

"You did this!" the ghost said in a chilly voice that sounded both hoarse and sharp at the same time. "You stole him away, and you're going to pay."

"M-M-Me?" Paris stuttered. "I think you have me confused with someone else."

"It was you!" the ghost screamed, not giving her much space.

Paris tried to scuttle back on her backside and elbows, but that invisible force pushed her down to the ground, and it was getting increasingly difficult to fight it. "I think there's been a misunderstanding and we need to go," Paris managed to say, angling her eyes down at Faraday in her arms.

He nodded and mouthed, "Use magic."

She knew a few combat spells that could work, but her limited mobility required her to say the enchantments. Paris opened her mouth to start the magic, and the ghost backed up a few inches, giving her some much-needed space. For a moment, Paris thought the spirit would let her go, but then the Lady of the Lake extended her hand in her direction.

"It's time you pay," the ghost said. "It's time that you die."

CHAPTER THIRTY

Paris tried to speak, but suddenly she couldn't breathe. She was suffocating from the invisible force as if it was sitting on her chest, crushing her.

Her hands shot for her throat as she writhed in pain. Paris was unaware of what was happening around her. She caught sight of Faraday momentarily going for the ghost as though he was trying to attack her. That made the Lady of the Lake retreat a few steps, which took some of the crushing pressure off Paris' chest. She was able to suck in a small sip of air and partially sit up.

Apparently, the presence of a squirrel running at the ghost had stolen her attention briefly, but she instantly dismissed him and turned her focus back on Paris. Knowing that every second counted, Paris held up her hand, ready to send a combat spell at the spirit when someone suddenly burst onto the scene in a blur.

Paris, not knowing what other dangers were about to assault her, backed up several yards on her hands and feet before rising to a standing position. She was shocked when she caught sight of Hemingway standing between her and the ghost, his hands extended in both directions between the two.

"Don't hurt her!" he yelled, and to Paris' shock, he was looking straight at her.

CHAPTER THIRTY-ONE

Paris was still shaking all over but managed to point at herself while looking between Hemingway, the ghost, and Faraday on the ground beside her. "M-M-Me?" she stuttered. "She's the one who was trying to kill me."

"Don't hurt her," Hemingway repeated, his chest rising and falling fast, his hands still extended between the ghost and Paris. The Lady of the Lake still regarded Paris with a murderous expression, but she didn't move, only hovered on the other side of Hemingway.

Paris glanced down at the squirrel next to her, wondering if he could offer anything on this.

He gave her a thoughtful look. "Are you okay?"

She nodded, glad to see that he seemed okay too after the tumble and more. Paris sucked in a breath, her lungs aching from being suffocated by the invisible force and the freezing temperature.

"She's the one," the ghost said in a shrill voice. "I have to kill her."

Paris reflexively threw up her hand, ready to defend herself again. Hemingway shook his extended hand at her. "Please don't hurt her. She doesn't know what's going on."

"Well, she apparently knows she wants to kill me." Paris didn't lower her hand, ready to defend herself and Faraday.

Hemingway whipped around, putting his back to Paris. "Go!" he yelled at the ghost with authority. "She's not the one you want. Get out of here! Leave her alone!"

The ghost glanced over his shoulder at Paris, that murderous expression making her look more like a demon than a ghost.

"Get out of here!" Hemingway screamed, throwing up his hands and stomping his feet.

The ghost redirected her attention to him, and to Paris' surprise, she softened, tilting her head. "I'm sorry," the Lady of the Lake mouthed, then spun and soared through the Bewilder Forest in a blur of white, taking the cold with her as she retreated.

CHAPTER THIRTY-TWO

"You have some explaining to do," Paris challenged, her hands on her hips as she faced Hemingway.

He looked her over, then Faraday. "Are you two okay?"

"Well, an angry ghost nearly suffocated me, so I'm going to go with not really," Paris huffed, trying to catch her breath after the adrenaline and cold.

Hemingway sighed with relief. "I told you not to come in here at night."

"I heeded the warning, but that one didn't." Paris pointed at Faraday, who held up his paw, his eyes large and an adorable expression on his face.

"I'm sorry," he said in his squeaky voice. "I was curious."

"Yeah, your curiosity is going to be the death of me," Paris muttered.

Hemingway nodded and pushed his hands through his hair on either side of his head. "Although the Serenity Garden is much better now that we've gotten rid of the flawed magitech AIs. That was overdue."

Paris pointed in the direction that the Lady of the Lake had retreated. "So what's going to be the benefit of us meeting the angry ghost?"

Hemingway dropped his hands, looking heavy. "Probably there isn't one."

"Well, maybe we can start with who she is," Faraday speculated, climbing up the side of a tree and perching on a nearby branch so he was more on their level.

Hemingway sighed, averting his gaze. "She's a ghost. There isn't much more to it."

"You're lying," Paris stated with confidence. She was an expert at picking up when people were lying after spending enough time watching bullies try to con their way in or out of things.

Hemingway turned, putting his back to them. Paris strode around him and propped her hands on her hips. "Why is it that when you challenged the mean ghost, she listened? Who did she think I was? Why did Mae Ling think me coming in here would provide useful information?"

Surprise covered Hemingway's face. "That's what she said to you earlier?"

"You were watching me?" Paris was somewhat offended. "Why?"

"Because I saw Faraday come into the Bewilder Forest and couldn't stop him in time. But I knew she wouldn't harm him. The Lady of the Lake doesn't care about animals. Only other women."

"Why?" Paris asked. "Who is she?"

"No one," Hemingway lied again, his right eye twitching.

"Well, she wasn't a fairy," Faraday mused from the branch. "She didn't have any wings, and I hypothesize that in ghost form, they'd show since she wouldn't glamour them."

"Good point." Paris was grateful to have the logical squirrel's help on this.

Hemingway rounded on the rodent. "Why do you say things like hypothesize? What kind of spell made it so you can talk? It would have to be incredibly powerful, and still, you'd speak like a squirrel. The last time I checked, they didn't sound like an educated scientist."

"It was a powerful spell," Faraday answered at once, not at all flustered.

"I don't believe the talking squirrel is the one I'm questioning right now, Hemingway." Paris strode between the two and gave him a challenging look.

"It's just that I think he's hiding something." Hemingway didn't take his eyes off the squirrel who remained causal.

"You're hiding something," Paris stated. "Mae Ling isn't concerned about Faraday, but she told me to come in here tonight. Then you showed up. So tell me what you know about this angry ghost who wants to kill me."

Hemingway pulled his gaze from Faraday and looked at Paris, regret heavy on his face. "The ghost didn't want to kill you. She wants to kill the woman who stole her husband."

"Oh, well, I guess I'd want to kill that woman too," Paris stated. "So she thinks that every woman is the one who stole her husband?"

He nodded.

"Why did she listen to you when you told her to leave?" Faraday asked speculatively.

"Because..." Hemingway sounded hesitant. "The ghost is my mother."

CHAPTER THIRTY-THREE

Of all of the answers Paris expected, that wasn't one of them. "That was your mother?" She pointed in the direction the ghost fled. "But..."

"I'm not a fairy," Hemingway admitted, filling in what Paris was about to say. "I'm a magician, but the headmistress put a powerful spell on me so that I have the energy of a fairy. That was one reason I sensed you were a magician from the beginning. You don't think or act like a fairy."

Paris nodded. That wasn't hard to digest. Hemingway was very logical, which was one of the many reasons she related to him of all those at the college.

"It's one reason I sympathized with you," Hemingway continued. "I know how hard it is not to be like everyone at Happily Ever After. I know how it is to be different."

"Why does the headmistress have to spell you to appear like a fairy?" Faraday's question earned a scolding look from Hemingway.

"It's complicated," Hemingway muttered, not looking as though he wanted to answer that.

"Why don't we start with why your mother is haunting the Bewilder Forest at night," Paris stated. "Also, I'm sorry for her death. I'm sure that's difficult."

Hemingway shook his head. "It's not, really. I didn't know her when she was alive." He sucked in a breath, stress edging his eyes. "You see, my mother was a Cinderella that a fairy godmother was charged to match with my father, a supposed Prince Charming. Apparently, everything went fine, and they were married. However, my father never loved my mother. The fairy godmother made a mistake. She matched the wrong man to my mother according to what I've discovered. But the fairy godmothers weren't adaptable then, just as they aren't very much now, although I hope that's changing. Anyway, my mother, believing in her fairy godmother, forced the marriage and became pregnant with me."

Paris gulped, sensing the sad ending that was coming.

"When very pregnant," Hemingway continued, "my mother discovered my father was having an affair with another woman."

"The one she thought was me and wanted to kill," Paris guessed.

He nodded. "My mother being pregnant and heartbroken earned the sympathy of the fairy godmother who had matched her with the wrong man. She brought her here, where she quickly gave birth to me. However, my mother was emotionally destroyed and went out one night, paddled to the middle of Mirror Lake, tied herself to an anchor, and threw it and herself into the water."

Paris gasped. "She drowned herself…"

"Yeah." He shook his head. "She couldn't get over my father or that he didn't want her. As the famous Hemingway said, 'the most painful thing is losing yourself in the process of loving someone too much, and forgetting that you are special too.'"

A chill, as if the ghost was still there, ran down Paris' back. "She's haunted the Bewilder Forest at night ever since?"

Regret filled Hemingway's eyes. "Headmistress Starr could free her. She's offered. Mae Ling has as well. But, I don't know how to let her go."

An ache erupted in Paris' throat. She could relate to Hemingway acutely. How could he want to let go of his mother when he never got to know her alive? Of course, he'd hold onto her ghost, even if she was vengeful and angry. It was all he had of her. Having lost her parents in another dimension, Paris knew that she'd hold onto anything of them that would connect her to them, even if that was their ghosts.

"So after your mother died, the fairy godmothers raised you," Paris guessed.

"Yes," Hemingway affirmed. "My father, who wasn't a good man and didn't love my mother, didn't want anything to do with me. The idea was to raise me until I was of age. Then I could enter the real world. However, when that time came, I asked to stay. Headmistress Starr had kept me a secret from Saint Valentine and the FGM Agency, knowing they wouldn't accept a magician living at the college. They've always thought that I was a fairy. When I came of age and didn't want to leave, she offered to continue to disguise me so I could teach here. So I could stay."

"If anyone ever learned that you were a magician..." Faraday's tone conveyed his question.

Hemingway's eyes widened. "I'd be done. Headmistress Starr would have to get rid of me. A half-fairy at the college has been met with enough push back by the board and FGM Agency and donors. If anyone found out that a magician was on the faculty, well, there'd be no chance I could stay."

"Don't worry, your secret is safe with us," Faraday reassured him.

Hemingway offered a small expression of gratitude.

"So, you've never left here. Other than our trip to LA. You've always been here," Paris stated rather than asked, remembering that he'd admitted as much when they first met. "Why?"

His gaze drifted to the side, shame in his eyes. "The world

outside Happily Ever After College broke my mother." He held his arm out in the direction of the Enchanted Grounds in the distance. "This place is all I've ever known. I can't imagine leaving here. I don't know who I am outside this bubble. The fairy godmothers are loving, for the most part, and my father was horrible. What possible good could come from being a part of a world where people break each other's hearts? I'd much rather be part of the world that mends them."

"But you're hiding," Paris said and instantly felt awful for the judgment. "I'm sorry. I can't imagine what you've been through—"

"No, you're right," Hemingway interrupted. "I'm a coward. The longer I stay here, the harder it is to leave. I've left for special events, but only for a few hours. I can't bring myself to try to live outside of Happily Ever After."

Paris nodded. "I understand. I spent almost all of my life on Roya Lane."

"Because you were spelled and being protected from the Deathly Shadow," he argued.

She nodded. "We all have reasons for staying in the same place. It sounds like you've never been able to be who you truly are. To be a magician, you'll be exposed and have to give up your place here. That can't be easy."

A tender expression crossed Hemingway's face. "It's not easy, but hiding who I am also isn't. I'd like to be a magician, but ironically, then I can't be who I've been."

Something suddenly occurred to Paris and her eyes darted to the bite on Hemingway's arm. "Moira. The mermaid. She didn't bite you because you were feeding her or got too close. It's because you're a magician."

He sucked in a breath and nodded. "Yeah, and I had her put in the lake to discourage anyone from ever drowning themselves in Mirror Lake again."

"Getting eaten alive by a mermaid does seem like a bad death option," Faraday cut in.

Paris lifted her hand without realizing it and rested it on Hemingway's arm. "Thanks for explaining this to me. I'm sorry about your mother. If you need help with any of this, I'm here."

He offered a pained smile. "Thanks. I think at some point, I might take you up on that. I don't know when, but I realize that I have to figure out how to let her go."

CHAPTER THIRTY-FOUR

News Source: The Times

Article Headline: Two Tech Companies Crash and Burn At Once

McGregor Technologies and Rose Industries had recently been neck-and-neck dominating a small sector of the tech business. However, in a strange and ironic turn of events, both companies have taken a sudden downturn as their stocks plummet.

It was recently leaked to the press that products sold by McGregor Technologies were responsible for numerous fires due to faulty wiring. One of these fires burned down a three-story office building. Others have caused thousands of dollars in damages and risked the lives of many.

McGregor Technologies' CEO, Mr. Grayson McGregor, wasn't available to comment on the claims regarding the faulty wiring of the company's products that allegedly caused the fires. However, silence in this incidence isn't golden and has caused many shareholders to sell off their stocks. Meanwhile, customers are erring on the side of caution and voicing hesitancy regarding buying the company's products.

Ironically, McGregor Technology's competition isn't benefiting from their decline. Recent discoveries show that Rose Industries is under citation for numerous dangerous working conditions in their facilities. The tech industry doesn't take these human resources issues lightly, and multiple lawsuits immediately slammed the company.

Rose Industries' CEO, Ms. Amelia Rose, was also unavailable for a comment on the matter, but consumers have an opinion. The current consensus is that shoppers would rather go without than support a company that mistreats employees.

Will these two tech companies weather this storm? Or will they find themselves a casualty, like so many tech niches that didn't do their due diligence before setting up shop? That remains to be seen.

Paris laid down the newspaper that had "magically" made its way to the top of her dresser that morning. She didn't feel good about having Wilfred plant the articles that started the wheels in motion to take down McGregor Technologies and Rose Industries. However, she stood by the plan. The way to get those two together was to ensure they worked together, and the way to do that was to destroy their current companies. Then they'd fall in love and start something better together...that was the hope anyway. Paris hoped it worked.

It was a very risky plan. The headmistress was relying on Paris. She was wagering a lot on a different way of doing things. If this didn't work, not only would the love meter suffer, but Willow would be under fire, and Paris could potentially be tossed out of Happily Ever After College. She was being scrutinized enough for being half-magician. If her plan failed, it would give donors the ammunition they needed to get her kicked out of the school. Paris knew a little about how Hemingway felt. Unlike him, she knew a life outside of Happily Ever After College. Similar to him, she wanted to stay no matter what. This felt like her home, and she didn't want to fail. Which meant she had to hope that the risks she'd taken paid off.

Paris was about to warn Faraday to be good and leave for breakfast when her phone buzzed with a message.

She glanced at it, hoping that it was her Aunt Sophia or Uncle John or anyone but who she realized the message was from.

She liked the person that the message was from but only in small doses. The king of the fae challenged her patience and her brain cells. However, when Paris read the text from King Rudolf Sweetwater, she instantly felt remorse for her judgment. He was in trouble. Or at least one of his daughters was. His message read:

Something has happened to Captain Morgan. Will you meet me at Heals Pills on Roya Lane? Then we'll go to the Fantastical Armory. Papa Creola has information.

Paris didn't issue a warning to Faraday to behave after reading the message. She hoped that the talking squirrel knew not to investigate things that he shouldn't after the night before. Even if he did, she was okay with it. They wouldn't have learned Hemingway's history if Faraday hadn't gone into the Bewilder Forest, and for some reason, it was meaningful to Paris.

She waved to the squirrel, hurried out the door, and headed for the Enchanted Grounds where she could open a portal to Roya Lane, the protective charm securely fastened around her neck along with the heart-shaped locket.

CHAPTER THIRTY-FIVE

One thing was certain a few moments after Paris had been on Roya Lane: the Deathly Shadow knew she was there.

The wind ripped through her hair and clothes, trying to yank the protective charm from around her neck.

I'm so done with wind, she thought, holding the protective charm and heart-shaped locket in her grasp as she ran through the cobbled streets. Paris veered around vendors and slow walkers with apparently nowhere to be, making haste to get to Heals Pills. She'd been by the shop hundreds of times, but for some reason, hadn't gone in there.

On her first time into the small shop, Paris burst through the door and slammed it behind her, pressing her back against it, nearly out of breath.

King Rudolf Sweetwater and another man glanced up from the register at the sight of her, curiosity on their faces. Thankfully the shop was empty. Even better, the Deathly Shadow didn't seem to have followed her inside, although she saw the violent wind whipping around Roya Lane, making magicians' hair fly into their faces, lifting skirts, and knocking over small carts.

Paris spun after checking the streets and sucked in a breath. "I was being followed by the Deathly Shadow."

The fae rushed over, looking out the glass at Roya Lane. "Did he have my daughter with him?"

Paris squinted at him, wondering if he was serious. "The Deathly Shadow doesn't have a body and currently is taking the form of invisible wind."

King Rudolf gave her a confused look. "Does that mean no? Remember, she's about this high." He held his hand up to his shoulder. "And she's gorgeous and really spoiled."

"If the Deathly Shadow had her, I didn't see, but I'm going to say no," Paris confirmed.

The fae nodded. "Yeah, I didn't think it would be that easy to find Captain Morgan, although according to Papa Creola, it's pretty certain that the Deathly Shadow has her."

"Why?" Paris instantly felt remorse for the king of the fae. It must be awful to have one of your children taken.

He pulled his phone from his pocket. "Well, I got this message from Captain Morgan before her phone stopped working." After scrolling through a few screens, he showed it to her. The message said, "Dad, this windy thing that makes me sad took me and is holding me prisoner. He keeps saying something about halflings and is the angry type. I'm in a cold warehouse that's worse than that one time I had to stay in a motel because I was trying to make it on my own. Find me. Hurry. I have a spray tan tomorrow."

Paris glanced up, her heart beating fast. "Why would he take her? He wants me."

"That was my question," King Rudolf said. "I was going to offer you in return, but when I tried calling Captain Morgan, her phone went straight to voicemail so she either dropped it in the toilet again or the Deathly Shadow realized she had it and confiscated it."

"Good to know I was a bartering chip for you," Paris said dryly.

"You're welcome."

"Don't you think that the Deathly Shadow allowed her to keep her phone until she sent the message?" Paris asked.

King Rudolf scratched his head while thinking it over. "That makes sense. I wondered why this evil and powerful entity who could trap my daughter—who has escaped from the mafia, like, three times—forgot about the cell phone."

"Do you think he knew that you'd tell me and I'd use this as an opportunity to track him down and fight him? And that's also why the Deathly Shadow was stationed on Roya Lane, seemingly waiting for me?" Paris asked. "I mean, the only way to get my parents back is to face the Deathly Shadow. He must know I'll want to track him down at some point, but he's trying to steal the advantage by taking Captain Morgan."

"That's weird," King Rudolf said. "That's what Papa Creola said, followed by 'why else would anyone annoy themselves by listening to Captain Morgan explaining the last ten seasons of Big Brother otherwise.'"

"Do you think that's what she's doing?" Paris had to ask. "Do you think she's talking to her captor?"

"Well, not right now." Rudolf pointed out to Roya Lane. "I mean, the Deathly Shadow is here, but don't worry, he can't get in here. There are similar wards on Heals Pills as Crying Cat Bakery. As long as you stay in here, you're safe."

"Cool," Paris chirped, annoyed. "The only problem is that you said we needed to go and see Papa Creola for further information at the Fantastical Armory. Oh, and there's that whole thing where I can't live the rest of my life here."

King Rudolf nodded. "Yeah, the lighting in this place isn't the best. You'd definitely get tired of this space after a year or so."

Paris refrained from rolling her eyes. "I hope that Captain Morgan is okay. We need to get to Papa Creola so we can figure out the next step. The Deathly Shadow is prowling the streets of Roya Lane, has your daughter, and we need to stop him, but we currently don't have any of the advantages. We need Father Time's help. How do we get to the Fantastical Amory with that angry entity waiting outside?"

The guy who had been quietly hanging out by the cash register strode over. "I think that's where I can help. My name is Ramy Vance, and I'll happily die today for this cause."

CHAPTER THIRTY-SIX

"Wow, thank you, but that's not necessary." Paris' eyes were wide as she took in the guy before her, offering to die to help her. He appeared normal with short curly brown hair and an honest face, but she hadn't met anyone who would make such a strange offer.

"No, it's totally necessary," King Rudolf said. "Yes, this is how you'll die today."

Paris shook her head adamantly. "No, I'm sure we can get to Papa Creola some other way."

"It's fine," the fae argued. "Ramy wants to do it."

The strange guy nodded. "Yeah, I want to do it."

Paris gulped. "What the hell do you sell here? Hallucinogens? Are you both taking them?"

"Yes," Rudolf answered at the same time that Ramy said, "No."

"This is Heals Pills," the king of the fae explained. "We sell an elixir made from dragon eggshells. I started it with your Aunt Sophia. Ramy here is our only store clerk, and he fell into the fountain of youth—"

Paris rubbed her hands over her temples. "Please tell me we're not playing the two truths and a lie game?"

"These are all truths," King Rudolf stated. "Anyway, Ramy can't die so—"

"Easily," Ramy interrupted, holding up a finger.

"Easily," the fae repeated. "Anyway, he can be killed and often is because part of the payment for him not being able to die easily is that he's accident-prone."

"How often do you die?" Paris blinked at the guy.

"Ten to twelve times," Ramy answered.

"A year?" Paris questioned, shocked.

"A day," he corrected.

Paris could only imagine how shocked she looked right then. "I'm sorry, this is the most bizarre thing I've ever heard of."

"That's the most bizarre thing?" King Rudolf asked. "Wow, I've got some stories for you. I mean, I can top that with some tales from a single week I spent in Cabo San Lucas."

"Please don't," Paris begged.

"Anyway, it sounds like you need a diversion to make it down to the Fantastical Armory," Ramy said to her. "So how about I put on a disguise that looks like you and stride out the opposite way down Roya Lane? That mean wind thing will follow me. Kill me. Meanwhile, you can get down to Papa Creola."

"Wow, are you serious?" Paris asked. "That would be amazing."

Ramy grinned proudly. "I'm happy to help. I hear you're pretty important and that if the Deathly Shadow gets you, we're all screwed."

"Yeah, it's going to be like that one time I had to go bowling because I lost a bet with a gnome," King Rudolf offered. "My hands felt greasy for a whole week."

Paris shook her head at him. "I think Ramy was referring to lights out for the world if the Deathly Shadow got a body and killed Father Time."

"Well, that would be sucky too," Rudolf agreed. "But seriously, have you ever been bowling? It's the grossest sport ever. The only thing worse than that is the knowledge that people eat chili cheese fries between frames. Like, do these weirdos not care about their lives and cleanliness?"

Paris stared at the fae for a long moment, trying to figure out if he was serious or not. Deciding not to give him any more attention, she turned her focus to Ramy. "I appreciate your help. I have to ask. If you can't be killed—"

"Easily," Ramy interrupted.

"Right," she said at once. "If you can't die easily, why don't you work somewhere that better utilizes your talents? Or use your lives to save the world? Or I don't know, do something really big?"

"Well, this shop saves lives every day," Ramy said proudly. "Heals Pills is a miracle drug. Because of that, the shop is constantly under threat. I die regularly having to defend it."

"Wow." Paris was shocked.

"Yeah, and I've been a bodyguard to the very best actors," Ramy said. "I've done lots of things. Although I could use my lives to save the world, unfortunately, when I've tried, I've made things worse. So this is a good intermediate position for my talents."

Rudolf nodded. "Ramy-Cans is right. He's a walking accident. Anywhere he goes, he creates problems. Send him in to disarm nuclear weapons, and he'll blow up the world. He's best doing lower-level jobs."

"Are you sure that being a diversion will be okay?" Paris was suddenly nervous about the plan.

"Yeah," Ramy answered. "All I have to do is look like you, run out of the shop the opposite way you have to go and die. Now, if there were one more part of the equation, I'd say you couldn't rely on me. Dress up as a girl, make an angry man chase me, and die? Well, I can do that all day long."

"And you'll come back?" Paris worried she was asking too much of this guy she'd just met.

He nodded. "For sure. I'll be back in time for the afternoon shift."

"Good, because you need to put away that new shipment," King Rudolf stated.

"You could add a please to that," Paris scolded.

"Right," the fae said. "Because I'd be pleased if you put away that new shipment. Right away. As soon as you awake from dying. No breaks. Okay." He turned to Paris. "How was that?"

She shook her head. "We have Captain Morgan to rescue. The Deathly Shadow for me to defeat. My parents who I need to get back. Let's get on with this. Thanks for your help, Ramy."

He winked at her. "I look forward to dying over and over again for you, Paris Beaufont, who I've seen many times on Roya Lane but couldn't speak to until now."

CHAPTER THIRTY-SEVEN

"Wow, I have..." Ramy's mouth popped open as he patted his chest after taking on the same appearance as Paris.

"Take your hands off my chest...your chest," she scolded.

His face flushed pink. "Sorry. I just don't get the opportunity to feel—"

"Please don't finish that sentence." Paris thought of plugging her ears.

Ramy grinned at Rudolf. "I like her. She's polite."

"She told you not to talk about your lack of game," King Rudolf stated.

"But she said please." Ramy held up one finger.

It unnerved Paris to see an exact duplicate of herself talking in front of her. However, she reasoned that if it were spooky to her, it would work to fool the Deathly Shadow. It wouldn't work for long, but hopefully long enough to give her and King Rudolf a chance to escape the shop and get down Roya Lane to the Fantastical Armory. It saddened her that Ramy would have to suffer and die for it, but he seemed happy to help.

"Okay." Ramy peered out the shop's front window. "When you two are ready."

"Ramy-Cans," King Rudolf began, putting his hand on the guy's shoulder. "You know that I'm very fond of you. You've worked for me for twenty years and helped to grow Heals Pills to the empire that it is. The company wouldn't be what it is without you. But so help me, if you screw this up, I will find a way to kill you for good."

Paris was about to scold her pseudo-uncle, but Ramy held up his hands as if in surrender. "I promise not to. I won't trip on the pavement and die prematurely. I won't get struck by random lightning although there isn't a cloud in the sky. I won't, yet again, get hit by a wrecking ball although there doesn't appear to be any demolition sites anywhere."

Rudolf gave him a stern expression. "You better not. You have one job and a very easy one. Run out of here the opposite way of the shop that we need to reach and let a deadly and evil entity murder you in the streets. It's not that hard. Don't mess it up."

Ramy nodded. "I'll try and make you proud." He glanced at Paris. "I hope to see you again soon. After I come back to life again."

Paris smiled. "Thanks for your help, Ramy."

Without another word, the guy who looked like Paris sprinted out of Heals Pills. She and Rudolf waited for a moment, but the clues that the Deathly Shadow had taken the bait were immediately apparent as a gust of wind streaked after the doppelgänger, sending newspapers and debris in all directions, knocking down people and creating havoc as it streaked after Ramy.

Paris felt bad for the guy who would no doubt feel pain from the weird death, but she shook that off when King Rudolf grabbed her hand and yanked her out the door and down Roya Lane.

CHAPTER THIRTY-EIGHT

Paris and King Rudolf didn't stop running until they burst into the Fantastical Armory. Although Paris wanted to believe that maybe the Deathly Shadow didn't do anything painful to Ramy, the screams behind her told her otherwise. He wouldn't have a protective charm and would be easy pickings for the evil entity. However, she relished the fact that they'd deceived the soulless monster.

Subner glanced up unhurriedly from his book when the pair burst into the shop. Papa Creola's assistant was sitting in the same spot behind the counter in the strange store when Paris and Rudolf entered. He'd pulled back his greasy black hair, and he wore the same scowl as before.

"Oh, I thought there was at least one distinct way my day could get worse." Subner blew out a sigh of frustration. "I should have realized there were two."

"Good to see you too, Sub," Rudolf chirped and glanced over his shoulder, checking the streets. It didn't appear they'd been followed. "How long has it been?"

"Not long enough," Subner answered.

"So he doesn't like you either," Paris said to the king.

"Subner loves me," Rudolf stated.

"You're the third-worst person on Mama Jamba's planet," Subner explained.

Rudolf flashed a proud grin. "See there? I beat out two horrible people. I can only imagine the losers who you loathe more than me."

"One of them is standing right next to you," Subner explained. "The first one spawned that halfling."

Paris rolled her eyes, then directed her gaze at Rudolf. "If you're wondering what I did to deserve such disdain, I have no clue."

"You were born," Subner grumbled.

"Well, I'm so sorry for my existence," Paris said.

"I don't think you really mean that," the elf stated dryly. "If you do and you want to do this world a favor, you should off yourself. Then the Deathly Shadow can't absorb you, get more powerful, and come after Papa Creola. That's the easiest solution to all our problems."

"He makes an excellent point," King Rudolf mused.

Paris' eyes widened with horror. "I'm not offing myself. That's not the solution. And we need to get Captain Morgan back. Aren't you worried about her?"

The fae shrugged. "Honestly, I bet the Deathly Shadow came to Roya Lane to get away from her. That girl can nag someone enough that they'd want to kill themselves."

"Sounds like the Captain and Paris need to spend a lot of time together," Subner offered, his eyes back on his book.

"Do you have to be here?" Paris asked.

"It's my shop, so yes," the elf answered.

Papa Creola strode through the door at the back of the shop, not surprised to find Paris and Rudolf standing inside the entrance. "Paris isn't killing herself to solve the Deathly Shadow problem. Mama Jamba wants her for things."

"What things?" Paris looked the father of time over. As before, he was in elf form and wearing hippie-type clothes—frayed jean shorts and a t-shirt that said, "If we all had a bong, we'd all get along."

"Things," Papa Creola repeated. "Captain Morgan is fine, although she's complaining incessantly about how the humidity is messing up her hair."

"Oh, I would be complaining too," Rudolf stated. "Where is she being held?"

Papa Creola shrugged. "I have no clue. It's your job to track down your daughter, now isn't it?"

"You know that Captain Morgan is okay, but you don't know where she is?" Paris questioned.

"You know how to put on your shoes, but I bet you don't know how to make them," Papa Creola countered. "There are always holes in knowledge. I can only see so much. Besides, part of this is you all figuring out where the halfling is ."

"Then we go and rescue her," Paris added.

Papa Creola shook his head. "No, that's exactly what the Deathly Shadow wants. He abducted Captain Morgan knowing there was a certain someone who would feel responsible for this and come to her rescue."

"Well, it is my fault," Paris argued. "The Deathly Shadow wants me. He's trying to draw me out and wouldn't have taken Captain Morgan if not for me."

"Sounds like you should off yourself and make everyone's life easier," Subner offered, indicating the many cases filled with swords and knives. "I can pick out a weapon for the job."

Papa Creola ignored his assistant. "I believe that the Deathly Shadow thinks you'll come after Captain Morgan. By allowing her to send that text message, he's made it possible for you to find him. At first, I thought he was rusty, but now it all makes sense. He's orchestrated this whole thing to trap you. The Deathly Shadow is betting on you, Paris, coming after Captain Morgan. That's when he'll make his final move. We must turn the tables on him and do things on our terms, or once again he'll have the upper hand and probably succeed this time."

"So you don't want us to go after Captain Morgan?" Paris asked.

"I don't want *you* to," Papa Creola answered. "She is her father's responsibility."

King Rudolf drew in a breath, looking defeated. "I don't know how to find her. I mean, if Saks Fifth Avenue isn't releasing this season's designer bags, I have no idea how to locate my daughter."

"Maybe the solution is to kill myself," Subner muttered, looking around at the wall of weapons as if searching for the right one.

"You know that you can't be killed." Papa Creola sighed.

Something suddenly occurred to Paris and she turned to King Rudolf. "The text message that Captain Morgan sent. It should give us a rough idea of her location if we reverse the magitech in your phone."

The fae retrieved the phone from his pocket and eyed it. "Can I find that option in the app store?"

Paris shook her head. "Take the phone to Uncle John at FLEA down the street. He should be able to find the information for you."

Papa Creola nodded. "That should get you an approximate location, but from there you'll have to do more investigating to find the Captain's exact location."

"Then I go after her," King Rudolf stated victoriously.

"No, then you have to wait," Papa Creola declared.

"But she has a spray tan appointment tomorrow," King Rudolf argued. "When that fades, well, she looks as white as a seagull and squawks loudly about it like one."

Father Time gave Paris a sturdy expression. "The timing of this has to be right. You can't face the Deathly Shadow until everything is in place."

"What do I need to do?" Paris asked.

"You'll need to lure him away from his location," Papa Creola explained. "He's picked it because it offers an advantage, so we have to turn the tables."

"Like when he tricked my parents into going through the vortex," Paris guessed.

"That's right," he affirmed. "The way to destroy the Deathly Shadow isn't complicated. It's the exact thing inside you that you'll have to use to overpower him. That's why ironically, the one he's wanted to recover is the only one who has ever had the chance of ending his reign."

"That all sounds very abstract." Paris suddenly felt defeated. "How do I use my inner strength to overpower him?"

"You'll figure it out," Papa Creola said matter-of-factly.

Paris slumped, realizing that she should have expected this answer but wishing that he had offered something—anything that helped.

"I can tell you that you're going to need something special to contain the Deathly Shadow," Papa Creola continued. "Unfortunately, because of what he did to himself, he can't really die. So your job will be to overpower him finally and put him in something that locks him away for eternity."

"What is this container?" Paris asked.

King Rudolf sighed. "I don't know, but when you find out, let's put the 1980s in there. That fashion and music don't ever need to come back."

"Only one person can make this container," Papa Creola explained.

Paris nodded and rolled her eyes. "That seems about right. Let me guess, they won't want to help me, and I'll have to defeat some monster to get them to do it?"

Subner started suddenly, looking like he'd awoken from a nightmare. He glanced around and sighed. "Oh, for a moment I thought Liv was here. Turns out that it's her daughter and she's inherited her tendency toward sarcasm."

"Actually," Papa Creola began, his focus still on Paris. "They'll want to help because they were one of your mother's closest friends."

King Rudolf pressed his hands to his chest. "I'm the one who has to make the container."

Papa Creola shook his head. "No, it's Rory Laurens."

"Rory Laurens, as in he might be related to Bermuda Laurens?" Paris asked. "I was going to seek her out for something."

Papa Creola pointed at Paris' pocket where her phone was. "The timing might seem perfect since Sophia messaged you about a meeting she set up for you with the author of *Magical Creatures*."

"Spoiler alert," Subner muttered. "He planned the timing."

Paris retrieved her phone from her pocket and saw a message from Sophia about a meeting she'd set up. "So I meet with Bermuda, and she'll help me find Rory?"

"Or I hand you a crossbow and we all leave you to do the right thing," Subner offered.

"If I were going to kill myself in your shop, I'd do it as messy as I could and get blood everywhere," Paris teased.

The elf shrugged. "I need to get new carpet anyway."

"Once Rory has made the container, then we can proceed to the showdown," Papa Creola explained. "In the meantime, King Rudolf, find your daughter's location. I'll work on finding the right place for the confrontation. That will be important. We must figure out how to draw the Deathly Shadow to us. More important than any of that is we need something that uses the container and the power of the Deathly Shadow to reopen the vortex he created fifteen years ago. He's the only one who can, and we'll only have one chance."

Paris thought for a moment. "Well, we'd use the Deathly Shadow's energy to pin down the right location of the other dimension. Then we need something to anchor onto that and open a vortex. It seems as though there's some magitech that we could use for such things."

"Good." Papa Creola sighed. "I hoped it wouldn't take you long to figure that out."

Paris laughed at this. "Or you could have simply told me."

"I can't," he argued.

"Because like Mama Jamba you're trying to empower me," Paris guessed.

He shook his head. "I'm not wired to be overly helpful. It gives me hives."

Another chuckle fell from her mouth. "You gods are so strange."

"Okay, we all know what to do." Papa Creola created a shimmering blue and green portal in front of Paris. "This will lead you to Bermuda Laurens, who is waiting for you. Be careful. Get everything ready as quickly as you can. This is finally our chance to defeat the Deathly Shadow, but we have to prepare perfectly."

CHAPTER THIRTY-NINE

The portal spat Paris out onto a beautiful green plain with rolling hills and trees every so often. It unmistakably smelled like a farm.

Paris glanced down at her boots to ensure she wasn't standing in the middle of a patty of cow waste. Thankfully she wasn't, but the odor was still all around her.

After nearly being trampled by a horse recently, Paris tensed when a large creature thundered in her direction from across the grassy hills. Well, it didn't thunder like a stallion. Instead, the wide animal with long hair trotted toward her, swaying from side to side. What was stranger than the beast that looked ready to slowly mow Paris down was the tower of giraffes that ambled toward her behind the creature.

Paris didn't feel that she was in any immediate danger of getting trampled until she turned to look over her shoulder and saw the biggest person she'd ever seen. Paris had seen many giants on Roya Lane. They had the worst tempers and thought they could bully easily due to their size. The giantess who strode across the green grass in Paris' direction was larger than the others, making them look like dwarfs of the species.

The giants on Roya Lane were usually about six-and-a-half feet tall. The rumor was that they were halflings of sorts because real giants would never live in actual society. The "real giants" all lived on the Isle of Man apparently, and they were huge. The one approaching had to be at least seven feet tall, and although she wore an olive green safari suit and hat, she didn't appear to be a welcoming tour guide based on the scowl on her face.

Paris glanced over her shoulder to find that the giraffes and the yak in the lead had paused. She glanced back to see the giantess had halted a few paces from Paris.

"You look like your mother, Guinevere," the woman said after measuring Paris up. "Let's hope for both our sakes that you don't act like her."

CHAPTER FORTY

"You're Bermuda Laurens?" Paris studied the giantess. She appeared both approachable and menacing. It was a weird combination. Paris expected her to try and eat her and bake her an apple pie at the same time.

"The one and only." She glanced over Paris' head to the tower of giraffes and the strange yak trotting along. "You're Guinevere Beaufont, the halfling who is both unique and rare in her combination and also desirability."

"I prefer to go by Paris," she muttered dryly.

"Then you accept this fate that you've received?"

"You mean the whole being rare and therefore hunted?" Paris shrugged. "Yeah, sure. Does that mean the rumors are true, and I'm the only fairy and magician ever to be born?"

"As far as I'm aware, you're the only creature with two magical species to ever exist," Bermuda stated stoically. "Mortals have been able to breed with giants, gnomes, and many others. It isn't easy, the more advanced the magical creature, like fae but—"

Paris laughed. "Fae advanced? Do you mean in abilities to make me want to kill them?"

"You are like your mother," Bermuda said flatly. "Although fae can be considered quite irritating in their behavior, they're also very powerful and one of the longest-living magical creatures on the planet. So yes, they're considered advanced."

"I'm the only halfling with two magical species?" Paris asked. "That's so bizarre."

"Well, you're not a result of science, as you know," Bermuda stated.

"No, I'm the result of a genie's sick joke," Paris muttered.

"Regardless, you exist, and you're unique." The giantess regarded her with new interest. "Really, you'd be quite fascinating to study. When analyzing a problem, do you consider how you feel about it or how you think about it first?"

"I don't know," Paris said honestly.

"When you have a decision, do you prefer the easy option even if it's less desirable or the harder one that will be more advantageous?" Bermuda asked.

"Strangely enough, I haven't done a lot of self-reflection in that regard," Paris answered. "I'm still getting used to the idea that I'm a halfling."

"Self-awareness is the first step to discovery."

"Right." Paris drew out the word. "I was here because—"

Something nibbling on her shoulder cut Paris off. She looked up and started to find the yak chewing on her jacket. She spun and was further surprised to see the tower of giraffes all gathered there, staring down at her with mild interest.

"It's not a surprise that Nevin came to you," Bermuda said.

"Nevin?" Paris asked. "Who is Nevin?"

"He's the yak." Bermuda leaned forward, closer to Paris. "He thinks he's a giraffe and isn't ready to face the truth, so don't tell him."

"Did you just tell him?" Paris looked between the yak and the giraffes, noting the obvious differences. "Can't he simply see that he's different?"

"He can't speak English."

"Well, I won't tell him since I can't speak yak." Paris stepped to the side, out of Nevin's reach.

"You might be able to. Have you tried?" Bermuda asked.

Paris shook her head, wondering if all her mother's friends were strange. She had a feeling that they were.

Bermuda blinked at her, annoyance in her gaze. "No, Nevin can't see the differences between him and the giraffes. Could you see how different you were from fairies before you knew you weren't one completely?"

"I am one," Paris argued. "I'm half."

"You're technically a magician because both your parents were," Bermuda stated. "But due to magic, you are half-fairy."

"Technicalities rule the world," Paris joked, not earning a reaction from Bermuda.

"Nevin thinks he's a giraffe," Bermuda explained. "He hangs with them instead of his own, like you. Even if he were to look in a mirror, he'd see himself as a giraffe, picking out those qualities he shares rather than his differences."

"Like the ears?" Paris teased, not finding any similarities between the large and fat gray beast and the tall brown and white giraffes.

"Like the personalities," Bermuda corrected. "There's a lot more to appearances than the way things look."

"Here I've had it wrong my entire life," Paris quipped.

"You didn't come here to study safari animals, I'm guessing," Bermuda snapped her fingers, and a large bag of feed materialized in one of her arms and a couple of containers in her other hand. She pushed one of the cups into Paris' hand. "I'm guessing that you've come to take knowledge from me like your mother. Magicians are always after information."

"An unruly bunch we are," Paris joked and sighed, looking at the empty cup.

Bermuda shook her head, not at all impressed. "Well, if you're going to learn anything from me, you'll do it while earning your keep."

"You're feeding me to the lions then?"

The giantess shook her head. "You're going to feed the animals."

CHAPTER FORTY-ONE

Bermuda Laurens plunged the second cup into the bag and held it out for Paris to take. She did, exchanging it for the empty one.

Immediately, the closest giraffe was her best friend sticking its mouth into the cup and nibbling on the pellets of food. It ate in quite the civilized manner, not at all forceful.

"They're so peaceful," Paris observed, never having been this close to such large animals and surprised that they didn't intimidate her. The giraffes lined up for their food and patiently waited their turn. She had expected to feel as if she was about to be trampled by the tallest animals in the world, as with the stallion at Happily Ever After College, but she didn't.

"That's because they aren't normal giraffes." Bermuda tossed out the food for the others to eat off the ground. "They're magical and known as peace giraffes."

"Because they make those around them calm," Paris guessed, definitely feeling relaxed and in a very noticeable way from before.

"Exactly," Bermuda affirmed. "They're great to have at mental hospitals and other places where stress and anxiety can be high."

"How can I get a support peace giraffe?" Paris asked.

"Do you have a million dollars?"

She shook her head. "I don't have a hundred dollars."

"Then you're not getting one." Bermuda tossed out more food. "The price of the animal isn't the only challenge. They also eat about seventy-five pounds of food a day."

Paris glanced at the large bag of feed, which was already half-empty from the giantess spreading it over the grass. "I hope you brought more food."

"I'll conjure more when we walk over to the other animals," Bermuda stated.

Paris refilled her cup, holding it out for Nevin.

"He won't eat from someone's hand," Bermuda explained. "You're better off throwing it out for him."

"What's his magical power?" Paris asked.

"He thinks he's a giraffe," Bermuda muttered.

"So an identity crisis is a magical power now, is it?"

"Of course. Believing you're something that you're not takes extraordinary abilities."

Paris shook her head, realizing that she had a lot to learn. The giraffes and Nevin had made quick work of the bag of feed, and when it was empty, they immediately became less interested in Paris, trotting off in the opposite direction.

Bermuda summoned another couple of bags that she set at her feet. Not seeing any animals nearby, Paris squinted into the distance where there were rows of trees, all of their low branches trimmed by the tall giraffes. She felt as though she was on the African plains and definitely could have been since Papa Creola had created the portal that brought her there.

"Where are the other animals to feed?" Paris questioned.

"They're coming." Bermuda held her chin high with a neutral expression. She had a broad face and prominent features. Paris thought that if she smiled, she might be pretty, but she was starting to get the impression that the giantess wasn't the smiling type.

"Are you going to ask me your questions now or are you still working up the nerve?"

"I'm not nervous about my questions," Paris protested, somewhat offended.

"Well, you did have the peace giraffes around you, but I sense your hesitation," Bermuda stated. "My guess is you're here because someone told you to seek out my expertise, but you're not sure you want to."

Paris stuck her hands on her hips. "Actually, two people did. One of them was Papa Creola so you can tell me where to find your son, and he can help me defeat the Deathly Shadow and hopefully get to live my life without fear. There's no hesitancy there."

"No one lives without fear," Bermuda chimed.

Paris suddenly realized that the Deathly Shadow might be able to track her down there, wherever they were, and searched the plains for wind. The stress she almost always felt when outside Happily Ever After College and potentially being hunted returned. The peace giraffes had made her feel better, and she suddenly wished they were still close by.

"You're safe at this park," Bermuda remarked, having sensed her sudden tension. "The protective longhorns keep this place safe from evil with their magic."

"Oh, well, they sound as helpful as the peace giraffes. Maybe I can take one of those with me unless they're a million dollars too."

"They aren't," Bermuda chirped. "But their horns are on average five feet long and can span up to ten feet from point to point, and they're dangerously clumsy with them."

"Oh, well, never mind then. I hope they keep their distance."

"They won't," Bermuda said. "It's their feeding time. Here they come now." She pointed in the opposite direction of where Paris faced, and the half-magician turned to see the most intimidating animals barreling in her direction.

CHAPTER FORTY-TWO

The protective longhorns were massive—and there were a lot of them. The reddish cattle with white spots had the largest horns Paris had ever seen, although she hadn't been around many horned animals. Attached to either side of their heads were thick, pointy horns that stretched out and up.

Paris immediately knew what Bermuda meant about them being clumsy with their horns. As they thundered in their direction, in proximity to each other, their horns banged into each other's making a *clicking* sound.

For a moment, Paris considered taking shelter behind the giantess, but that seemed like the cowardly thing to do.

"Ummm...any advice for dealing with these guys who have clearance issues?" Paris asked Bermuda, watching as the protective longhorns approached at a rapid trot.

"They're extremely gentle," Bermuda answered. "If they poke your eye out with their horn, it's not because they meant to. Hold out the cup of feed and pour it into their mouths."

"That doesn't make me feel much better that they're well-intentioned," Paris quipped, filling her cup and holding it as far from her as she could.

"Well, if it makes you feel any better, they won't be here long." Bermuda indicated something farther away behind the herd of longhorns. "The bison are on their way, and they always run the protective longhorn off."

"Because…" Paris dared to ask.

"Because they're so much bigger," Bermuda said matter-of-factly.

"You don't sugar-coat things, do you?" Paris deadpanned as the first of the protective longhorns approached, their hooves kicking up dirt. Since Paris wasn't as tall as Bermuda, she couldn't see the approaching bison in the distance, but she had enough to fill her attention.

The protective longhorn did seem somewhat civilized, stopping a safe distance from Paris and holding their mouths open for her to feed them. They stretched out their long tongues, and as though using them as fingers, it curved back around and pointed at their mouths as if they were saying, "Put the food in my pie hole, please."

Paris found herself giggling as she emptied a cup of food into one of their mouths. He backed up and chewed, making way for the next one as she refilled her cup. Paris was constantly aware of the long horns that rattled around her head as she leaned over. However, when one came close to her, she pressed the side of the steer's face, and it got the hint and backed up.

"So you said that two people told you to search me out," Bermuda began, making quick work of feeding the longhorns. "Who was the second?"

Paris was slimed many times by the snotty noses of the cows as they jostled for food. "That's way gross," she remarked, sliding her hand covered in snot down her pants.

"If you touch one of their tongues with your finger, it gives your entire family seven years of good luck," Bermuda explained.

Paris eyed the pink curvy tongues all around her as the animals encouraged her to feed them. Sighing, Paris decided that it couldn't hurt. After everything her family had been through, they could use the extra good luck.

After emptying a cup into a protective longhorn's mouth, she quickly touched the long tongue and shrank away to refill her container.

"The other person told me to find you because you might know something about my friend." Paris laughed at the longhorns that were all standing around her with their mouths open.

"That's the part you're hesitant about," Bermuda guessed.

"No, I'm not as concerned about my friend as other people. I trust him," Paris explained.

"What's wrong with this creature?" Bermuda asked.

Paris was surprised when the longhorns backed up, looking over their shoulder. She guessed that meant the bison were coming. "There's nothing wrong with him. He's really smart and talkative."

"And?" Bermuda questioned.

"He's a squirrel," Paris muttered.

The giantess nodded as though she'd expected this. "Animals shouldn't be able to talk. There's strong magic at work if they can."

"That's what my other friend said who told me to consult with you on this," Paris explained. "But Faraday, the squirrel, said it was a spell and that he's always been curious, soaking up knowledge and enjoying learning about science."

"Squirrels don't talk and aren't interested in science," Bermuda said plainly. "Are you sure that Faraday is a squirrel?"

"Well, he has a tail and looks like one."

"I know a cat that looks like one, but he's actually a lynx and can talk," Bermuda stated. "He can't be trusted. Lynx are notorious for being secret-keepers."

Paris gulped, wishing she had an animal to feed, but all the protective longhorns had moved on. In the distance, she spied the huge dark bison approaching, their faces large but thankfully their horns much smaller. After feeding the longhorns, she found she wasn't as nervous about the bison. Instead, she filled up her cup, ready to feed them. "What's magical about the bison?"

"Nothing. Sometimes things are what they are."

Similar to the protective longhorns, the bison didn't try to trample Paris. She guessed that they reasoned if they did, they wouldn't get fed. They circled her and the giantess, their mouths open and an insistence to be fed heavy in their dark eyes.

"I've also known a talking alligator named Smeg," Bermuda continued.

"What's wrong with him?" Paris asked.

The giantess shook her head. "Nothing. All the lizards related to Godzilla can speak. He just is never quiet and makes fishing really difficult."

"Maybe you should stop inviting him on these fishing trips," Paris offered.

Unimpressed, Bermuda pursed her lips. "I never invite him. He always seems to show up."

"There's nothing wrong with this Smeg, so maybe there's nothing nefarious about Faraday," Paris reasoned. "Maybe he's related to Rocky or Slappy the squirrels."

"I don't know them," Bermuda said.

Paris emptied another container of food into a bison's mouth. "They're cartoons."

"Then I don't think that's why Faraday can talk," the giantess said quite seriously. "My advice to you would be to be leery of a squirrel who can. Yes, someone could have used a spell, but it would have to be incredibly powerful. Then I'd expect him to talk like a squirrel, which means he'd be interested in gathering nuts and not science."

"Faraday is allergic to nuts."

Bermuda side-eyed Paris. "That's even more reason to be suspicious. Squirrels are supposed to eat nuts."

"Fairies are supposed to be obsessed with romance," Paris argued. "I'm not."

"That's because you're half-magician."

"I'm just saying, there are exceptions to every rule," Paris countered.

"Then you need to find out what this exception is that makes your friend not behave like a squirrel." Bermuda finished off the last of the feed, and the bison were immediately disinterested in them.

Before they could trot off, the same as the other animals, Paris patted one of the largest bison on the head, finding that she wasn't as intimidated by them anymore.

"That's Mike Bison." Bermuda indicated the one she was petting. "He has an anger management problem, so I'd be careful."

Paris pulled her hand back at once. "Kind of like the boxer he's named for."

"Boxer?" Bermuda asked. "He was named after his father, not a boxer."

"Oh." With the bison having moved off, Paris noticed some elegant gazelles approaching. She glanced down at the empty feed bag. "Looks like we need more food."

Bermuda shook her head. "We don't feed the thieving gazelles. They prefer to steal their food and just about everything else."

"They're thieves?" Paris was fascinated by all the strange attributes of these magical animals.

"Yes, so hold onto anything you don't want taken."

Paris' hand instinctively went to her protective charm and the heart-shaped locket, both fastened around her neck.

"You can find my son, Rory, in Los Angeles. I'll give you the address, and you can open up a portal in a moment, as soon as this lot passes. We wouldn't want one slipping through the portal. They'd steal everything in a one-mile radius that they could before someone properly stopped them." Bermuda indicated the thieving gazelles as they passed, a shifty look in their eyes. "I'll warn you that Rory should be very busy right now. It's April fifteenth, and that's his busiest day of the year."

"He's an accountant?" Paris was shocked that a giant who was the only person to forge a container to hold the Deathly Shadow was an accountant.

"He used to be," Bermuda answered. "He still does taxes for his friends. Now he's wasting his life away writing books."

"Don't you write books?" Paris questioned. "You're the author of *Magical Creatures*."

She grimaced. "My son writes about things that aren't real and haven't happened."

"You mean fiction?"

Bermuda nodded. "It's a wonder why people would use their time reading that stuff when there are books about real things and places to educate them."

"Yeah, or books on tax codes," Paris joked.

The giantess shook her head, a look of disapproval on her face. "That sounds like something your mother would have said."

"Did you not much like her either, like Subner?"

"Liv was hardly ever serious, overly employed sarcasm as a form of communication, and never brushed her hair," Bermuda stated.

"Oh, well…" Paris didn't know what to say about all that. It pretty much sounded like her.

"She was also the bravest warrior I've met and the reason that magic still exists," Bermuda said in a low voice. "When you meet her again, and I hope you do, don't ever tell her I said that first bit about her. She'd surely throw it in my face and make insinuations that I like her."

"We can't have that," Paris teased.

"No, we definitely can't," Bermuda imparted quite seriously as the last of the gazelles passed. Paris thought that the herd would pass without incident when one of the larger ones circled back.

Before she knew what was happening, the thieving gazelle grabbed the cup in her hand with its teeth and ran off.

The giantess shook her head. "You can't trust those guys. They take things even if they don't want them."

Paris laughed, glad that they only got away with the cup and not her charms or leather jacket.

Bermuda held out her hand, a piece of paper in it. "That's Rory's address. You can portal close to that location, but then you better hurry since I suspect the Deathly Shadow will pick up on your presence and be after you. That evil entity won't stop until he has you or he's stopped, I'm afraid. I hope that my son can help you—for all our sakes."

"I'll be safe once I'm on Rory's property?" Paris asked.

"Yes."

Paris eyed the address and created a portal to as close to it as she could. Before stepping through, she offered a smile to the giantess. "Well, thanks for all your help and advice."

Sternly, Bermuda nodded. "Keep an eye on that squirrel of yours. Animals who can talk are either covered in secrets or the work of powerful magic. Either way, you may not want to get mixed up in it."

CHAPTER FORTY-THREE

The sun was as bright in Los Angeles as it was wherever she'd been with Bermuda Laurens. Paris had stepped out into a quiet neighborhood that looked as if she'd stepped back in time. The street was wide, and large trees lined the sidewalk. The houses were one-story little bungalows with large porches.

Paris smiled at a couple in a swing on their porch, then the black and white cat in the yard. Remembering what Bermuda had said about getting to Rory's property fast, she glanced at the address in her hands again and the street number on the house with the porch swing.

The couple was still lounging there, but the black and white cat had disappeared. Paris was a block from Rory's house, it appeared, which made her feel more at ease since she had her protective charm. However, she wasn't going to dawdle, not that she was a dawdler.

She hurried down the sidewalk, making quick progress. It was more likely for Paris to cry while watching a sappy romantic comedy movie than dillydally and the odds of either of those were extremely low. Paris had always felt as if she had a place to be and there was no reason to stroll to get to said place.

"To dither is to die," Paris remarked to herself, looking over her shoulder, trying to stay aware of her surroundings and more importantly any strange wind that came her way.

"I used to know someone who talked to herself often," a strange voice said in front of her.

She whipped around, tense and ready to fight, but there was no one standing in front of her, as she'd expected. Glancing down at the yard beside her, she found the black and white cat she'd seen a few houses back.

Pausing, she looked around for the source of the voice but didn't find anyone.

"I think I'm hearing things, kitty," Paris related to the creature, which was mostly white but had large black spots and a black tail, save for a white tip on its end. He wore a curious expression.

"Like what?" the cat asked, quite seriously. "It could be a sign that you're going crazy."

Paris backed up, wondering what the hell was going on. "You spoke..."

"So did you," the cat remarked.

"Cats aren't supposed to speak." She thought that maybe she should run after what Bermuda Laurens had said about talking animals.

"I'm not really a cat...not like you're used to."

Then Paris remembered something else that Bermuda said. "Are you a lynx?"

"I am."

"I learned about you and that you—"

"Can't be trusted and I'm notorious for keeping secrets," the lynx interrupted, completing her sentence.

"How did you know that's what Bermuda Laurens said to me a minute ago about lynx?" Paris backed up again.

Casually, the cat lifted his paw and licked it as if he didn't have a care in the world and wasn't concerned that Paris looked ready to start running. "I know things."

"You were spying on me a minute ago...wherever I was with Bermuda," Paris accused, her eyes narrowed.

"Spying is such a harsh word," the strange creature said in a refined tone, sounding a little like Wilfred for a moment.

"You..." Paris said with a gasp. "You're the cat who saved me from the Deathly Shadow in Beverly Hills, aren't you?"

"As I already mentioned, I'm not really a cat," the creature said in answer.

Paris remembered that she was standing in the middle of a very quiet neighborhood and glanced around. Thankfully no one was watching her talk to a cat or whatever it was. Still, she realized that she shouldn't stand around where the Deathly Shadow could get her.

"You're safe," the animal said matter-of-factly.

"How?"

"Because," he answered simply.

"Who are you?" Paris asked. "Uncle John seemed to know about you."

"I'd say," the creature said.

"Were you a friend of my parents?" Paris didn't feel nervous about the lynx despite what Bermuda Laurens had said.

"Your mother," he said. "She was my...best friend."

"You were her familiar," Paris said with a gasp, suddenly full of so many questions. "You *were* the one who saved me in Beverly Hills, then."

"My name is Plato, and I thought that it would be a disservice for me not to offer my input after your lecture from Bermuda."

"She says animals shouldn't be able to talk," Paris offered and added, "You already know that because you were watching me...somehow."

"Bermuda Laurens knows a lot about magical creatures," Plato began. "But she doesn't know everything. Talking animals are rare, as they should be. In most instances, it's not a cause for concern. It's simply rare magic. Unfortunately, when something is rare, it is feared. I think that in time, you'll find that to be true for you—and I'm remorseful for that."

"Do you mean that because I'm the only magical halfling, others will fear me?" Paris questioned.

"Unfortunately, this world likes things to be the same. Uniqueness is rarely celebrated before it is feared," Plato explained. "In the giantess' instance, for all Bermuda's knowledge, that which she doesn't understand, she believes is wrong."

"You believe it's okay that Faraday can talk?" Paris thought she'd lost her mind if she was seeking advice from a lynx.

"What did your Uncle John say when you asked him about me?" Plato countered.

"He turned the question around on me and asked me what my instinct on the matter was." She remembered the conversation clearly.

"What was it?"

"Well, I thought you'd saved my life, and usually someone who does that is okay." Paris laughed.

"What's your instinct on Faraday?" Plato asked.

"Well, I've liked him from the beginning, even if he's really strange for a squirrel. He'd be considered strange for a person too."

At this, Plato's tail flicked.

"So my mother had a talking lynx as a pet?" This new development fascinated Paris.

"I think of her more as my pet."

Paris laughed. "You were probably spelled not to talk to me or tell me anything."

Plato shook his head. "Such things wouldn't work on me, and Papa Creola knew that. I simply kept my distance until you were ready."

"But you've been spying on me and protecting me as of recently," Paris remarked.

"I've been watching you since you were born."

Paris didn't know what to say, which was probably why her mouth fell open as she stared down at the lynx.

"I mean, not like a weird stalker," Plato added. "I needed to keep an eye on you."

"Because I'm the one who was supposed to bring my mother back?" she asked.

"My interests in protecting you aren't only because you'll bring back Liv."

Paris considered the lynx for a long moment. "So are you saying that I shouldn't listen to Bermuda's warning about talking animals?"

"I wouldn't dare tell you to trust me," Plato countered. "Know that anyone who tells you to trust them can't be trusted. Those who can, earn it, not ask for it."

Paris tried to think if Faraday had asked for her trust.

Plato continued, "Although I think that Bermuda is a supreme source on magical creatures, she doesn't know everything or understand all things. For as smart as the giantess is, she is still very shortsighted. This is a person who never once laughed at your mother's jokes."

Paris grinned. "Was my mother funny?"

A fond expression crossed Plato's face. "She was the funniest person I've ever known, and I've known a lot of people. Pretty much all of them."

"Oh," Paris replied, pride filling her chest.

"Of course, if you tell her that I said that once she's back, I'll end you," the lynx threatened.

"So you've kept me alive all this time to kill me for passing along a compliment to my mother?" Paris was amused.

Plato shrugged. "Pride is a strong thing."

"Well, I better get on my way and stop dawdling." Paris suddenly felt like she was stalling, but how could she not want to spend time with her mother's best friend...although it was starting to feel like everyone was her mother's best friend. Maybe she was that type of person. It was beginning to feel that way.

Plato gave her a thoughtful look. "Richelle E. Goodrich said, 'life may dawdle along in minutes, but don't be deceived, for it will spring by in years before you notice.'"

That made Paris think of something. "The last fifteen years without my mother, I'm sure it's been difficult for you as her familiar."

Plato's gaze slid to the side. "These last fifteen were the hardest years I've lived, and I've lived a very long life."

"Well, I'm going to get her back and my father," Paris said with conviction. "And I'm going to end this Deathly Shadow, once and for all."

"I believe that," Plato stated. "You should know that when you face the Deathly Shadow, that—"

"That I have to do it alone," Paris interrupted, thinking of what her Uncle Clark had said.

However, Plato shook his head. "Your Aunt Sophia can't help you. Neither can your uncles. You really wouldn't want King Rudolf there. Another *human* can't accompany you. Otherwise, I fear that the Deathly Shadow won't come for you. He'll think it's a trick. More importantly, I firmly believe that you have to be alone to defeat him. There's something about believing we have no backup options that makes one pull on the strength they didn't know they had."

Paris nodded and chewed on her lip. "Yeah, that makes sense."

"However, remember how I said that rules didn't apply the same to me…" Plato let the sentence trail off with a strange hint in his voice.

"Does that mean you'll be there?"

"As I said before, I've always been there, watching you. I'm always here for you."

The smile that sprang to Paris' face quickly disappeared when a gentle breeze made leaves tumble down the road behind her.

Instinctively she turned, checking over her shoulder, then remembered that Plato said she was safe right then. Realizing that the breeze was merely that, she sighed and turned back to the lynx.

However, to her surprise, he'd disappeared.

Paris shook her head, realizing that she should probably get used to people giving her advice and support, then vanishing.

CHAPTER FORTY-FOUR

Thankfully, even after the lynx disappeared, the gentle breeze didn't pick up and turn into the presence of the Deathly Shadow. It was so strange to Paris to think that her mother's best friend was this unassuming black and white cat. However, she sensed that Plato was very powerful and he'd said he'd lived a long life. Also, Paris wasn't sure what had gotten rid of the Deathly Shadow in Beverly Hills, but she'd sensed it was something mighty at the time—it was Plato.

The fact that Liv had so many loyal friends made Paris proud. She was excited to meet Rory, hoping that he was as interesting as the others she'd met. Of course, if he were anything like his mother, she'd be in for a treat.

Paris was relieved when she found the modest blue bungalow with the lush yard and oversized front porch. When she stepped across the property line, she felt the energy charge indicating that she stepped across a magical boundary. It was a security system of sorts—an alarm that would tell the residence there'd been trespassing.

For that reason, Paris should have been unsurprised when a

giant as big as Bermuda Laurens burst through the front door, his eyes narrowed and a threatening look on his face. He had a mop of dark unruly curly hair and bright green eyes and dressed like a lumberjack.

Paris held up her hands and was about to declare who she was, but she didn't have to because the threatening look on Rory's face instantly transformed to one of relief. He shook his head, running his eyes over her with a sigh of surprise.

"You look exactly like her," he murmured.

CHAPTER FORTY-FIVE

"Apparently, I'm as much of a pain in the ass." Paris brandished a wide grin.

"Guinevere," Rory murmured, staring at her as if she was a ghost.

"I go by Paris."

"I'd heard that you knew the truth, but...well, I didn't expect you to come here." He strode off the porch, looking around. "Are you okay? You weren't followed?"

"By a black and white cat, but I think he's harmless."

Rory ushered Paris toward the house, looking over his shoulder. "Plato is the least harmless creature I know, but he'd never hurt you. That's an animal you want on your side."

Paris halted on the garden path, looking up at the giant with kind eyes. "So you trust Plato? Your mother doesn't. She's the one who told me where to find you."

"My mum doesn't trust anyone if we're honest," Rory answered. "She's mad at Plato because he owes her money, abandoned her in the desert, and made fun of one of her hats."

"Not one of her hats," Paris said with an exaggerated gasp.

He nodded. "She takes her hats very seriously."

Rory opened the door to his house, and Paris was instantly flooded with a savory smell, reminding her that she hadn't eaten in a while. The home he led her into was warm and comforting. Similar to Happily Ever After College, it reminded her of a grandmother's house.

"Are you hungry?" Rory strode across the living room to the dining area. "We didn't have a proper introduction. I guess you know who I am."

She nodded. "Yes, and I'm Paris. I've come to ask for your help because I hear that you were a friend of my mother's. I'd love a sample of whatever is cooking."

He sniffed the air. "I have a chicken pot pie that just came out of the oven. A venison chili on the cooker and some ribs in the smoker. Which of those do you want?"

"Are you feeding an army?" she had to ask.

He shook his head. "No, it's normal fare."

"Oh, well, I'd love whatever you're offering."

He indicated a seat at the table. "Make yourself comfortable, and I'll be back with some offerings."

Paris did as instructed, going to take a seat and finding a warm gray cat curled up in the chair.

"June Bug, would you make room for our guest?" Rory scolded, watching over his shoulder as the cat vacated the seat, looking quite put out.

"Oh, sorry, kitty." Paris watched as the giant disappeared into the kitchen. A pressed cloth covered the already set table. Little figurines decorated the cabinet on the far wall, and hand-painted plates graced the near wall. It felt like she'd come home to grandma's house.

"So you met Mum?" Rory asked from the kitchen.

"Yes, I needed to find you and ask her about a talking squirrel," Paris answered.

Rory poked his head around the corner of the kitchen. "A talking squirrel?"

"He's allergic to nuts," Paris added with a nod. "Bermuda thought that you might be busy because of your side accounting business."

The giant shook his head as he returned with a full plate of assorted options. "She knows I write books."

"She mentioned that too."

He laid the plate in front of Paris. "How much did she grumble when she did?"

Paris laughed, her eyes wide at the array of colors and smells as she took in the delicious plate of food. The crust of the chicken pot pie bursting with vegetables looked perfect. Chef Ash would have been impressed. The small cup of chili had so many spicy notes hitting Paris' nose. The smoked ribs dripped with a rich barbeque sauce.

"You cooked all this?" She was impressed. "Thank you."

He shrugged. "Just whipped it up with leftover ingredients."

"I think I'm enlisting your skills when I need tutoring for cooking classes at Happily Ever After College."

Rory took the seat opposite her. "I heard you were training to be a fairy godmother. It's a great opportunity for you. I think you're what that college needs."

"We'll see about that." Paris picked up the utensils and tried to decide where to start.

"So you need my help?" Rory crossed his hands in front of him.

It felt weird that Paris had skipped many of the formative conversations with all these meetings, having to jump right to business. Still, time was of the essence, and she needed to fight the Deathly Shadow. Deciding that if she survived this duel, she'd catch up with Rory then, she laid down her fork before taking a bite. "Yes, I'm here because I need you to create a container that can hold the Deathly Shadow. Apparently, according to the father of time, Papa Creola, you're the only one who can do it. So no pressure. And I need it right away. So definitely no double pressure." She winked, but he quickly averted his eyes.

Rory ran his hands through his hair, his head down and a sigh falling from his mouth. Paris was pretty sure this was when her luck ran out, and he told her it was impossible, or it would take a long time.

Instead, when the giant looked up, there were tears in his eyes. "Then it's true, isn't it? You're going to bring her back...finally."

CHAPTER FORTY-SIX

"I'm going to try," Paris answered, not needing Rory to clarify who he meant.

"This is great news," Rory said with relief in his voice. "Now, please eat."

Paris dug into the chicken pot pie for a second time. "Thanks again." She stuck the fork in her mouth and instantly sank back from the perfect combination of flavors. The carrots were still firm enough, the peas snapped in her mouth with fun little bursts, and the chicken was perfectly juicy and tender. A flaky crust and a thick creamy gravy wrapped all of it.

"You need a container," Rory supplied when Paris opened her eyes.

She nodded. "Yes, according to Papa Creola, I can't kill the Deathly Shadow. I can only overpower it and stick it in a container, which only you can make."

"It would make sense that you can't kill him since he's not technically alive anymore," Rory said gravely. "It would also make sense that only something giant-made could contain the Deathly

Shadow since we work with the strongest of metals and use enchantments that reinforce them better than anyone else."

"You must be the very best." Paris took a bite of the chili, suddenly torn between whether she liked that more than the chicken pot pie or not. It was a toss-up at this point, but she was seriously considering proposing to one of the two dishes.

"I learned from my grandfather, and he was the best," Rory argued.

"I'd guess he's not living anymore, making you the best," Paris stated boldly.

The giant nodded.

"I'm not sure what I'll need to contain the Deathly Shadow since this is my first soulless monster to fight," Paris continued. "However, it should be small enough that I can attach some magitech to it to open the vortex."

"That's how you're going to bring them back?" Rory looked stunned. "That could work."

Paris smiled and picked up the sticky ribs. "Let's hope it does. Yes, then we defeat an evil beast, open the vortex and have a welcome home party."

"Do you remember much about your mother?" Rory asked, his gaze low.

Paris shook her head and took a bite of the ribs. She wasn't much for getting messy while eating, but she'd also never had ribs as good as these.

"Yeah, I guess the enchantments Papa Creola put on you made it so your early memories were fuzzy," he reasoned. "Liv was as casual as you when talking about facing giant evils. I think she did it to keep herself sane when entering a battle. Probably a good strategy. Then there was her sense of humor and sarcasm."

"Your mother and Subner didn't seem to like those parts of her." Paris wiped her mouth with a pressed napkin.

"They might not have, but I'm certain it kept her alive," Rory offered. "She had the hardest job of anyone I knew, and most would have burned out after a year or so. Liv's easy-going attitude and flippant nature kept her going. It usually made me roll my eyes, but I know it kept her alive."

"You two were close?" Paris dug back into the chicken pot pie.

"Liv was my best friend in this world," Rory admitted and held up a finger as if in warning. "But when she comes back, don't tell her that, or she'll try and hug me or something."

Paris laughed. "Why does no one ever want to tell my mother how great she was or is and how much they love her? That's the third time today that someone has confessed their affections for my mother but warned me not to tell her."

"There's no way that Liv couldn't know how much we all adore her," Rory said, affection in his eyes. "Wait until you meet her. You'll be captivated like the rest of us."

CHAPTER FORTY-SEVEN

Not only was the plan to take down McGregor Technologies and Rose Industries working, but the next steps of the strategy were falling into place effortlessly. All the fairy godmothers had to do was break up Grayson McGregor with his fiancé, then do the same with Amelia Rose and stick them together. The falling in love part would be a little tricky, but it always was. However, Paris thought that part of the plan would be simple enough—all they needed was the perfect setup.

"That's where you come in," Paris said to Chef Ash, who for once had dressed in regular clothes instead of his chef's uniform.

He rolled up the blueprints that he'd been working on meticulously since being assigned part of the project. "Constructing an escape room has never been a dream of mine until now. This is going to be a lot of fun." ‘

"The key is to make it different from other escape rooms." Christine winked. "Ensure that the participants can't escape."

Chef Ash nodded. "I'm on it."

Paris glanced at Christine. "Are you ready to look like a hottie?"

Not wearing the usual blue gown that changed her appearance,

Christine was sporting her red hair and freckles. "Yeah, give me tattoos. I hear some girls find them sexy."

Paris grimaced. "Tattoos aren't my thing, but to each their own."

"Then you can't date me because I have two tats," Christine admitted.

"Let me guess. You got the first one when you were eighteen to rebel against your parents who wanted you to be a good little lady and attend fairy godmother college," Paris guessed.

Christine grinned. "It's as if you can look into me and see my soul."

"You'd have to have a soul for that," Chef Ash joked, amused by their banter.

"Nice one, Chef Ashton." Christine grinned, glancing at Paris. "Yes, I got a tattoo on my eighteenth birthday to upset my parents."

"Did it?" Paris asked.

Christine shook her head. "No, because they thought the two sparrows I got tattooed on the side of my stomach were to represent them."

"Was it?" Chef Ash inquired.

She frowned. "No, I got them because I thought they were cute when I saw them on Pinterest. I don't like birds."

"Is it because of the killer doves that Professor Shannon Butcher released on Valentine's Day?" he asked.

Christine shook her head. "No, this was before that. I've been afraid of birds most of my life."

Paris blinked at her with confusion. "How are you afraid of pretty little sparrows?"

She shrugged. "I don't know. I just am. And bunnies. They scare the hell out of me."

Paris and Chef Ash laughed. "You're so very weird, Christina."

"Bunnies seem all cute and innocent—"

"Because they are," Paris interrupted her friend.

"Yeah, but their teeth never stop growing," Christine continued. "That's just wrong."

"So no to birds and bunnies," Paris stated. "Anything else on the list of deadly animals that aren't deadly that scare you?"

"Maybe ladybugs or butterflies," Chef Ash supplied.

Christine shivered with disgust. "Yeah, that's a big no thank you to those bugs. Although I happen to like bees. I'm thinking of keeping a hive at some point if Hemingway allows it."

Paris shook her head. "So no to fluffy bunnies, sweet sparrows, and flitting little butterflies. But you want to keep something that can sting you?"

"Not only something," Chef Ash added. "She wants to keep several hundred of them."

"Go big or go home," Christine sang. "Now make me look like one of those guys on the cover of a steamy romance novel."

Paris lifted her finger, thinking of the right look for this disguising spell.

"But have her wearing a shirt," Chef Ash insisted.

"Nothing with long sleeves," Christine stated. "I want to show off my sleeve of tattoos."

Paris nodded and flicked her finger at Christine. The redhead immediately disappeared, replaced by a tall guy with a broad chest, a dashing smile, and slicked-back hair. He wore a tight-fitting t-shirt that showed off his muscles and two sleeves of various tattoos.

"Nice." Christine admired her arms. "I think I'll say my name is Colt. That sounds like a romantic lead in this steamy romance book I've jumped out of."

"Great, Colt. You'll be Michelle Bordeaux's new assistant since I decided that I needed to fire my deadbeat son." Paris flicked her finger at herself, taking on the appearance of the short and chubby designer she'd used the first time she met Grayson McGregor.

"You're great at disguising spells," Chef Ash gushed, impressed.

"Thanks," Paris said. "My Aunt Sophia gave me some tips. She's really good with them."

Christine crossed her tattooed arms over her muscled chest. "Another benefit of being you. You have the magic of a magician and the looks of a fairy. It simply isn't fair."

"Did you forget that whole part where she hasn't known her parents her entire life?" Chef Ash asked.

Christine rolled her gorgeous eyes. "That's the perfect setup for an interesting life. Everyone knows the most awesome characters are orphans. Harry Potter, Superman, Daenerys, Annie, Cinderella, Peter Pan—"

"Your sympathy on this whole thing is overwhelming," Paris said dryly.

"I mean, I'm sorry that your parents are stuck in another dimension," Christine said. "Mine are stuck in their youth, and my dad wears shorts that are too short, and my mother still has bangs. Bangs! Can you believe it?"

"I can't." Paris giggled.

"So things could be worse," Christine continued. "At least you have a chance of recovering your parents. No matter how many times I drop subtle hints about how no one should have bangs ever, my mother insists they frame her face. You know what else frames someone's face? A bonnet. You don't see those coming back, do you?"

Paris and Chef Ash laughed.

"Well, I think I'll leave the fashion advice up to you. I'll pretend to be a designer." Paris looked at the guy beside them, not in disguise. "You'll be my architect and carpenter. Are we ready to go build an escape room and break up a relationship of a failing CEO?"

"Absolutely," Christine sang. "Let's go make Grayson McGregor's life even worse."

Chef Ash grinned with a nod. "Then we'll make it better than ever."

CHAPTER FORTY-EIGHT

As Paris had expected, Grayson McGregor's fiancée Tee had barged into the meeting, her overly made-up face red with fury.

"I can't believe you're still going along with this stupid escape room," she fumed, making everyone in the empty basement look up suddenly. The area was as it was the first time that Paris and Christine had visited it with the CEO of McGregor Technologies.

Grayson stood from the makeshift table that he'd set up for Chef Ash to show off the blueprints he'd put together. "Tee, we discussed this. If the company goes down, I'll start another one. However, replacing employees isn't as easy, and that's who the escape room is for."

"It's for you, and you know it," Tee accused, crossing her arms, her eyes flicking to Christine disguised as a cowboy-rebel type. "Well, and who are you?"

"My name's Colt, sweetheart," Christine said with a flirtatious smile and a southern drawl, completing the cowboy disguise. "What's your name?"

"Tee," she replied, quickly putting her hand with her engagement ring behind her back. "Tee Sharon."

Colt, also known as Christine, held out his hand for her and when Tee extended her non-ring hand, he lifted it and kissed the back with a heated look in his eyes.

Grayson shook his head. "This is Michelle's assistant. He'll be around a lot as we work on the escape room. I bet you're okay with it now, huh?"

She shot him a scolding look. "Apparently, I have to get over it because of that contract you signed."

"A contract is a contract," Paris chirped, tapping the documents they'd had Grayson McGregor sign right before they leaked the information about his products, sabotaging the company and making the stock plummet.

"Even if McGregor Technologies files bankruptcy?" Tee questioned.

"It's not that serious, is it?" Paris asked Grayson, trying to keep any hint of victory out of her tone.

He nodded and pushed his hands through his hair. "I'm afraid it could be. It will depend on how the lawsuits go, which doesn't look like it'll be in McGregor Technologies' direction."

"Which means that constructing a dumb escape room isn't a good idea," Tee said smugly. "Not now or ever. When this company fails, we should turn the office building into a Pilates studio."

"Are you a Pilates instructor?" Colt asked. "You look like one." He ran his eyes mostly over Tee's chest, which a tight vest framed.

"I am." She batted her fake eyelashes at him.

"I'm not turning the building into a fitness studio for snotty socialites who are more concerned with the size of their waist than making the world a better place through advanced technologies," Grayson spat and glanced down at the blueprints again, seemingly to shake this off.

"Maybe if you spent more time concerned with yourself, the company wouldn't be facing litigation," Tee argued boldly.

"Really, does making the world a better place involve starting fires?"

"Get out!" Grayson exclaimed loudly, his face flushing red.

Paris and Chef Ash tensed, but Christine used this to her advantage. She, as Colt, held out her arm to Tee. "Would you mind showing me the first floor? I need to get an idea of what's above here for planning the escape room."

"You don't." Paris pretended to be annoyed by her flirty assistant. She then gave Grayson a pointed look, feigning confidence. "Still, it would be good if we could concentrate on these plans, and these distractions aren't helping. My time is very valuable."

Grayson sighed. "Tee, why don't you take Colt up to the first floor and tell him all about how you want to redesign the laboratories into spin rooms."

She held her nose high into the air, narrowing her eyes at her fiancé, no affection in her gaze. "I'd love to. It's a perfect space for it and wouldn't be a failing business." Tee took the arm that Colt had extended, and the pair trotted across the basement's concrete floor, disappearing a moment later.

Grayson's jaw flexed as he shook off the stress. "My apologies. Tee and I don't see eye-to-eye on certain things. We obviously have different ideas of what to do with this building, but I'm creating this escape room."

Chef Ash, who was going by Ashton for this mission, offered a consoling look. He glanced around the blank space. "You know, David Allan Coe said, 'It is not the beauty of a building you should look at; it is the construction of the foundation that will stand the test of time.'"

Grayson looked out on the empty basement with a heavy expression. It seemed evident that the carpenter wasn't talking about the foundation of McGregor Technologies.

"So the plans?" Paris asked, recapturing Grayson's attention. "Do they look good to you?"

The CEO nodded. "Yes, let's start construction right away. Ironically, I have a feeling that soon I'm going to need a place to escape to and not out of."

CHAPTER FORTY-NINE

Paris wasn't granted a moment of rest after returning from McGregor Technologies before she received a series of messages. Everything was falling into place for the Deathly Shadow's showdown, which filled her with dread. Whether she was mentally and physically ready for this fight, it was going to happen. It needed to be soon because every day was one where Captain Morgan was held captive. However, there were a few key pieces to complete and they couldn't be rushed. The good news was that it appeared that King Rudolf knew his daughter's location.

Thankfully there wasn't any assaulting wind when Paris hurried to the Crying Cat Bakery where the fae said he would meet her. She entered the magical bakery to find the strange assassin baker and King Rudolf arm-wrestling at a small table in the corner. Lee was barely trying while the fae's face was pinched and red. He was using what appeared to be all his strength to press the baker's wrist back on the table, but it wasn't budging.

"Do you want me to end this?" Lee asked Rudolf.

"I...won't...be...defeated," Rudolf said between breaths.

Cat, who was carrying a tray of rainbow-colored scones, shook her head. "I was defeated this morning trying to get dressed."

"I was today years old when I learned that I could in fact put my pants on one leg at a time," Rudolf offered, putting his shoulder into the effort, but it wasn't working to his advantage.

"Before today, were you jumping into your pants?" Lee appeared bored by the arm-wrestling contest.

The king gave her a look of offense. "I don't put on my pants. I have people for that."

Lee nodded and glanced at Paris. "Are you here to collect census information? I'm a legal citizen, and my wife is illegal and should be arrested and deported."

Paris laughed. "I'm here because King Rudolf told me he'd found his daughter's location and we need to discuss the plan."

"So you can't have my wife arrested?" Lee asked, still easily holding King Rudolf's arm up.

Ignoring her, Paris glanced at the fae. "Uncle John was able to find the location from where Captain Morgan sent the text?"

"Yes," he grunted. "He wants you to meet him at the Fantastical Armory after this. Apparently, there's a problem with the vortex-thingymajig."

Paris sighed. "Okay, well, I should get to that quickly. That's important. Where is Captain Morgan?"

"Strangely enough," Rudolf said through clenched teeth. "She's in Paris. We've narrowed it down to a few potential buildings."

"Oh, I'm guessing that the Deathly Shadow has his reasons for that location," Paris observed, watching the pair continue to arm wrestle.

"There's significance in names and locations," Cat said in her thick French accent. "If I were going to absorb someone's power, I would choose a place that had a strong relation to them to strengthen the whole thing."

"You never seem to care where you are when you're sucking out my soul," Lee commented over her shoulder to her wife.

Cat batted her eyelashes at Lee and strode for the back. "Try not to die when in Paris. I happen to like that city and don't want you dying there ruining it for me. Actually, that might be the way for me to like it more, so maybe do die there."

Lee chuckled, amused by the threat.

"You're going to help to rescue Captain Morgan?" Paris was grateful that the king would have help—he appeared to need it.

"I'm going to help him if he can beat me in arm wrestling," Lee corrected.

Paris pointed her finger in the direction of the pair and used a simple combat spell. A second later, King Rudolf's arm overpowered Lee, sending her hand down on the other side of the table.

Triumphantly, Rudolf thrust his fist into the air and rejoiced. "I'm the winner!"

"That was cheating." Lee rolled out her wrist and narrowed her eyes at Paris. "I like you more than I did before, which wasn't that much, but still."

"I think that two people rescuing Captain Morgan is better than one," Paris stated. "I'm going to draw the Deathly Shadow away before then, but there could be a trap. I suspect there will be."

"I sure as hell hope so." Lee stretched to a standing position beside King Rudolf, who still looked quite proud of his win even if he didn't earn it.

"So you two will narrow down where the location of Captain Morgan is," Paris affirmed. "Then I need you on standby, ready to go when I have everything in place to fight the Deathly Shadow."

Lee glanced at Rudolf and pursed her lips. "She's a bossy little thing, isn't she?"

He nodded proudly. "Yep. Just like her mother."

CHAPTER FIFTY

Paris found Uncle John and Subner with their heads together, bent over the counter, working on something when she entered the Fantastical Armory. They both looked up when she came through the door. One of them smiled fondly at her. The other scowled.

"You know if you keep that look on your face, it will stick like that," Paris said to the angry elf, repeating what Uncle John often said to her when she frowned.

"That's the idea," Subner answered. "I'd prefer not to give off a welcoming appearance."

"Is that the vortex opener thingy?" Paris pointed at a metal claw-looking thing sitting between them.

"Yes." Uncle John sighed in frustration. "Rory sent me the plans he's using to create the container for the Deathly Shadow. The idea is that once you trap it, you fit this onto it and pull on the Shadow's energy, finding the right location for the vortex."

"That's key because you can open over a million different vortexes," Subner muttered.

"Which is why no one has been able to keep trying to open them and get back my parents," Paris guessed.

"Well, and your mother is a pain in the ass, so if it requires only having to try and open one vortex, then I wouldn't do it," Subner stated.

Uncle John chuckled, apparently used to the unhappy man's sour disposition toward Liv. "We're guessing that the Deathly Shadow hasn't opened another vortex since he tricked Liv and Stefan so pulling on his energy, you should be able to open the last one he created. I'm not going to lie, it's very unstable magitech, and I'm not sure that I can get it working properly."

"Which means we should forget about this whole bring back Liv and Stefan thing and focus our energy on something more worthwhile," Subner grumbled.

"I'm missing something with the coding," Uncle John continued, ignoring the hostile elf beside him. "Subner and I have been trying a few things, but I don't think they'll work."

"Is it possible that I contain the Deathly Shadow and when you have the vortex locator thingy working, then we use it to get my parents back?" Paris asked.

Uncle John shook his head. "Rory says that the way the container will work, there will be a small window when we can harness the Deathly Shadow's energy to find the right vortex location."

"Figures." Paris groaned.

"Don't worry," Uncle John consoled. "Papa Creola says he has a solution that should work."

"Oh, that's hopeful. Where is he?" Paris looked around the large shop as if expecting the father of time was hiding behind one of the glass counters. He wasn't.

"He'll be here," Subner answered.

"When?" Paris was antsy to get things going—nervous energy building in her chest.

"Now," Papa Creola answered, striding through the door at the back. His hair was unkempt as usual, and he looked grumpier, although he was wearing a t-shirt that said, "Being happy is what life is all about."

"Oh, good timing," Paris joked, earning a laugh from Uncle John and two scowls from the elves.

"You need more information to make the vortex opener work," Papa Creola answered. "I'm sending you to the Great Library."

"What makes this library so great?" Paris was excited about the potentials of this place after recently discovering her love for books. "Does it have a slide?"

"Having a slide doesn't make a place great." Subner tinkered with the vortex opener.

"I wholeheartedly disagree," Paris argued.

"You're five minutes old and know nothing," he retorted.

She stuck her tongue out at him. "I'm five-and-a-half minutes old."

"The Great Library, a place that you would visit in your second year at Happily Ever After College," Papa Creola began in an even tone, "houses every book ever written. New editions get added as they are updated."

"So it's a fairly large place then," Paris said in awe.

"Seriously, why don't you open the vortex to the other dimension and join Liv wherever she is," Subner muttered. "Then problem solved and you two can live annoyingly ever after in someone else's world."

"But I miss you so," Paris gushed, putting her hands together beside her face and giving him a look of mock adoration.

"You're fortunate that you're a fairy godmother," Uncle John said to her.

"In training," Subner cut in.

"You have to poke holes in things, don't you?" she asked him, to which he nodded.

"The Great Library is restricted," Uncle John continued. "Only fairy godmothers and those in training, dragonriders, House of

Fourteen members and royalty and some chosen few are allowed in there."

"Why?" Paris asked, somewhat offended. "Shouldn't knowledge be for anyone?"

Subner sighed. "It's thinking like that which will destroy the planet."

Papa Creola nodded. "Subner is right. Knowledge is power, and many of the books inside the Great Library could be dangerous in the wrong hands. There are spells on everything from time travel to necromancy. Access to the Great Library is restricted to keep the wrong knowledge out of bad people's hands."

"Oh, well, I guess that makes sense," Paris reasoned. "So you need me to fetch a book?"

Papa Creola shook his head. "No, I need you to meet with someone."

"Oh, well, although the Great Library sounds fun, why can't this person meet me here? Or at the pizza place on Roya Lane?" Paris asked. "I haven't had time to eat, and I'm starving."

"The reason you have to meet this person there is that they're coming from another dimension," Papa Creola explained.

"What?" Paris asked. "Like my parents?"

"That's right," Papa Creola affirmed. "However, it's easier for this person to travel between realms because he's not really alive."

"Oh, wow," Paris said in awe. "Like the Deathly Shadow?"

"Differently," he answered. "This person retained his soul but cheated death. It was quite irritating to me, broke hundreds of rules, and made Mama Jamba mad. His stunt nearly broke the fabric of time and destroyed the Earth.

"Wow, this sounds like a bad man," Paris observed.

Papa Creola pursed his lips. "He's a good guy but smart enough to figure out how to break the rules he didn't want to follow. I couldn't fault him entirely since he did figure out how to die and also not die. He lives in a parallel dimension. Because of the way the Great Library works in that it is in this world and every other one, he can meet you there."

Paris blinked, overwhelmed by all this new information. "This is complex. So the Great Library is in every world? Why can't we find my parents through there? Wouldn't they know to search out the place in their dimension and meet up there?"

"It doesn't work that way, Einstein," Subner criticized.

"The Great Library, having all books ever written, exists in all worlds," Papa Creola explained. "But just like how things work in parallel realms, we only see those in our dimension."

"Oh, so even if my parents went to the Great Library, we wouldn't be able to see them," Paris guessed.

"Not to mention that there are other complications," Papa Creola went on. "Finding the Great Library isn't easy if one doesn't have a portal door there. It can take months and even years to follow the Fierce to the Great Library's location."

"The Fierce?" Paris asked.

"A fairy who one has to find and follow to discover the library's location," Papa Creola answered. "Then there's also the issue of time. We have no way of knowing how time moves in the dimension where Liv and Stefan are. Even if we could get through by way of the Great Library, figuring out the timing would be impossible. It would be like setting up a meeting with two parties but not knowing what time zone which one was in."

"Okay, so I need to meet with this not-dead guy because?" Paris questioned.

"He's going to give you the equation and piece of information that John will need to fix the vortex opener," Papa Creola answered. "I don't think this information is in a book, but because he's figured out how to move between dimensions without frying his brain or mixing up all his body parts, he's in the best position to tell us what we need for the device."

"All right, how do I get to the Great Library?" Paris rubbed her hands together, eager to get to the next step of the plan.

"I'll open a portal," Papa Creola answered. "You'll return through the fairy godmother door to the college."

"Great. Who exactly am I looking for in the Great Library?" Paris questioned. "Since it's a big place, I'm guessing, how am I going to find him?"

"The Great Librarian will help you find who you're looking for." Papa Creola opened a shimmering blue and green portal in the middle of the Fantastical Armory. "The man you're looking for, who is our only hope to open the right vortex to find Liv, is Ren Lewis. Try not to piss him off, or he might not help you."

CHAPTER FIFTY-ONE

Piss *him off?* Paris thought as she stepped through the portal to the Great Library. She wondered if, like Subner, this Ren Lewis was grumpy and had some grudge against her based on who her mother was.

Her concerns about offending this stranger disappeared at once as awe overwhelmed her. As she'd expected, the Great Library was huge. Standing in the middle of a wide row flanked by tall shelves, Paris blinked, trying to figure out how far the building went on. Miles, it seemed.

The Great Library was two stories tall with the second story open like a loft. The archways that ran the length of the library were dark wood, as were the floor and shelves. The wood was a nice contrast to the floor-to-ceiling windows that flowed down the space on either side of the row, bringing in natural light.

Paris had never been in a library before, having not been interested in books due to Papa Creola's spells. However, she instantly was in love with this place and all the potential adventures she could have exploring books. The smell of the pages, the way the light reflected off the shelves, the quiet—it was all so magical.

For as far as she could see through the banks of windows there was brown. The flat city that lay around the Great Library was so monochromatic that at first, it hurt Paris' eyes. She initially thought she'd time-traveled into the past because the city streets weren't filled with cars and traffic lights but rather donkeys and carts.

"Where is this place?" Paris muttered aloud, feeling as though she was yelling in the quiet place.

"The Great Library is in Timbuktu," a man said at Paris' back. She turned to find a guy wearing long black robes and a thoughtful expression regarding her. He had a dark beard, and his hands pressed together in front of his chest.

"Hey, are you Ren Lewis?" Paris whispered, although there was no one around them. The Great Library appeared to be empty.

The man shook his head. "I'm Paul, the Great Librarian, but Ren is down here waiting for you. You'll be Paris Beaufont."

She nodded, looking around at the massive library. "So this place really exists in multiple worlds? Does that mean you have to have multiple phone plans?"

"It might if I had a phone." He snickered, thankfully finding her joke funny.

"It seems that those in high positions aren't that into technology," Paris remarked, having noticed that Papa Creola, Mama Jamba, and the fairy godmothers didn't seem reliant on it like most everyone else.

"Books are my passion," Paul stated. "So I'm naturally not interested in technology or phones, and honestly, I don't have anyone I need to keep up with. My job here at the Great Library keeps me plenty busy."

"Yeah, I'm sure that reshelving the checked-out books takes forever," Paris joked.

"I have an assistant," Paul held out his arm, and right on cue, something soared down from one of the high shelves and landed on him. "This is Beatrix. She's a gryphowl and incredibly good at finding things, such as books."

The magical creature was quite large even resting on his arm where it folded its snowy wings into its body and regarded them with majestic eyes. The gryphowl appeared to be a cross between an owl and a large cat. It had the wise face of an owl with brown and white feathers. Under its large wings were four sets of legs that resembled those of a jungle cat. It also had the large pointy ears and striped tail of the large jungle cat.

"She sounds like a very helpful assistant," Paris remarked. "My animal companion usually only gets me into dangerous situations and is way too literal. That's Faraday's superpower."

"Faraday, you say?" Paul looked curious.

"Yeah, why?"

He shrugged. "Just wondering." The gryphowl took off suddenly, flying ahead in the long row that stretched before them. "Beatrix will lead us to Ren. I'm not certain of his specific where-abouts since as you've noticed, the Great Library is extensive, and it's easy to lose track of people."

Paris nodded and started forward, following the gryphowl. "I can only imagine. From the outside, does the Great Library take up a large portion of the city?"

"It looks like a modest dwelling," Paul answered. "It's tiny, and none who pass it are the least bit interested in what's inside."

"Wow, so you don't get any solicitors," Paris teased.

"Only those who are looking for the Great Library and are invited can enter," he explained.

"And follow the Fierce," Paris added, remembering what Father Time had said.

Paul strode beside her, his long robe billowing behind him. "That's right, but as a fairy godmother, you can go through the portal in the Serenity Garden. The door to return is at the front of the Great Library, and I can lead you there after you meet with Ren."

"Thanks." Paris looked down each row as they passed. "I could see getting lost here."

Beatrix landed on a shelf a few paces ahead. "It looks like we've found Ren Lewis. I'll leave you here to make your introductions. When you're finished and ready to return to Happily Ever After College, Beatrix will lead you back to me."

Paris nodded, gulping, finding herself suddenly nervous about this man she was to meet. He sounded very powerful if he cheated death and could pop between parallel worlds. She hoped that he was more good-natured than Bermuda and Subner, who didn't laugh at any of her jokes, but she had a feeling that he wouldn't since Papa Creola had instructed her not to piss him off.

Preparing herself mentally for the next phase of this mission, Paris rounded the corner to find a man with red hair and a mischievous glint in his green eyes standing in the row, a book open in his hands. He glanced up at her with an irritated expression and ran a speculative gaze over Paris, sizing her up quickly.

"You're a bit underwhelming, aren't you?" the man commented, his accent British and tone refined.

Paris sighed, thinking that they were already off to a great start.

CHAPTER FIFTY-TWO

Paris glanced down at her leather jacket and all-black outfit, wondering if she'd missed the memo on the dress code. Ren Lewis wore an expensive suit and tie, his short red hair spiky and perfectly neat.

"Didn't know I was supposed to wear a formal gown," Paris retaliated. "I can put on a disguise if you like, but I draw the line at combing my hair."

He rolled his eyes and closed the book. "I meant that you're a bit underwhelming in appearance as the only magical halfling in existence in this world or any other that I'm aware of."

Paris again glanced down at her clothes. "Yeah, well, I don't know what you expected. Horns? Claws or talons? I have wings and a bad attitude."

Ren sighed. "I know that you're half-magician and half-fairy, not part demon and falcon. I can see your wings."

Paris glanced over her shoulder at her wings. They were always there but were glamoured not to appear and be out of her way. Otherwise, they'd constantly knock into things and give her clearance issues like the protective longhorns.

"I think I am part demon," Paris remarked, remembering the story of how she came about. A demon had bitten her father. Her parents feared the demonism would pass to her, which led to a genie turning her into a half-fairy.

"That would explain the goth outfit." Ren indicated her clothes.

"Cool, now that we've discussed my lack of fashion sense and how underwhelming I am with first impressions, I hoped you could help me since you're apparently a multiple world dimension expert."

Ren shook his head and looked at the ceiling. "Why is it that young, entitled blonde brats are always annoying me and expecting me to help them out?"

"I'm not sure that question reflects well on you," Paris joked. "Are these young girls asking for ice cream money or a ride home because you're always lurking around the skating rink or the mall?"

He flashed her an amused grin, one of his pointy canines showing. "Oh, looky there. Someone can dish it out and take it. And here I thought this meeting would be a bore-fest."

"Do you often get bored when you have to meet the only half-magician, half-fairy in the universe in the Great Library to explain to them how to pinpoint a vortex location?" Paris pretended to be seriously interested in the answer.

He faked a yawn. "I'm sorry, I fell asleep. What was the question?"

"I'm Paris Beaufont, and you're Ren Lewis, and Papa Creola says you can help."

"I thought we were past introductions, love," Ren quipped. "Let's not shake. I really don't want to know what drivel is going on in your head."

"I wasn't going to tell you," she retorted, amused by this character, although she remembered that Papa Creola warned her not to piss him off. However, it seemed more likely that he would offend her first. Good thing she wasn't easily offended. Otherwise, she might have already clocked the guy. She still might...after he helped. He seemed like the bully type, although strangely helpful.

"I have telepathy linked to touch," Ren explained, holding up his hand.

"That's a fun party trick," Paris joked.

"So is the mind control I could employ to get you to do the chicken dance."

She laughed. "I don't need you to use mind control for that. Do you want me to do the short version or the deluxe one?"

"I'll take a rain check on both," he answered. "Yes, the father of time in your world says you need to know how to open a specific vortex harnessing the energy of an evil entity."

"Yeah, a piece of cake, right?" Paris asked dryly.

"I've had harder tasks," Ren related.

"How did you cheat death?" Paris was too curious not to let the question spill out.

He tipped his head back and forth. "I used science, technology, philosophy, and religion to find clear loopholes in the system. It wasn't really that hard."

"And now you're alive but not really?"

"That's absurd," Ren retorted, offense jumping to his eyes. "I'm totally alive. I simply don't exist in your dimension. If I did, bad things would probably happen. Papa Creola and Mama Jamba would probably nag me incessantly about all the rules I supposedly broke, but really, the blame was all on them. Close the loops if you don't want a skilled person such as myself to find ways to break your rules."

"You don't have a lot of friends, do you?" Paris asked.

"You'd be surprised," Ren answered. "Before I nearly destroyed the planet you currently call home while defying my death, I saved it a few times. Everyone loves a hero."

"So even though you have a bad attitude, you *are* a good guy," Paris observed, remembering what Papa Creola had said about how Ren wasn't evil although he broke the laws of time and space.

"Well, you admitted to having a bad attitude, and I'm sure you think of yourself as good so the two aren't mutually exclusive, now are they?"

"Good point," Paris chirped. "So the technology to harness energy to open a specific vortex? Can you please help me with that?"

"For sure," Ren answered but didn't say anything else.

Paris lowered her chin. "Will you?"

He held up a finger, pausing her. "I will, but first you have to make me a promise."

"Why?" Paris wondered who this bloke was that he'd require a promise from her. They were pretty much strangers.

"Because I happen to like this world and don't want it turned into a scrambled egg. There's a reason I didn't write down or publish the way I cheated death. Then it would have shown up here, and some idiot would try and replicate it. Interdimensional travel is probably the most tricky thing anyone can ever do."

"So it's okay for you to defy death, break laws, and move between realms, but the rest of us can't?" Paris challenged.

He flashed her a grin. "That's right, love. I'm Ren Lewis, and rules don't apply to me. I didn't destroy the world when I did what I did. I can't say anyone else would be so lucky...and by luck, I mean utterly perfect in execution."

"Your modesty is simply inspiring," Paris joked.

"I've been told," Ren stated. "Anyway, you have to make a promise, and if you go back on it, I will hunt you down, haunt you from my dimension—which will no doubt make you look like a loon—and within a few short months, I'll break your sanity."

"What's this promise?" Paris stated.

"I'm going to give you what you need," Ren stated. "You'll give it to your magitech guy to fix the vortex opener. Then you're to destroy the instructions and after your mission, demolish the vortex opener. Papa Creola knows what opening a vortex to another dimension will do to the fabric of time and apparently believes it's worth the risk in this case. However, if you do it again, you risk creating all sorts of problems here, in my realm, and thousands of others. They're all connected but separate, and that's for an important reason. Doors aren't supposed to be open between them. Each time it happens, we run the risk of everything crashing down for all of us."

Paris soaked this all in, the magnitude of what she had to do to get her parents back really settling in. They must have been incredible people for Papa Creola to take such a risk. What Ren was asking made sense. It was smart, and she was happy to comply. "Yes, I'll destroy everything."

Ren nodded and pulled a piece of paper from the inside pocket of his suit jacket. "That's written on special paper with special ink, meaning that the information can't become the property of the Great Library. I enjoy this place more than anyone, but some things don't need to be on these shelves."

Paris took the piece of paper and opened it to find it filled with equations and information that didn't make sense to her, but she guessed that Uncle John, Subner, and Papa Creola would be able to figure it out. "Thanks for this."

"Destroy it and the device when you finish," Ren warned. "I'll know if you don't. I'll feel the vortex when you open it and if another one opens, then remember..."

"The haunting," Paris filled in his words. "I get it. My sanity is at stake. I'll do as you wish."

"Good." Ren backed away. "I'd say good luck on your mission, but it seems as though you're going to need a lot more than that. It sounds like you're going to need a bloody miracle, but unfortunately, all you have is magic and your bad attitude. I hope that's enough."

Paris gulped and nodded. "Me too."

CHAPTER FIFTY-THREE

It was strange to exit a door at the front of the Great Library and step through the stone wall into the Serenity Garden at Happily Ever After College. Paris turned to find only a small seam that indicated the door to the library. Otherwise, it was hardly noticeable.

The Serenity Garden appeared totally different than the last time Paris was there, after the magitech AI ruckus. Hemingway must have been busy getting the space cleaned up so the students had access to it again.

Paris' belly rumbled when she strode into the mansion, reminding her that she hadn't eaten in...well, she couldn't remember how long. She stopped off at the kitchen, hoping to grab a snack since it was a while until Chef Ash would serve a meal. She found him in there, as usual, several pots and pans simmering and stirring themselves—the many aromas instantly intoxicating.

"Can I steal a sandwich?" Paris pointed at a tray of cream cheese and cucumber sandwiches sitting on the closest work-station.

Chef Ash turned, a surprised smile springing to his face. "There you are. Yes, you can have all the sandwiches. Do you want me to whip you up something hot? I can make lentil soup or chicken curry or just about anything you'd like. I bet you're hungry after all your adventures and pulling off those disguising spells."

Paris nodded and sat on the barstool she often occupied when visiting with Chef Ash. "I'm starving, but sandwiches are perfect. Thank you. How is the escape room coming along?"

"Oh, it's great." His face transformed with excitement. "I have it almost done thanks to some help from Hemingway."

"Great news," Paris said. "Then we'll be ready to move to the next phase of the plan."

"I'd say," Chef Ash chirped. "Christine was brilliant at breaking up Grayson and Tee."

"She did it!" Paris exclaimed. She'd had to rush off to Roya Lane, then to the Great Library straight after the meeting at McGregor Technologies, and hadn't gotten a proper update.

He nodded proudly. "She's brilliant in the field and owned the role as Colt. I think that made Grayson fester with resentment and on top of everything else, it seemed to push him over the edge."

"That's great news," Paris said.

"Yeah and when I was there today working on the escape room, Grayson mentioned that something I'd said made him rethink the engagement."

"Oh?" Paris questioned. "Was it another one of your wise quotes on building and architecture?"

"Well, I did quote John Ruskin, saying, 'When we build, let us think that we build forever.'"

"I can see how that would make someone rethink marrying a train wreck like Tee." Paris laughed.

"Yeah, that was the idea," Chef Ash agreed. "However, it was something else I said."

"Which was?" Paris questioned.

"Well, when Tee yelled at me for the third time for the noise the power tools were making, I said to Grayson that I'd rather hear the racket from an electric saw for the rest of my life than her nagging."

A laugh burst out of her mouth. "That's simply brilliant."

Chef Ash beamed. "Thanks. It's fun working in the field. I've never done it before, always just teaching and cooking. As a bonus, I've gotten to flex my carpentry skills—all thanks to you."

Paris blushed and ate a bite of her sandwich. "Well, I'm glad you're enjoying, and it seems we're on track. We've destroyed two companies, one relationship, and now we have one more to go."

He chuckled. "I never thought that taking down companies and ruining relationships would make me feel proud."

She nodded, feeling a little demented for relishing it. "Think of all the good that's going to come from this. Now all we have to do is break up Amelia and Bryce, and we'll be ready for the last part of the plan."

Chef Ash flashed a proud grin while retrieving something from the refrigerator. "I had an idea about that and thought I'd get it ready. I know you're so busy with the Deathly Shadow business, I wanted to take some of the stress off you."

"Thanks." Paris tried to look over his shoulder as he pulled something from the industrial-size cooler.

Chef Ash turned, presenting a large white box. He set it down in front of Paris. On the top was a card addressed to Amelia Rose. She opened it and read:

Ms. Amelia Rose,

I wanted the chance to apologize for the feud that's gone on too long between us. Will you please meet me tonight in the basement of McGregor Technologies? I hope that we can finally come to a truce. I really think that if we start working together, we'd both be more successful and I'd much rather have someone as talented as you on my side than against me.

Sincerely,

Grayson McGregor

Paris opened the box to find decadent chocolate-covered strawberries, which instantly made her mouth water. She jerked her head up, her mouth wide open.

"Wow, this is perfect," Paris said in awe of her friend. "Bryce is going to flip when Amelia gets this. He was already so jealous of Grayson when we spied before."

Chef Ash nodded. "Then Amelia, too curious not to, will show up where Grayson will be working on puzzles and planning in the escape room. He was excited when I left earlier and said he was going to work on it all night."

Paris beamed. "At that point, we've done all we can, and the rest is up to fate."

"I don't believe that fate has much to do with two people falling in love," Chef Ash related. "Two people who are meant for one another need to be given the opportunity for the spark to ignite. Those two, with the obstacles removed from their lives, will fall headfirst."

"I really hope you're right." Paris' phone stole her attention. She retrieved it and gobbled down the rest of her sandwich. Not only was the Amelia and Grayson mission coming to a head, but so was her mission.

The message was from Rory. He was done with the container for the Deathly Shadow, meaning that she was one step closer to bringing her parents back.

CHAPTER FIFTY-FOUR

It was strange to see so many people inside the Fantastical Armory. Paris hadn't spent a lot of time in the shop, but every time she'd been in there, the large space was mostly empty. Now there was a giant, two elves, a fae, the assassin baker, and her Uncle John.

"You're late," Papa Creola called when Paris strode into the shop.

"I literally just got the message from Rory." Paris was still wiping cream cheese from the corner of her mouth.

King Rudolf gave her a commiserating look. "Don't you know that when Papa requests a meeting with you, you're supposed to time travel to five minutes before and show up promptly?"

"Time travel is illegal, Rudolf Sweetwater," Papa Creola scolded. "If I catch you doing it again, I'll have all your assets frozen."

The fae let out a high-pitched scream of panic. "No, without money, I'll be like a commoner and have to drive a used Tesla."

"Commoners don't drive Teslas," Lee corrected.

"Or drive," Rory added.

"And why would you drive when you have portal magic?" Uncle John asked, his brow scrunched up as he worked on the device in front of him.

"Driving around makes me sleepy," Rudolf stated. "That's how I get ready for bed at night, taking a late drive until my eyes nearly shut."

"Sounds safe," Lee snarked.

"Let's be glad Teslas can drive themselves," Uncle John added.

"They can?" King Rudolf questioned. "Oh, that makes so much sense now. I thought I was controlling the car with my mind."

Papa Creola shook his head and refocused on Paris. "Did you meet with Ren Lewis?"

"Yeah, that guy is a piece of work," Paris answered.

"You didn't make him mad as I warned?" Papa Creola asked. "He's very temperamental."

Paris laughed. "You can say that again. No, but he insulted me a few times." She retrieved the piece of paper that Ren had given her and handed it to Uncle John, who was still tinkering with the vortex opener.

"Does that make sense to you?" Paris watched as he scanned the page.

His eyes widened, and his mouth popped open. "Of course. That's exactly what I was missing."

He showed it to Subner, and the elf nodded. "That should do the trick. I should have realized that it was a decimal issue."

"Isn't it always?" Lee asked, earning a contemptuous glare from Subner.

Rory held up a small silver container made from metal that had to be enchanted. It looked like a clamshell with hinges on one side and opened in the middle on a seam. "The container for the Deathly Shadow is ready."

"Do you think he'll fit in there?" King Rudolf asked. "I heard he used to be a chunkster when he had a body."

"He doesn't have a body anymore," Papa Creola stated tersely.

"He's just energy and space won't matter. We only need something that will hold him."

"The vortex opener will fit around that?" Paris' nerves built in her chest again.

"It should," Uncle John answered. "I just need a bit longer to do the reconfiguration on it, and with the new formula, it ought to work."

"Okay, and you two are ready to go after Captain Morgan when I set off?" Paris asked King Rudolf and Lee.

"Yeah, but I think I'd rather face the Deathly Shadow than my daughter," the fae related. "After missing her tanning appointment and her ten facial treatments a day, she's going to be a raving mess."

"Paris is the only one who can face the Deathly Shadow," Papa Creola said matter-of-factly.

"About that," Paris began, her tone wavering. "I have the container to put the creep in. I have the magitech to open the vortex. But I'm confused on one tiny, little bitty thing."

"What?" Papa Creola asked simply.

"That whole overpowering him to put the Deathly Shadow in the container," Paris answered.

Everyone looked at Father Time, awaiting his answer.

"You're going to have to figure that out on your own," he stated to her disappointment. "We can't do everything for you."

"Right." She drew out the word.

"I've secured a location for the showdown," Papa Creola continued. "The ideal place will be Death Valley in California."

"Because of the name?" Paris remembered what Cat had said about names of locations and significance, which was why the Deathly Shadow had picked Paris, France, to hold Captain Morgan.

"That's right," Papa Creola answered. "Now we have everything that we need to proceed. Tomorrow morning, you'll portal to Death Valley, remove your protective charm, and wait. Remember that you have to do this alone, Paris. Whatever happens when you face the Deathly Shadow will affect everyone on this planet. Everything for the last twenty years has been building up to this moment."

The room was silent for a long moment.

"You can do this." Uncle John offered Paris a look of encouragement.

"If anyone can, it's you," King Rudolf chimed.

"But if you think you're going to fail," Subner began. "Consider offing yourself before the Deathly Shadow overpowers you."

"Whatever happens, there will be no stopping it." Papa Creola's voice suddenly sounded heavy. "The events that will come to pass tomorrow have been coming for a long time. There's no stopping them at this point. We just have to hope that this story ends in our favor."

CHAPTER FIFTY-FIVE

A melia Rose was shaking when she stormed into McGregor Technologies that night. She didn't know what Grayson was up to. Maybe he did want a truce after sending the chocolate-covered strawberries, but it wasn't a gift that went over well with Bryce.

Things had been tough with Bryce for a while...well, from the beginning, if Amelia was honest with herself. She'd always thought of him as a friend. Then he wanted more, and she told herself that he loved her so much, she'd be stupid not to reciprocate. However, she'd never been in love with him, as much as she'd pretended—trying to force the feelings.

Amelia had convinced herself that she was supposed to love someone if they were madly in love with her. That's why she'd accepted his proposal. When things started to fail with Rose Industries, her relationship with Bryce also deteriorated more. Now she reasoned that when there wasn't a foundation of true love, there was nothing to keep things strong when life got hard. She and Bryce had a foundation built on conveniences and his obsession with her. That wasn't enough.

That afternoon Amelia had decided to disband her company, unable to recover from the harmful accusations about working conditions in Rose Industries' facilities. She didn't understand where all of this had come from or why it felt impossible to fight no matter how much she tried. It was almost as if magic was at work, although she wasn't sure she believed in such things.

After the heavy afternoon of feeling like a failure, Amelia had gotten the note and gift from Grayson, requesting the meeting at McGregor Technologies. That hadn't gone well with Bryce. It was as though he'd been looking for a reason to explode at her. Then he'd issued his ultimatum, and that was the last of it for her.

"If you go and meet with that corrupt businessman, we're over," Bryce had said an hour before.

Amelia didn't respond well to threats. Grayson's company had failed too. Maybe he did want to resolve things. No matter what, Amelia knew that she needed to meet with Grayson and figure things out. Closure after everything was what she needed most. So she pulled off the gaudy engagement ring Bryce had given her and left it on his desk before storming out.

McGregor Technologies was quiet when Amelia descended to the basement. There was no security, as she would have expected, but the company was about to declare bankruptcy. A meeting in the basement was strange, but maybe that's where Grayson's office was.

As she strode out of the elevator, Amelia got the impression the space had recently been under construction. The smell of paint and new carpet was heavy in the air.

Unsure where to go, Amelia strode one way down the long hallway, then the other. There was only one door. She paused in front of it, reading the sign: "Only the pure of heart should enter, ready to be lost and found."

Amelia blinked at the weird message but shook off her confusion. She turned the knob and pushed the door open. After sticking her head through, she glanced back and forth and saw a small room that looked like a study with bookshelves and lounge chairs. One of the built-in bookshelves at the back of the room wasn't completely flush with the wall. Looking around and not seeing any other rooms to look for Grayson, Amelia cautiously moved over to the bookcase.

She grabbed the side and pulled back the hidden door to reveal another room. This one resembled a billiards hall with several pool tables and all the balls scattered as if someone had been playing a game.

She glanced around, wondering why Grayson would want to meet down here and also wondering what all this was.

At the back of the hall was another door. Sitting in front of it was the black and white eight ball used in a billiard game. Her curiosity piqued, Amelia bent and retrieved the eight ball, wondering why it was sitting beside the door. She tried the handle, but it was locked.

Amelia sighed, feeling like this was a waste of her time, but also intrigued and reluctant to abandon this. She really did want to find out what Grayson wished to say to her. If she was honest with herself, Amelia hadn't been able to quit thinking about him since that meeting on the Underground. Maybe it was because that first interaction had been so volatile, but it felt like there was more to it than that.

She absentmindedly turned the eight ball over in her fingers while thinking. That's when she noticed a key taped to the other side. It seemed like a strange place to keep a key, though.

Fueled by something inside her, Amelia removed the key from the eight ball and fitted it to the lock. It slid in without an issue and turned at once. Amelia pulled back the door, again poking her head through.

In the next room, she heard something break the silence. It was a small bistro with soft music and lighting. There were a few tables set with tablecloths and flowers.

"Grayson," Amelia called, looking around. She stepped into the room, leaving the key in the door. She was both confused and intrigued, unaware that the door behind her had closed and locked.

In a corner booth, Grayson perked up from where he'd bent over what looked like plans. He gave her a confused look as though trying to place her face in that location.

"I'm here," Amelia offered with a neutral expression.

"Okay…" He drew out the word.

"Well, what is all this?" Amelia motioned to the bistro decorations. "Why did you want me to meet you here?"

He tilted his head and squinted. "I'm sorry, I have no idea what you're talking about."

CHAPTER FIFTY-SIX

Paris was unsurprised that she wasn't hungry at dinner. She didn't think it was because she'd had the cream cheese cucumber sandwich and it ruined her appetite. Paris thought it was because she had to face a treacherous evil the next morning and still didn't know how she would overpower the Deathly Shadow.

Maybe sensing her stress, most at the dinner table kept their distance from her, not engaging her in conversation. Christine and Chef Ash had taken off to monitor the Grayson and Amelia situation in case more intervention was necessary.

Paris turned the page of the notes that Uncle Clark had given her on the Deathly Shadow, hoping that something jumped out at her and gave her an idea of how to defeat him. She'd read through the comprehensive details multiple times, and so far, nothing had occurred to her.

The notes detailed many of the horrible things that the Deathly Shadow did to lose his soul and body. Then he'd learned of the prophecy of the halfling and waited, knowing that he needed to absorb Paris' powers to come back in full—well, better than before. As informative as that was, it didn't tell Paris anything that she thought she could use to defeat the monster.

Aunt Sophia had sent some encouraging messages and stated that she and Lunis would be stationed close by if things got dire. However, Papa Creola had made it pretty evident that Paris needed to do this alone. That was the only way it would work. Still, it made Paris feel somewhat better to know that she wasn't entirely alone.

Still, whether she had an army or the container and vortex opener, none of it mattered if she couldn't overpower the Deathly Shadow.

"Can I offer you something that's helped me when facing situations I didn't know how to overcome?" Penny Pullman asked, sitting next to Paris.

She'd been so far off in thought that she hadn't realized the other girl was there and watching her.

"How do you know I'm facing something I don't know how to overcome?" Paris looked at the girl with kind eyes.

"I recognize the look on your face," Penny admitted. "I've worn it many times and see it reflected in the mirror constantly."

"Oh, well, I'm definitely up against a challenge that I don't know how to overcome," Paris confided.

"I can't tell you how to defeat what you're facing tomorrow," Penny began thoughtfully. "I don't think any of us want to be in your shoes."

"Well, besides Christine who thinks this is all so cool," Paris interrupted.

Both girls laughed.

"Yes, besides Christine," Penny agreed. "But I can tell you that the best weapon anyone can ever employ is to believe in yourself. I know that sounds like fluffy advice that won't really help, but at the end of the day, it's going to be you against the Deathly Shadow. All you have is you, and I think the key for you to win is to believe in yourself no matter what. As ominous as things get, you can't let your faith in you waver because that's when you'll fail."

Paris thought for a moment, considering the wise words. They didn't sound like fluff. She knew that in life, the answers to the biggest problems were simple. Belief was everything. All the self-doubt was only making things worse. It was time for Paris to give herself a pep talk, get some rest, and get ready for the showdown. It was that simple and that complex. It was that easy and that hard. She felt ready for what she'd face the next day. She didn't know how she'd overpower the Deathly Shadow, but she knew that she would—and all the rest were details that she'd figure out when the time came.

"Thanks." Paris offered a smile of gratitude to her friend.

"I believe it's going to work out," Penny stated with a rare confidence in her voice. "I mean, you should too because when you believe that, you see opportunities. The alternative is believing that it won't work out. Then you see only obstacles."

Paris drew in a breath, feeling a renewed courage that she desperately needed for what came next. "It's going to work out."

CHAPTER FIFTY-SEVEN

"You asked me to meet you here." Amelia Rose wished she'd taken the note on the top of the box of chocolate-covered strawberries.

Grayson McGregor shook his head. He looked tired, albeit cute in a blue sweater, his hair tousled. "I'm sorry, I think you're confused."

"The box of chocolate-covered strawberries you sent," Amelia shook her head.

A nervous laugh emerged from Grayson's mouth. "What? I didn't send anything of the sort."

Amelia scratched her head, completely confused. She suddenly wondered if this was a trick, looking around at the strange bistro and remembering the other weird rooms. She indicated the tables. "What is all this?"

He glanced around, appearing disoriented too. "It's an escape room...well, it's going to be. It's still in the works."

Amelia was intrigued that Grayson was building an escape room in the basement of his building. "So you didn't send me a note telling me to meet you in the basement of McGregor Technologies?"

His head snapped to the side, obviously not prepared for that question. "Basement? Me? What? No, I didn't."

"Well, then I have no idea what's going on," Amelia said, looking around. "And the timing couldn't be worse."

He nodded. "I agree. I don't feel like fighting with you after the last couple of days I've had."

"Fight?" Amelia nearly yelled. "Your note said you wanted to talk and come to a truce."

"I didn't write that note and didn't know anything about it," he stated adamantly.

"Then who is playing this game on us?"

He shook his head. "I have no clue, but why would I invite you down to my unfinished escape room? That's absurd, especially after everything we've been through."

"Yeah." Amelia chewed on her lip, disappointment suddenly billowing in her chest. "This is so odd."

"Really odd," he admitted. "We'll have to figure out who's behind this trick."

"For sure." Amelia wished he'd sent the note and the chocolate-covered strawberries, then grew frustrated that she felt that way. Still, that was the truth that she'd only admit to herself. "Well, I guess I better be on my way. Sorry for bothering you."

"You weren't bothering me, but yeah, I understand." Grayson sighed.

Amelia could have sworn disappointment surfaced in his eyes too, but she pulled her gaze away, turning for the door. Her heels made clicking noises on the tiled floor as she crossed the space.

To her surprise, when she tried the door handle, it didn't budge. She tried it again. It was locked.

"What's wrong?" Grayson sensed her stress.

Amelia spun and pointed at the door. "It's locked."

CHAPTER FIFTY-EIGHT

"Locked?" Grayson frowned. "No, that's impossible. That's the only way out of here."

"What?" Amelia's hands planted on her hips. "How is that possible?"

"Well, we're still under construction," Grayson explained, moving around her and trying the door handle. It didn't budge. He glanced over his shoulder as if he was missing something.

"How is there no other way out?" Amelia pointed at the far wall. "What's that door for?"

"It's a bathroom and closet, but that's it," he stated.

"So this is a dead-end? How is that possible?"

"We have to build the next rooms. And there are no emergency exits yet."

"Don't you have a key?" she asked.

"It was taped to the bottom side of an eight ball," he answered. "Where is it now?"

She pointed at the door. "It's in the other side of the handle."

He threw his hands up. "Oh, great. So we're locked in here."

"No, we're not," Amelia argued while pulling her phone from her pocket. Her eyes widened. "I don't have reception."

"No, you wouldn't." He sounded annoyed. "We're in a basement, and it's an escape room where I don't want people cheating on the puzzles."

"So we don't have the key to get out of the only exit to this room and no phone access," she began. "When do you expect your cleaning crew to be here or anyone else?"

"Well, since I'm declaring bankruptcy, I haven't been wasting money on such frivolities as cleaners."

"But you had an escape room built?" she argued.

He nodded. "I had a contract. And to answer your question, the construction crew isn't supposed to return until tomorrow morning."

She narrowed her eyes at him. "So you didn't send me a package of chocolate-covered strawberries and a note to meet you in this basement, then lock me in here with you? And now it sounds like I might have to spend the night in here with you?"

He held up his hands. "Look, I didn't send you anything. I don't know about this at all. It's a mystery to me, and I obviously don't want to be locked up in here tonight either."

Amelia felt ready to explode, but then she realized something important about what he said. Grayson hadn't said that he didn't want to be with her. He had only said that he didn't want to be locked up.

She directed her gaze around the room, looking for escape options. Finally, she laughed, realizing the silliness of the moment. "Is it ironic that we're locked up together in an escape room that we can't get out of?"

Grayson chuckled and nodded. "I was thinking that same thing."

"So there really isn't a way out of here?" she asked. "A vent where I can sneak through a false wall or something?"

He arched an eyebrow at her. "I admire your ingenuity, but no.

As I said, the room is still under construction, but we should be safe here for the night. There is ventilation and airflow. It just isn't large enough for a human to shimmy through."

Amelia slumped, looking down at her pencil skirt and blouse, realizing she'd be in these clothes the rest of the night. However, she was determined to make the most of it.

Grayson flashed her a smile to her surprise. "Well, if we have to be locked up all night, you at least want to make the most of it?"

She tilted her head with a skeptical expression. "What does that mean?"

"That means that the props on the table are real." He lifted a bottle of red wine off the table and held it up. "Are you up for a drink? I'm up for drinking away my problems."

Amelia nodded and laughed. "Yeah, I really could use a drink or two. One for each of my problems, at least."

He winked at her and grabbed a couple of glasses. "Great. Go ahead and grab the corner booth. I hear it's the best spot in this place and fills up fast."

CHAPTER FIFTY-NINE

Leaving the comfort and safety of Happily Ever After College to portal to one of the most dangerous places in the world felt like a cruel irony. Staying in bed wasn't an option for Paris. Hiding inside Fairy Godmother Estate wasn't going to work. And putting off the inevitable meeting wasn't smart.

Paris' fate was tied to the Deathly Shadow. It always had been since before she was born. He needed her to come back into power. She needed him to have the only thing she never knew she wanted—her parents. Avoiding him and using protective charms would only work for so long. Paris hadn't been able to live a full life, and she was tired of running and hiding. Obviously, she didn't want to die but she would rather that than live a half-life. Of course, her death would mean the Deathly Shadow came into full power, so she needed to avoid that at all costs.

Preparing to open the portal to Death Valley on the Enchanted Grounds, Paris looked at Faraday beside her. "Are you sure you want to go with me?" she asked the squirrel.

"I've never been to Death Valley," he said in reply.

Paris rolled her eyes, which were still adjusting to the growing sunlight as morning dawned across the grounds. "That's your reason? This isn't a field trip to fulfill something on your bucket list."

"Did you know that Death Valley is the hottest place on Earth?" Faraday mused. "Because of that, it's home to a whole host of unique animals, an ecological atmosphere like no other, and so many different scientific phenomena."

"Rattlesnakes," Paris sneered.

"You mean the genera Crotalus and Sistrurus of the subfamily Crotalinae?"

"No, I meant rattlesnakes you dorky genius," she muttered. "I hear you can stumble upon huge nests of hundreds of rattlesnakes in Death Valley. If that's not a sign that it's the pits of hell, I don't know what is."

"Actually, the Badwater Basin where we're going is the lowest point of elevation in all of North America," he offered, his tone teeming with excitement.

"Great, so I'm going to the literal pits of hell," Paris remarked. "To meet someone whose history makes the devil sound like a tame school girl."

"It's going to make for a great story at a dinner party," Faraday offered.

She shook her head. "Great, when I'm hosting my weekly game night, in between Karen talking about her trip to the zoo and Melanie gossiping about the neighbors, I'll be like, 'Did I ever tell you all about that time I met Satan's mentor in Death Valley? Please pass the sour cream and onion dip.'"

He shook his head. "I hope you'd have better sense than to serve sour cream and onion dip at a dinner party. It's not a football game. There are standards."

Paris actually laughed, grateful for the stress relief. "What's the scientific family name for squirrels?"

"I'm a member of the family Sciuridae," he answered at once. "It includes squirrels, chipmunks, prairie—"

"No, you're a member of your very own weird family. It's called the Weirdest Weirdos," she interrupted. "Any other facts you want to pass along about Death Valley before I portal to see Mr. Angry Pants?"

"I don't think in his current form that the Deathly Shadow can wear pants," he countered.

Paris laughed again. "No, that's why he wants me. So he can finally wear those cargo pants he bought from Gap."

"I am certain that cargo pants aren't in fashion anymore," he objected.

"How would you know?" Paris questioned. "Since you don't wear pants." Her mouth popped open suddenly. "Oh, that would be so cute. We should get you little pants and maybe a suit jacket. Oh! What about a top hat?"

Faraday shook his little head, not at all looking amused. "I don't like hats."

"Of course that's your response to my awesome idea," Paris grumbled. "I think you've missed the point."

"That you want to dress me up like a little dollhouse critter," he muttered. "No, I didn't miss it. I'm simply going to ignore such a ridiculous idea."

"Well, although this conversation is fun and making me question my sanity, I think I'll pop off to Satan's lair," she joked. "I'll bring you back a refrigerator magnet as a souvenir."

"I don't have a refrigerator," he muttered and folded his tiny arms over his chest.

"Fine, I'll get you a key chain," she offered.

"Well, don't drink the water," Faraday advised when she was about to bite the bullet and create the portal to Death Valley.

Paris paused. "Say what?"

"Don't drink the water in the basin. It's poisonous."

She sighed as if the interruption was an inconvenience but was secretly grateful for the delay. Hurrying off to fight a devasting evil wasn't something she wanted to be early for. "What gave it away? The Badwater Basin part?"

He nodded. "I'm glad that wasn't lost on you."

"Although I'm portaling off to the pits of hell without a sporty water bottle, I doubt that I'd get there and be like, oh I'll take a quick drink from this stream before the devil's predecessor shows up."

"It's more like a pool than a stream," he corrected.

"Noted. Thanks. Well, I'm off. Water my plants while I'm gone." All out of jokes, Paris opened a portal to the Badwater Basin in Death Valley, California, feeling more like she was sleepwalking at that point than fully aware of what was happening.

She took a step toward the portal and noticed the squirrel scurry beside her, keeping up. Like the first time they met, Paris paused and regarded Faraday. "Are you following me?"

"I said I was going with you," he insisted.

"This isn't really the opportunity for you to tag along for a science adventure."

"I know. You said that humans weren't allowed to accompany you because it might prevent the Deathly Shadow from showing up, but I'm not a human. Only a strange squirrel hanging out in the desert. I won't disrupt your meeting with DS."

Paris laughed at the acronym, wishing they'd employed it earlier. "According to Plato, I'm supposed to do this on my own because as Penny said, it's about believing in myself."

He nodded. "Makes sense. When you don't have a backup option, then you pull on strength and power that you would never have harnessed. I'm guessing it will be something stronger than an army could have mustered."

"We will see." Paris chewed on her lip.

"Anyway, I'll be there just in case," he offered. "Like, if you need help identifying some rocks or a mountain range."

"You do realize I'm not going on a nature hike, right?"

"I get it." He regarded the shimmering portal in front of them.

"I'll stay out of the way and a weird squirrel accompanying you shouldn't take away from your need to believe in yourself to do this. You still have to do it on your own."

Paris considered this, really surprised that Faraday wanted to go with her for this. Still, Plato had also mentioned that he'd be watching, so she reasoned it was okay for the squirrel to be there. As he said, he wasn't human, so it shouldn't count against her for the DS.

She gave in with a sigh. "Okay, fine. But don't get in the way or bore me with archeological facts about Death Valley or I'll drop you in a pit of snakes."

He grinned, facing toward the portal. "You got yourself a deal."

CHAPTER SIXTY

Amelia swirled the Bordeaux around in her glass, enjoying the way it ran up the sides and crawled back down. She set it down on the white tablecloth, looking up at Grayson and realizing he was watching her from the other side of the booth.

"So McGregor Technologies is declaring bankruptcy?" she asked him. Neither of them had spoken since they sat.

He nodded and sipped his wine. "It seems inevitable at this point."

"If it makes you feel any better, Rose Industries doesn't look like it will recover from the allegations about employee mistreatment," she offered.

He frowned. "Your failure has never brought me any good feelings."

Amelia drank, enjoying the warmth from the red wine. "So you didn't make the false claims about the conditions of our facilities causing the initial investigations and slander?"

Surprise sprang to his face. "Of course not. But it crossed my mind that you leaked the information about the faulty wiring of McGregor's products to the press."

"Well, I didn't," she stated firmly. "We might have had bad blood from the beginning, but I only wanted to beat you fair and square."

He laughed. "You just about did. Pretty impressive for just starting Rose Industries. Maybe I should have hired you when you first applied. I guess when I thought lack of experience was a factor in success, I was wrong."

She grinned and crossed her legs under the bistro table. "I didn't know what wasn't possible, unlike some jaded veteran in the industry."

"So you exceeded the goal quickly with Rose Industries instead of thinking of the perimeters," Grayson observed. "It's kind of poetic."

Amelia nodded. "When you don't know the restrictions, they don't apply to you as much. No one told me what wasn't possible so I did it."

"And in record time, you created a company that took over the market."

She sighed and took another drink. "It's all gone now. It sullied the brand, but that's okay. I'll start again."

He nodded, his eyes bright across the table. "That's what I said. The difference between the mediocre and those inherently successful is the latter doesn't quit. A failed venture means that we'll know how to do it better the next time."

"It's true." Amelia smiled. "A loser says, well, I've failed so it's time to quit. A winner says I've failed so now I know how to succeed."

"I am sorry about Rose Industries," Grayson offered with a meaningful expression in his eyes.

"Me too," she admitted. "But I already have ideas for my next venture."

He smiled slightly. "Me too."

She returned the smile. "Good. It sounds like we're both going to land on our feet."

Grayson lifted his wine glass, "Then how about we say cheers to new ventures."

Amelia raised her glass and clinked it against his. "Cheers to that."

CHAPTER SIXTY-ONE

Paris felt as if she'd stepped through the portal to another planet. Death Valley was unearthly. If she survived, she had to ask Mama Jamba what she thought when she created such a strange place.

She stood on the flatlands on a desert floor that stretched out for miles in all directions. The cracked ground created a strange, crusty hexagonal design.

Distant mountains surrounded them, making Paris feel as if she was sitting in a bowl. The air was dry, and although it was early, the temperature was already creeping up, replacing the night's chill.

Paris reasoned that Happily Ever After College, wherever it was, had to be in a similar time zone as the West Coast. Or for this event, Papa Creola had arranged for Paris to portal here in the morning. She was grateful that it wasn't blistering hot and definitely didn't want to stick around until the sun was blazing overhead, heating up lava flowing under the ground in this hellish place.

"Isn't it fascinating that Death Valley is an example of the viciousness of nature?" Faraday asked, having stepped through the portal beside her. "There are volcanos, craters, extreme temperatures on both ranges and—"

Paris glared down at him.

As if surrendering, the squirrel held up his paw. "Sorry. It's habit. I won't talk about any of my scientific observations."

"Be a squirrel," Paris suggested, trying to suck in a breath to release the tension in her chest. She didn't know how long it would be until the Deathly Shadow, which apparently was attuned to her energy and could track her down, would find her. When she was outside Happily Ever After College or another protected location, it never took very long.

"I'll try," Faraday said. "Be a squirrel. I can do that."

"Good." Paris sighed, realizing what she had to do next. Her fingers were shaking when she went to remove the protective charm around her neck. That would help to alert the Deathly Shadow to her location. Moreover, in protecting her, the talisman also blocked some of her energy, which she'd need to overpower the Deathly Shadow—however, she wasn't sure how she would do that when the time came.

Her fingers knocked against the other necklace she had fastened around her neck. Paris left the heart-shaped locket on as she removed the protective charm. She ran her fingertips over the smooth coolness of the locket, grateful to have something from her family with her, even if they couldn't be there to help her.

The etching of her initials reminded her that she was named for a fierce warrior—Guinevere Beaufont. She hoped that wherever her grandmother was, she was loaning her strength or courage or whatever Paris needed to get through this.

The words on the other side of the locket ran through Paris' mind. Words she'd read for what felt like most of her life and never understood: You have to keep breaking your heart until it opens. –Rumi

She didn't know what the words meant or why they were on

the locket that apparently protected her identity and now had other purposes, although she had no idea what they could be. Maybe the words didn't have any symbolism, but for some reason, she didn't entirely buy that.

There was no wind in Death Valley. It was eerily silent. As the sun peeked over the mountains to the east, Paris stayed vigilant, looking for any sign of the Deathly Shadow.

The scratching noise at her feet stole her attention. She glanced down to find Faraday kicking the crusty sand. "What are you doing?"

"I'm behaving like a squirrel."

"Are you digging?"

Faraday shrugged. "Yes, but I promise that my digging isn't leading to any scientific observation."

"Good," she chirped, searching the plains.

"I'm bored," he admitted. "Did you bring a sudoku or something to do?"

"Yeah," she retorted with an amused sigh. "I've come to meet a deadly creature and thought to pack activities for you. Would you also like a snack too?"

"That would be delightful," he agreed, his eyes large with excitement. "Do you have any fruit gummies? Those are a smart snack on the go."

Paris shook her head and pointed toward the closest set of mountains. "Why don't you go over there and explore? If I don't know you're making scientific observations, I won't care."

He glanced longingly in the distance, his curiosity obviously making him want to explore. "Okay, but I won't go far. If you need anything, holler."

Paris rolled her eyes and watched as the squirrel ran for the mountains, his brown form camouflaging him into the desert. As soon as Faraday was gone, a strong gust of hot wind swept across the Badwater Basin, making Paris flinch. The sand hit her in the face, forcing her to close her eyes for a moment. The howl that screeched past her ears sent a shiver streaking down her spine.

When she opened her eyes, it was almost as if the sun had changed its mind and decided to set rather than rise. Darkness mostly cloaked everything, but Paris' eyes adjusted immediately, seeing everything around her clearly.

She didn't have to see the black smoky form to know that the Deathly Shadow had arrived. Paris could feel him like a nightmare that had gripped her soul and was fiercely holding on for dear life. She ignored this and sent the signal to the others, pressing a single button on her phone before glancing back at the monster tied to her fate.

CHAPTER SIXTY-TWO

"It's time." King Rudolf lowered his phone after receiving the message from Paris Beaufont.

"Cake time?" Lee asked, leaning against the outside of the warehouse where they were stationed.

"After we rescue Captain Morgan," he answered. "If she finds out that we had cake without her, I'll probably never hear the end of it."

"Or, what would be better than showing up to rescue her with cake?" Lee suggested, drawing out the first word. "If you ever have to rescue me, which I highly doubt, you better bring cake."

"It's a good thought about bringing her cake, but Papa was pretty clear that as soon as the Deathly Shadow showed up to meet Paris, we had to swoop in and save Captain Morgan. We don't know how long we have."

Lee shrugged. "I guess it depends on if Paris dies quickly or slowly."

"She's not going to die. It depends on how long it takes her to defeat the Deathly Shadow." Rudolf hurried for the side door that they'd mapped out would be the best entrance into the place where Captain Morgan was held captive.

Lee ran to keep up with him. "Excuse me for considering all the outcomes. She could die."

"Well, I'm trying to only focus on the positive, desired outcome," Rudolf argued, then pressed his ear to the cold metal wall, listening for other guards. Their surveillance hadn't noted any, but he didn't want to be unpleasantly surprised.

Lee pulled out a sword that Rudolf didn't realize she'd brought with her. "Well, no offense, but an inexperienced half-fairy and half-magician who can't bother to brush her hair, might not stand a chance against an all-encompassing evil who eats demons for breakfast."

He rounded on her. "You can underestimate Paris, but I won't. She is a Beaufont and strength, courage and skill run in their blood. When the time comes, Paris will rise to the challenge. She's going to swallow that stupid shadow-thingy and bring back my best friend. I don't believe in a lot of things like gravity and calories, but I believe in Paris Beaufont."

Lee nodded, smiling victoriously. "Good. You passed the test."

"Test?" he questioned. "What do you mean?"

"I believe not only will that halfling have to believe in herself to be successful," Lee began. "There's a collective consciousness and what we all think has power. We all have to believe she will be successful for her to do it. Any doubt will be her downfall."

Rudolf grinned wide. "Well, I've never believed in anyone more…besides Batman. I believe in Batman."

Lee held up her sword, a twinkle in her eyes. "Well, then half our job is done. Are you ready for the next half?"

Rudolf nodded with confidence. "Let's rescue my little girl."

CHAPTER SIXTY-THREE

Amelia didn't know when she'd laughed that hard. After she and Grayson cheered their future ventures, the conversation rolled easily. Before too long, she was telling him about the time she accidentally tucked her skirt into her underwear and waltzed out of the bathroom at a chic club, hoping to get the attention of her ex-boyfriend who was sitting at the bar, chatting up another girl.

"I was halfway into the club when a Good Samaritan ran after me to tell me that my butt was on display for all to see," she said through a laugh, her eyes watering.

Grayson had then confessed to a series of funny mistakes that led him to where he was then. The two swapped story after story as they finished off the first bottle of wine.

Grayson was opening the second bottle of Bordeaux when Amelia pulled off her high heels and tucked her feet up beside her, deciding to get comfortable. She reasoned that if they had to spend the night there, she might as well settle in.

Grayson's eyes flicked up to meet hers while he poured her a new glass of wine. "It seems that all our mistakes have led us here so in a way, maybe we should be grateful for them."

"How so?" She wondered what he meant.

"Well, as we said, we're wiser now and in a better position to make good decisions," he supplied.

Amelia nodded and pulled the full glass of wine to her. "Yeah, although I probably could have gone without the last decision I made. Not sure what I'll learn from that."

"You mean the working conditions litigations?" He sipped his wine.

She shook her head, starting to feel tipsy but still lucid, as always. "No, I allowed my judgment to be clouded and accepted a proposal I shouldn't have."

His eyes darted to her hand lying on the bistro table. "Oh, I read in the newspaper about you and Bryce Tyler. You aren't…"

Amelia took a drink to cover her nervous expression. She felt ashamed. Not for breaking off the engagement, but for accepting it, knowing Bryce wasn't right for her. "I told him I couldn't marry him and gave him back his ring. I don't know what I was thinking before."

"Well, maybe you had to know what wasn't right for you, to know what was," he offered, a thoughtful expression on his face. "I mean if we're learning from mistakes, why limit them to business ones?"

"Yeah, I hope so." Her cheeks flushed with warmth. "Anyway, I also heard about your engagement. Congratulations."

He pressed his lips together, his gaze falling to his hand lying beside his wine glass. "I broke things off with Tee."

"Oh, I'm sorry." Amelia tried to sound like she meant it, but something deep inside her rejoiced.

Grayson shrugged. "We'd never really gotten along, but I'd learned how to take her in doses."

"That's not really how marriage works." Amelia laughed at him. Thankfully, he joined her.

"I know. Can you imagine the years of misery we would have had? Separate bedrooms and silent dinners. We really couldn't have been more different."

"You fell into the relationship and couldn't figure out how to fall out of it," Amelia offered, speaking from experience.

He nodded. "Then before I knew it, things had gone so far, I didn't know how to back out of it."

"And you tell yourself that if they want you, that you might as well want them back," Amelia added.

"That's exactly right." He sat up. "I convinced myself that I was the problem. I was too much into my company. Too distant. What if it was only that we didn't have the spark to make me interested and want to put in the effort?"

Amelia felt something unfurl in her chest, like a feeling connected to an idea. "I think you have to have that spark, that chemistry, or the foundation will never be there to keep you interested."

"My carpenter who created this escape room recently quoted David Allan Coe. I think it went, 'It is not the beauty of a building you should look at; it is the construction of the foundation that will stand the test of time."

"Sounds like a wise carpenter," Amelia agreed.

Grayson nodded. "He really was. Strangely enough, it was other things he said that made me realize no matter what I did or how I changed, Tee was never going to be right for me. So I broke off the engagement. I should give the guy a raise." He laughed at the notion.

Amelia's thoughts trailed back to earlier when the note and present arrived, and she saw Bryce for who he really was—insecure and controlling. It truly was the small things that triggered big events—little phrases from a random person or a chance meeting.

She held up her wine glass this time. "Well, then, should we toast to the lost relationships that hopefully teach us what the right ones look like?"

He grinned at her, holding up his wine glass. "Absolutely. I'll cheers to that."

CHAPTER SIXTY-FOUR

Cold and hot at the same time, Paris felt as if the wind was about to rip her in two. She didn't waver though. Instead, she stood firmly in the mostly dry Badwater Basin, staring at the dark shape in front of her as it grew more solid...somehow.

The voracious wind sent sharp bits of sand into Paris' eyes. It hit her in the face, scratching her cheek. Made her hair whip her as if it was using her parts against her. However, she didn't turn away or shield herself. Didn't stand down from the fight that had been building since the moment of her conception.

Suddenly, while staring at the transparent figure of the Deathly Shadow, something occurred to Paris. She was part-magician. Part-fairy. Still, she couldn't forget that regardless of what a genie did, she had demon blood in her. She was more like the Deathly Shadow than she had ever wanted to admit...until then.

Maybe that wasn't such a bad thing, Paris thought.

What would it take to overpower the Deathly Shadow? He was a demon who had gone farther than any other, who had ingested his own, who had lost his body, unable to survive the acts he'd done in his immortal form. He was seemingly unstoppable.

The Deathly Shadow had believed the prophecy. What he needed was the power from the only magical halfling to ever exist to regain his body and strength. The foretelling had said that was a half-magician, half-fairy, and it wasn't wrong. It only left out one part.

Guinevere Paris Beaufont wasn't only a halfling.

She had the blood of a demon.

That was what would end the Deathly Shadow. Because sometimes what you needed to get rid of evil was a little evil mixed with good.

As the Deathly Shadow took form, using all of its reserves to have a shape, Paris balled up her fists, remembering the part of her Uncle Clark's notes that had been the most helpful:

"You are good at your essence," Clark had written. *"My sister Liv had ensured that with her wish to the genie. However, it couldn't entirely erase your blood. You will always carry the blood of a demon passed onto you from your father. It didn't corrupt Stefan as many feared. Instead, when he fought evil, he was unrelenting, fueled by his demon blood to crush that which was inside him.*

"I don't know this to be true, but my gut tells me that what you need to defeat the Deathly Shadow is that darker part of you. The Deathly Shadow will try and draw out the power connected to you as a magician and a fairy. Let it. Then hit it with the part it never knew about. Hit the Deathly Shadow with what it is, swallowing that demon whole. No matter what, I believe in you."

Paris gulped while looking at the semi-transparent figure in front of her. The Deathly Shadow didn't have a body, but for this showdown, he'd given himself a form. That was for the best because she wanted to look at the man she was about to erase from this planet forever.

CHAPTER SIXTY-FIVE

Nearly doubled over from laughing, Amelia pulled her long brown hair out of her ponytail holder, knowing that it was a mess after all the time she'd run her hands through it.

She shook out the strands and saw Grayson straighten across the table, his laughter freezing.

"What is it?" She looked at him quite seriously, wondering if she'd done something wrong.

They'd had some wine. However, she didn't think that's why the conversation had been so easy or the laughter overflowing. Sometimes, with some people, things flowed. You didn't have to force it, and the clock didn't tick. It was as if magic had taken over and replaced all the things that made other relationships before so difficult.

Grayson shook his head, seeming to try and shake off the magical spell he was under. "I was thinking of the first time we met."

Her smile faltered. "Oh, that was…"

"I was a jerk," Grayson said at once, cutting her off.

"I was nervous," she added quickly. "I had the job interview."

"Which you didn't get to," he added.

"And we both missed our train," she replied.

"Then you hated me," he supplied.

Amelia couldn't argue with that. She did, and it had fueled her to build Rose Industries. "Now, here we are. Two unlikely adversaries, having wine and stuck together for the night."

Grayson swirled his wine in his glass while regarding her. "I never hated you."

"No?" she asked coyly.

"Not at all." He shook his head. "I had too much ego and you—"

"I was what?" she challenged him.

"I wasn't ready for someone like you yet," he admitted, suddenly quite serious.

"What does that mean?" She suddenly realized that they were both leaning across the table in each other's direction. Closer than ever before. His hand was inches from hers. His face a breath away.

"That means I think I realize now, after everything—after McGregor Industries and failed relationships—what I was searching for."

"What?" Amelia's mouth hung open, wondering what was happening so suddenly on that strange night.

"It feels," he began slowly, his eyes flicking to her lips, then her eyes, and back to her lips. "It feels like I've been searching for someone like you."

"Someone like me?"

"You," he repeated more fervently. "I feel as if, looking back, and being here and knowing what I know, and feeling everything that you've made me feel tonight, that I've been searching for you, Amelia Rose."

CHAPTER SIXTY-SIX

"I've waited a long time for this, halfling," the Deathly Shadow said in a hoarse voice that sounded as if it sought to cut Paris in two.

She remained standing tall, not allowing the monster's haunting tone or his wiggling, smoky form to unnerve her. The Deathly Shadow's image was primarily black but resembled the shape of a man. Details filled in moment by moment, making him almost look human, although he couldn't fool her. He was undoubtedly a monster.

Paris faked a yawn. "I didn't brush my hair for this meeting so I think one of us cares more about this than the other."

"You don't stand a chance against me," the Deathly Shadow stated, his face materializing for the first time. It was that of a demon, red-skinned with horns—as she had expected.

"Well, then I should have stayed home," she continued to joke, knowing that was keeping her calm and hopefully unnerving him with her semblance of being unafraid of him. In truth, she was terrified, but hopefully, that didn't show.

"Others have claimed you can defeat me," the Deathly Shadow

rasped, standing in the dark Death Valley before her, only a few feet away. "You've been counseled. However, I deceived your parents, and those you trusted don't know how powerful I am—how powerful I've always been."

Paris shook her head, pretending that he was wrong and trying to convince herself he wasn't right and telling the truth.

"This was always fated," the Deathly Shadow stated. "Nothing is more powerful than me. Nothing could stop me from what I want. I've only been waiting for this moment. To absorb your power. Now is the time. Get ready to die but know that it's for a good purpose."

"Why?" Paris challenged. "So you can take over the world?"

He laughed, his black mouth and white teeth a strange contrast to his red face. "No, I never wanted to take over this world. I'm not from this world, haven't you heard? How else did I know how to survive and break all the rules? How else did my body die when I survived? It couldn't withstand your atmosphere here. But I did survive."

Paris blinked at him, trying to understand. "So you're not from Earth? Where are you from?"

"How else could I open a vortex to another world if I wasn't from another place?" he asked.

Paris knew that Ren had, but he was an exception. "I don't know," she finally said.

"Obviously, you don't," he stated with conviction. "No, I never desired to conquer this world. My goal has always been simple. To destroy it." The Deathly Shadow extended his hand in her direction. "All I need to do that is you, halfling."

CHAPTER SIXTY-SEVEN

"Daddy! Where have you been? I'm late for my tanning appointment," Captain Morgan complained when King Rudolf and Lee barged into the locked room.

Finding the half-mortal, half-fae hadn't been difficult. The Deathly Shadow hadn't left guards or traps, apparently not worried about keeping her secured if he wasn't there and Paris wasn't the one trying to release her. The locks in the warehouse had been easy enough to bypass with magic and Lee's sword.

The room that the Deathly Shadow had kept Captain Morgan in wasn't too bad. It was dark, cold, and minimalist, but there was a bed, a toilet, and water. King Rudolf had spent a week in a place much worse...that place had plaid bed sheets.

"Are you okay, Captain Morgan?" As soon as he and Lee unlocked it, King Rudolf rushed over to his daughter, sitting in the corner of her cell.

She glanced up, her face smudged with dirt and her lip quivering. "I'm cold, Daddy."

He nodded, took off his coat, and wrapped it around his daughter's shoulders. "I'm so sorry, my love. You're safe now."

"And the darkness," Captain Morgan continued, her teeth chattering. "It made me feel so alone."

King Rudolf hugged his daughter tightly as Lee stayed by the door, guarding it and staying out of the way of the reunion.

"You're safe now," the king of the fae consoled. "I'm going to take you home. You're safe, and I will take care of you."

"Thank you, Daddy." Captain Morgan peeled away from her father. "There is a positive in all this."

"Yeah?" King Rudolf continued to look his daughter over.

She nodded. "I haven't eaten in a few days and think I can fit into that dress I got, making my other sisters look like bloated slobs."

He grinned down at his daughter. "I love that you always see the positive."

King Rudolf hauled his daughter to her feet, led her past Lee, and through the warehouse to safety.

The assassin baker shook her head.

Lee knew that King Rudolf and his family were dimwits, but they were also full of love and goodness. If the world were full of more people like that, she wouldn't have to kill so many.

CHAPTER SIXTY-EIGHT

Now, this all made sense. The Deathly Shadow had confessed the one secret that Paris didn't think anyone else knew... not even Papa Creola.

The Deathly Shadow wasn't from Earth—from this world. That's how he'd been able to sell his soul and exist with such power. It somehow, someway, made sense why the Deathly Shadow wanted to destroy their world. However, Paris wasn't going to allow it, and thankfully she had one secret left to reveal that he didn't know.

"Oh, well." She kept her voice ultra-casual. "I guess if some alien from another world comes here, we better let him take control. Should I lay down and give you my power or what?"

He narrowed his black eyes at her. "Don't play with me, little girl. I know you think you believe you can overpower me. I'm not stupid."

"You look stupid with those horns," she insulted. "Like, think about the clearance issues. I hope if you get a body, you pick something with small ears to make up for all that overcompensating you probably had to do."

"I know what those who have advised you have said," the Deathly Shadow exclaimed, ignoring her words. "You believe you can overpower me, but let's save ourselves the banter and tiresome chatter and get on with things. I'm here for you, Guinevere Paris Beaufont. Give me your unique power, and I'll be on with things."

"To destroy the planet I love so much," she stated.

"The one that I need to overpower, after taking you, to rule my planet," he countered.

She nodded. "Now we've boiled down to your final motivation. Well, why didn't you tell me this was about conquering one planet so you could rule your home? I would have rolled over then."

He narrowed his soulless eyes at her. "Don't play with me, girl. It's sad that you've been what's stopped me for so long. But I'm patient, and here we are. Now make this easy and submit, or I will overpower you. All those who advised you were wrong. A half-magician, half-fairy can't win against me."

She nodded. "You're right. You can win against a halfling."

The Deathly Shadow grinned, his pointy white teeth contrasting with his red face. "Good girl. Now do not make this harder than it has to be by resisting."

"However," she tilted her head back and forth, pretending that she hadn't heard him. "I'm more than a halfling. Good thing no one mentioned *that* when you were spying. You must have missed it when Papa Creola told me."

"What?" he asked, his eyes wide and teeth clenched.

"I'm half-fairy and half-magician with a tiny bit of demon." For the first time, Paris' eyes flashed red as she threw her hand into the air, attempting to harness the power of the Deathly Shadow before her using the strength that had flowed in her all her life, but she'd never felt until then.

CHAPTER SIXTY-NINE

The tiny bit of demon inside Paris hadn't surfaced before now, and it didn't scare her presently. She could feel it coursing through her, separate but part of her. Instinctively she knew that she could control it as her father could and used it to fuel him against evil.

Also at that exact moment, she realized that her father's demon blood couldn't be erased entirely but rather only diluted with fairy blood, which was the perfect way to overpower it. There was nothing more opposite from a demon than a fairy, which was all about love and goodness. So Paris wasn't only a halfling. She was something much more than she ever conceived. Now she knew why Papa Creola couldn't tell her how to overpower the Deathly Shadow. She would have freaked if she knew that she was still part-demon. Discovering it like this, well, it made her feel powerful. Paris had all the power of the demon, like her father, without all the corruption.

She held up her right hand and with it, the Deathly Shadow's form raised into the air, writhing as he screamed, suddenly seeming to beg. She wasn't going to bow to pleading, though. This was her fight, and she would win it on her terms.

Decisively and with a power that she'd never known, Paris knelt and slammed her hand down on the desert ground, and with it the Deathly Shadow flew to the crusty sand while crumbling to bits, his form breaking to smoke again.

She'd activated the demon inside her though, and she hadn't finished with the Deathly Shadow. This entity had destroyed her family for all her life. He would pay before she contained him. Then she would bring back her parents.

Paris thrust her hands in front of her, holding her palms out. With a power unlike she knew she possessed, the bits and pieces of smoke that were the Deathly Shadow were sucked into her hands, rolling into a ball—circling one another. A mass of pure energy.

She gathered it up, trying to decide how best to make this beast pay, feeling the power building in her like a volcano about to erupt. Feeling victorious against the one monster who had dictated her life, Paris flung her hands out. Smoke and bits of black sprayed out in all directions, and with them, screams of pain from a bodiless voice.

Paris would have taken that moment to gather her strength. To rejoice, but a blaring noise in her pocket caught her attention. She grabbed her phone and looked at it. The message was from Aunt Sophia. It simply said,

That's enough. Heroes put the bad guy out of the misery they were born into.

Paris slid her phone into her pocket. From her leather jacket, she gathered the container that Rory had created for her. It was time to contain the beast and bring back her parents.

She pulled the metal container from her jacket and held it out, ready to lock up the Deathly Shadow now that she'd overpowered him, but then fire erupted in a circle around her making her suddenly hot. Very hot.

Something had suddenly gone wrong…really wrong.

CHAPTER SEVENTY

Something strong and violent yanked Paris' feet out from under her, straight down to her back, knocking the air out of her. Her head hit the ground, which was harder than she expected.

She looked up, disoriented for a moment at the blackish sky around her, trying to remember where she was.

Death Valley.

What had gone wrong that there was a circle of flames licking at her now? Why was she lying on her back, feeling as if a force was about to push her into the earth? Had she been unable to control the demon part of her? She didn't know.

She felt the cold metal of the container in her hand, but she didn't know where the Deathly Shadow was. Then, as if cued by her thoughts, streaks of black darker than the sky circled overhead, creating wind and a roaring sound so loud her eardrums felt close to bursting.

"Thanks for breaking me back apart," the Deathly Shadow said, his voice all around her, making the ground under her back rumble. "I wasn't sure how to defeat someone with demon blood as well as a halfling in my cumulative form. You helped me out. I needed to be spread apart for this last bit to work. Shall we commence?"

Paris writhed in pain as she tried to fight the invisible bonds holding her down. Her face felt on fire from the flames all around her. She tried to sit up but couldn't move too much, as if chained to the earth.

The black swirling bits in the sky twirled until they became one. The Deathly Shadow was growing more powerful. He was close to overpowering her. Paris had lost her chance. She had him using her demon blood but let it corrupt her, thinking she was conquering him—making him pay.

She reached for something, anything, looking all around but only seeing the flames encircling her. Desperate and scorned by her failure, she pulled her hands into her, and one instinctively went to the locket around her neck. She often grabbed it when she felt desperate or alone. Right then, she'd never felt more of those two emotions.

To her surprise, the locket was cold although she felt on fire. Stranger still, she heard a voice in her head that didn't sound like hers.

"I've always been in your heart, ready to help you," the voice said. She instinctively trusted it. Almost seemed to recognize it.

That made no sense to Paris, though. However, it was hard to think with the growing heat and the roar of the Deathly Shadow. He was building in force, ready to overwhelm her.

What did the voice in her head mean? she wondered in a panic. What had always been in her heart, ready to help?

"You have to keep breaking your heart until it opens," a voice shouted in her mind.

Paris' eyes sprang open, burning because of the smoke and fire. Then there was the roar and power of the Deathly Shadow pressing down on her. Paris didn't care about any of that. She lumbered to her feet, staying low, and stared at the circle of flames caging her.

Black spiraled around her, seeking to make her dizzy and disoriented, but she ignored it. Instead, she yanked the heart-shaped locket from her neck, breaking the chain. Then she did something that she would never have considered before that moment.

Paris threw the locket with her initials onto the ground and raised her foot, slamming her boot down and crushing it with deliberate force.

Almost instantly, as if waiting for eternity to be free, something bright and brilliant flew from the locket under her shoe. At first, it was hard to make out the strange shape as it went from tiny to large. The figure, which was full of color in the black sky, flew around the circle, extinguishing the flames caging Paris with the beating of its wings. Paris blinked, trying to understand what she was seeing. Her eyes took in the image, and she made out the figure of a lion with the head of the goat on its back and the tail of a serpent. It was magnificent.

The chimera that had belonged to Uncle John didn't stop after it freed Paris from the circle of flames. Instead, it flew in a spiral until it gathered all the parts of the Deathly Shadow, corralling him into one massive ball of blackness once more. Only then did the chimera turn and look at Paris before vanishing in thin air. That was fine because she knew what had to happen.

The next part was up to her. It was solely her job to contain the Deathly Shadow.

CHAPTER SEVENTY-ONE

Feeling unsteady on her feet but mustering strength from a place she didn't know she had, Paris gripped the small clam-shaped metal container in her hand.

She held it out to the spiraling blackness, not knowing what happened next but purely operating on instinct.

She pulled on her demonism. On the part of her that was a magician. On her fairy half. Paris allowed them all to combine, and words she'd never said—never heard before—fell from her mouth, creating a spell that she knew for certain was never spoken by anyone. It was a language she'd not heard, but it effortlessly flowed from her mouth.

A scream from a bodiless form touched her ears, but it didn't hurt, although she knew it was supposed to harm her.

The ground shook, but Paris stayed standing, although she knew she was supposed to fall from the assault. These were the Deathly Shadow's last attempts, but she didn't stop speaking the ancient spell she knew by heart.

No matter what happened, Paris continued to recite the words that flowed from her consciousness, believing that she could do this. Her uncle's chimera had come to her rescue. Her father's demon blood had assisted her, breaking down the Deathly Shadow.

Now it was her turn to take over, doing what only she could do —believe that she could.

The sky grew bright and dark again as if the Deathly Shadow was trying to blind her, but Paris didn't waver. Instead, she spoke the spell that was in her heart. In her soul. Little by little, the bits of the Deathly Shadow seeped into the metal container, which she now realized was open in her hand.

The blackness gathered, accumulating with sounds of protest. Paris' words were louder and drowned out the Deathly Shadow. She wouldn't allow him to win. She wouldn't permit this creature from another world to destroy the one she loved. All she had to do was contain him, then…well, she'd get there when it was time.

The skies slowly started to turn pink, then blue, and the blackness disappeared as the rising sun shone once more when the last of the Deathly Shadow accumulated in the metal container. Paris wasn't sure how long had passed. A day. Days. A year. Years. It could have been a century for as parched and drained as she suddenly felt, as if everything had passed in an instant.

Paris staggered as the metal container shut in her hands and locked. She'd contained the Deathly Shadow. She'd finally done it.

As the sun rose over Death Valley, Paris felt her first ray of hope in a long time. In what felt like a lifetime.

She held the metal container out, letting the light of the sun catch it. All she had to do was put the vortex opener on the container, and she'd finally find her parents. She knew that time was crucial so she'd have to work fast.

Paris reached into her pocket, staggering from the energy it took to fight and contain the Deathly Shadow. Then she toppled over, and her face hit the sand as she suddenly passed out, drained and exhausted from her efforts.

CHAPTER SEVENTY-TWO

Something small jerked on Paris' shoulder. She really wanted to sleep longer. If only that gentle but annoying shaking would stop.

"Would you wake up already," Faraday said in her ear, his whiskers tickling her skin.

Paris groaned and rolled over, thinking maybe she could buy another few minutes before class. However, the ground was hard...and hot...and gross. It suddenly occurred to her that she was in Death Valley—with scorpions and tarantulas and rattlesnakes and—

"The Deathly Shadow!" she exclaimed and bolted to her feet in a burst of sudden energy. She looked around at the scorched desert, trying to reconstruct what had happened while blinking to clear her vision and her mind.

As if realizing that she needed a recap, the squirrel at her feet started pointing and talking rapidly. He first indicated the metal container at her feet. "You contained the Deathly Shadow, but by my calculations, you have two minutes to use the vortex opener. If you don't, you'll miss your window to pinpoint his energy."

He pointed a few feet away. "That's over there where you dropped it when you passed out from expending too much energy."

Then he pointed at her face. "So you know, your eyes are glowing red like a demon's, but I'm not judging you. Just hoping you don't steal my soul."

Paris shook her head, feeling the fire extinguish from her. She grabbed the container right away, then the vortex opener, and went straight to work without wasting a second. She fitted the vortex opener onto the container as instructed. "Okay, so I need to put this on like so then use the spell that Papa gave me and…" Paris put everything together, muttered the incantation, and pointed the container outward, fully expecting to create a vortex using the Deathly Shadow's energy.

Nothing happened.

She looked at the container encapsulated by the vortex opener. "I point it outward. Then I use the spell." Paris tried again.

Nothing happened.

Paris grunted. She didn't know if she had enough time to call Uncle John to figure out what was going wrong with the device.

"Put it down," Faraday encouraged from the ground.

"Why?" She was confused.

"I'm going to fix it."

"You're a squirrel."

He nodded. "Now put it down here, and I'll fix it. Then you can bring back your parents and get back to napping as you'd like to."

She sighed with relief. The squirrel knew exactly what she wanted, a very long nap. Well, first her parents, followed by sleep.

Paris set down the device and stood back. "Make me proud, squirrel. Otherwise, I'm returning you."

"To where?" He was already tinkering with the vortex opener.

"To wherever I got you when I hallucinated, and this whole weird dream started."

CHAPTER SEVENTY-THREE

It felt like forever as Paris hunched over Faraday, watching as he did different things to the vortex opener. It all could have been rocket science for all she knew, and it probably was. She didn't understand a single bit of it. And to make things harder to understand, her head was clouded from containing the Deathly Shadow and realizing she had some demon inside of her and doing all that she had.

However, when the squirrel stepped back and held out a paw at the vortex opener attached to the container, she was fully aware.

"It should work now, but you have limited time, so hurry," Faraday urged.

"How?" she asked, scooping the device up into her hands. "How did you get this to work when my Uncle John couldn't?"

"I had to fix a few things he didn't have calculated right, even after Ren's equations," Faraday explained as she pointed the device outward and started the spell again. This time something was different. A light glowed from the container, building up and radiating outward second by second.

"How, though?" Paris looked sideways at him as the device vibrated in her hands.

The squirrel stared intently at the container and vortex opener, then her. "When we get through this, I'll tell you my secrets, but you have to promise not to tell anyone else, ever."

Before Paris could answer, two things happened simultaneously. The vortex opener exploded in her hands, not harming her but sending cold air in all directions. The explosion created the most beautiful thing she'd ever seen. It was a perfectly round blue hole directly in front of her. Although it resembled a portal, she knew it wasn't one. Paris blinked at the large blue hole and looked at Faraday, wondering if he was witnessing what she was, but at that same moment, he disappeared—simply vanished.

She looked between where the squirrel had been and the opening, wondering what was real and what wasn't. Maybe she'd imagined it all. Perhaps she was still passed out. Maybe this had all been a strange dream, and none of it was real. Perhaps she wasn't real.

Then, as if dreams could come true, two shadowy figures materialized in the round blue portal-like shape, and for some reason, they looked like home.

CHAPTER SEVENTY-FOUR

For a moment, the light from the large blue opening was too blinding, making Paris throw up her arm to cover her face. She waited until her eyes adjusted, feeling the heat of the desert reminding her that she was in Death Valley.

The blue opening gave off a smoldering heat that burned her skin. However, the sun overhead was also beating down on her.

The radiating power before her suddenly lessened like someone turned down a loud noise. Or a light being dimmed. Paris lowered her arm to find that the opening to another world had closed. Standing there in the desert and looking around quite confused were two people: a man and a woman.

Paris instantly felt as though she knew them while still wanting introductions. These were her parents. They had to be, but it didn't feel real yet. She was in shock and hardly able to take in the moment fully.

The couple was younger than she expected, but she really couldn't pinpoint how much time had passed for them.

The figure who stepped forward first was a short, lean woman in her early thirties. She had long blonde unkempt hair and wore a black cloak over an all-black outfit and combat boots. Paris instantly approved of the ensemble.

The guy behind her was far more guarded, looking around as if expecting a demon or monster of sorts to jump out. He had jet black hair and the most piercing blue eyes.

Both of them regarded her with hesitancy when they realized she was the only one standing in the middle of the desert.

"You're safe." Paris watched their expressions as they took in their surroundings.

"Where are we?" the woman asked.

"Death Valley, but I can get us to someplace where there are fewer rattlesnakes," Paris joked, always needing to rely on her sense of humor to save her sanity. She didn't move but instead stayed frozen, running her eyes over her parents, realizing that she was staring at them although she didn't care.

"No thanks to rattlesnakes." Liv finally glanced down and looked herself over. "We were in that weird multi-universe with demons long enough. I need a shower."

Stefan nodded, checking his wife for injuries and sighing with relief. "But we're back now."

"Thanks to this one." Liv pointed at Paris. "You opened that vortex, didn't you?"

Paris nodded. "So you realized you were in another world and not through a portal."

"Yeah, but it was confusing at first," Stefan explained.

"We thought we'd stepped through a portal, but that damn Deathly Shadow fooled us." Liv scowled and looked around. "When I get my hands on him, I'm going to give that guy a body so I can strangle him to death."

Paris couldn't help but laugh. That did sound like something she'd say, just as everyone had said about her with her mother.

Both of her parents gave her confused looks for laughing.

"There's no need to worry about the Deathly Shadow," she explained. "He's gone."

"He was here," Stefan argued. "He opened the vortex. He tricked us."

"I got rid of him." Paris gulped, not sure how to explain the next part and knowing she had to.

"So you got rid of the Deathly Shadow and brought us back from that weird world?" Liv was totally in awe. "We owe you the biggest debt of gratitude ever."

Stefan nodded, relief flooding his face. "That's incredible. How did you do that? More importantly, who are you?"

"M-M-My name is Paris."

Both warriors tensed.

Stefan gulped. "That's weird…"

Liv slapped his arm playfully. "Not so much. Many are naming their kids Paris these days. It's a coincidence." She offered Paris a smile. "Sorry, it's just our daughter's middle name is Paris."

She nodded, not knowing what else to say…how to tell them… wanting to hug her parents but not wanting to freak them out. This was going to be weird…it *was* weird.

Liv looked at Stefan, ignoring that Paris was staring at them with her mouth wide open. "You know, I really miss that kid. I mean, it's only been a day, but a day without Guinevere is too much."

Paris sucked in a breath. It had only been a day for her parents.

Her father nodded at his wife. "I know what you mean. She's my heart."

Just like that, the tears fell from Paris' eyes. A sob escaped her mouth. She felt like crumbling. Her parents, not knowing who she was, gave her a look of confusion.

"What's wrong?" Liv looked her over as if she must be hurt. "Are you okay?"

Paris sucked in a breath. "It's just that you haven't been gone from this world for a day. You might have only been in the other one for a single day, but it was much longer here where the passing of time is different."

"We haven't?" Stefan stepped forward. "How long were we gone?"

"I'm sorry, but you've been gone for fifteen years." Paris choked on her breath between words.

Both Liv and Stefan tensed, visibly in shock. Liv's hand reached out, grabbing her husband's arm—horror in her eyes.

"Y-Y-You're," Stefan stuttered, the realization seeming to hit him, although he didn't seem to be able to finish his statement.

Paris nodded, swallowed, looked between them, let out a breath, and forced a smile. "Yes, I'm Guinevere Paris Beaufont. I'm your daughter."

CHAPTER SEVENTY-FIVE

"Being reunited feels so good." King Rudolf hugged Captain Morgan tightly. She didn't seem as excited about the experience but allowed it.

"I'm so glad that we can relate," the king of the fae said, looking at Paris across the counter in the Fantastic Armory.

"Although I'm sorry you and Captain Morgan were separated, my parents were apart for fifteen years, not a few days." Paris slumped to the side, wishing that she had her parents to hug right then.

"I kind of hoped for fifteen years," Captain Morgan grumbled. "If the lighting in my cell was better and I could get manicures, that is."

"That's not nice," Subner scolded. "Parents aren't something that you should take for granted, even if something with the IQ of a watermelon is raising you."

"Thanks, Sub," King Rudolf chirped.

Liv and Stefan had immediately gone into shock after the news that they'd been gone for fifteen years and rescued by their daughter. Paris brought them straight to the Fantastical Armory as instructed, and Papa Creola had taken them down to his office for examination. Apparently, traveling to different worlds could result in trauma and all sorts of other problems. Paris hoped that they recovered and when they looked at her again, it wasn't like she was a stranger.

Uncle John rushed into the Fantastical Armory, his eyes frantic, followed by Aunt Sophia and Uncle Clark. They all looked around with worry and anticipation.

"They're being examined for warts," King Rudolf said in a bored voice in answer to the questions on their faces. Captain Morgan had abandoned him to check her Instagram to see what she'd missed in her absence.

"They are being examined by Papa Creola because they traveled through a vortex to another world," Subner corrected matter-of-factly.

Uncle John sighed. "They're okay?"

Paris nodded.

Aunt Sophia hurried over and grabbed her hand. "What? What's wrong?"

She looked up, realizing that the dragonrider had sensed the stress in her. Paris bit her lip and let out a breath. "It's been only a day for them. They were only gone in that other world for one single day."

Clark choked on a cough. "Only a day…"

"I know," King Rudolf said. "Liv is going to look younger than me."

"She is younger than you," Clark fired back, irritation flaring on his face.

"Well, still, she's always had that mature look," Rudolf argued.

"But they are okay?" Aunt Sophia asked Paris.

"I guess," she answered. "I mean, how would I know? I don't know them. I explained that the Deathly Shadow was gone and told them who I was. They promptly went into shock, I brought them here, and that was it."

"The Deathly Shadow is really gone?" Uncle Clark asked, always serious.

"Yes," Subner answered, saving Paris the trouble of having to do so. "The container has been dealt with. The technology that opened the vortex was destroyed. All of you can forget that other worlds exist. It's best if you do."

"In turn, you'll get a sense of humor, right?" King Rudolf asked.

"Doubtful," Subner answered. "Maybe in another world, the version of me is cheerful."

King Rudolf turned to his daughter and patted her shoulder. "I vote we get that Subner from another world."

Captain Morgan ignored him, too busy checking her Instagram.

Papa Creola interrupted all that when he came through the back door of the Fantastical Armory, looking around at the many faces all standing at attention.

He let out a breath of relief. "They are fine. Well, they will be. They need to rest."

"Well, maybe next time an attack will take them out." Subner sounded disappointed in him.

"However," Papa Creola continued, ignoring his assistant. "They'll need much time to recover. In that interim, I don't want too much stimulation that overwhelms them." He gestured at the crowd. "You all are too much stimulation. Seeing your faces after fifteen years apart could throw them into a shock they won't recover from, so we're going to keep you away."

There were many voices of protest, but when Papa Creola threw up his hands, everyone went silent. "However, there's one person who Liv and Stefan must see. The only person who will help them heal, rather than cause them confusion and trauma." Then the father of time pointed straight at Paris and waved her forward. "Come with me, child. Your parents need you with them."

CHAPTER SEVENTY-SIX

Paris didn't know what she expected. Maybe she thought she could walk through the door at the back of the Fantastical Armory into Papa Creola's private office. She didn't expect to have to climb down what felt like a million stairs.

She was nearly winded by the time she got down the bazillion flights to a warm basement-type room where two strangers who weren't supposed to be strangers were curled up together on a sofa in front of a fire.

"She's as slow as you are," Liv said to her husband as Paris approached.

He glanced at Liv and smiled. "Well, she also has my eyes and charm."

"But my hair and sass," Liv argued.

Paris took the seat opposite her parents and cleared her throat to get their attention, although she thought that shouldn't be necessary. She still couldn't believe they were here. It would take time to process this. The reunion was definitely not going as she had envisioned.

Her parents didn't look as on edge as before when they'd stepped through the vortex. They looked drunk and ready to pass out.

"Sorry, I'd be clobbering you with kisses, but Papa gave us something to make us sleep." Liv was lying in Stefan's arms with a blanket stretched across them. "That dumb dork thinks we need to take a few days off."

"You've been gone from this world for fifteen years," Paris admitted, looking them over, still not sure if that moment was real.

Stefan looked over his shoulder at the stairs. "I don't think you're allowed to say that. Papa thinks it will upset us."

Paris nodded, feeling much more nervous than she expected.

Liv's eyes closed partway, but Paris noticed how pretty she was. She could stare at her mother for days. She had nice features that weren't too pronounced or too understated. Her father, well, he was a knockout, if he wasn't her father. Although they were her parents and gone for fifteen years, their time in the vortex had done a weird number on them, and it seemed they hadn't aged a day.

"I'm sorry." Liv opened her eyes. "All I want is to learn more about what happened. About your last fifteen years. To apologize. To see everyone. But stupid Papa has other plans for us."

Paris smiled at her exhausted parents, who had a lot to learn and assimilate. It would take time and would no doubt be overwhelming. "It's okay. All you need to know is that a lot of people worked really hard to get you two back. Apparently, you're a big deal."

Liv shook her head against Stefan's chest. "The only thing awesome about us was you. I'm so sorry we missed so much of your life."

"You didn't." Paris leaned forward. "My life is just starting, especially because you're both back."

That seemed to wake both of her very sleepy parents, who were struggling so hard to stay awake in each other's arms.

"Guinevere," Liv said and blinked as if suddenly realizing something. "You don't go by that, do you? You said your name was Paris."

Paris nodded. "Uncle John calls me Pare."

Her mother smiled. "Pare, I'm sorry we missed so much, but now that we're back, we're going to make the most of it. We want our life with you."

Paris nodded. "Yes, that's all I want." She stood, feeling as if her parents were about to fall asleep again and wanting to give them peace. There would be time to catch up properly. Hopefully, there would be a lifetime together.

Stefan reached out for Paris when she tried to tip-toe past them, his grace breath-taking. "Pare, did you become a Warrior for the House of Fourteen in our absence?"

She shook her head. "No. I'm becoming a fairy godmother."

Paris wasn't sure what she expected, but both her parents smiled, closing their eyes and holding each other. "That sounds perfect for our child," Stefan said, pressing Liv close to him. "Bringing love to the world is the best job I can think of."

Liv nodded. "I knew you'd make us proud, Pare. Will you turn out the lights and have waffles ready in the morning, please?"

"Yes." Paris tip-toed to the stairs, rather giddy that her life was so weird and so awesome. She really wouldn't have it any other way.

Paris thought her parents were asleep, but when she took her first step up the stairs, her mother said, "We love you."

Her father quickly added, "So very much."

"Familia Est Sempiternum," Liv said, on the verge of passing out, but still evoking passion into the phrase.

Stefan nodded. "Familia Est Sempiternum."

Paris smiled, feeling her chest warm like something deep inside her was slowly being repaired. "Family really is forever."

And with the conclusion of her words her parents fell asleep at once.

That felt like the perfect ending to a very long chapter in Paris' life. Short, sweet, and leaving it open for so much more to happen.

CHAPTER SEVENTY-SEVEN

"Love recovered that much, so quickly?" Paris asked, looking at the love meter on the wall in the headmistress' office in Happily Ever After College. It was at nearly thirty percent, which was much better than the day before, or the week before, or any time before that Paris had seen.

She didn't feel recuperated after the long night, but she needed to find out how things went with her big mission. If she was honest, Paris probably wasn't going to sleep for a while after all the new excitement in her life.

"Well, Grayson McGregor and Amelia Rose fell in love tonight," Willow Starr explained.

"They fell in love," Paris said, so excited and also overwhelmed.

"Everything fell into place," Mae Ling stated. "It was as if someone knew what they needed and put it all into place." She gave Paris a pointed look.

"And their companies?" Paris asked.

"They're dissolving them and already in talks about starting one together," Chef Ash said on the other side of Paris. "Think of the great things they'll do with a company together."

"Think of their kids," Christine gushed. "Those will be some hot children."

Everyone laughed.

"I had my doubts," Headmistress Starr began. "However, this proves that sometimes we need to use untraditional methods to fix problems or create matches. You brought us this plan, Paris, and it worked. For a long time, we've tried to teach match-making from old methods. More and more, I feel that we have to approach things with new thinking. The problem is, I don't know what that is. Fortunately, I feel as though I have resources."

She looked at the three sitting in front of her desk. "I'm not saying that you all get to run missions," the headmistress continued. "But I want you all advising. I want this college to take a bold turn. If it works, then great, the love meter recovers. If it doesn't... well, I'm not sure we have much to lose at this point. Love has never been at an all-time low before or recovered so fast."

"I think," Mae Ling began in a speculative tone, "that means sometimes we need something unexpected to put us on track. Who knows? Maybe that means we can achieve successes with love that we've never experienced."

The fairy godmother looked straight at Paris, and she couldn't help but feel like the other woman was charging her with a new unsaid responsibility. No matter what. No matter what her family life brought or the new world she'd experience, she'd accept. Paris wanted this. She wanted to be a fairy godmother more than ever. How could she not want to bring more love to this world when she saw her parents and how much they loved each other and her? She wanted that for everyone.

CHAPTER SEVENTY-EIGHT

Paris and Faraday were quiet for a long time in her room before she broke the spell and spoke.

"You going to tell me these secrets?" Paris finally said from her bed, the perfect amount of moonlight streaming through her room in the Fairy Godmother Estate.

"I get that people are crazy about donuts, but I don't get them," Faraday said from her sock drawer. "There. I said it. Gosh that felt good. Donuts are weird."

Paris laughed. "Seriously, you strange-ass squirrel. That's the secret you had to confess?"

Faraday sighed. "No, but I have lots of secrets. Weird enough, most of them are about food. Like, butter. Why is everyone obsessed with it?"

"You are the weirdest." Paris pulled the covers up to her chest and finally felt sleepy, almost as if Papa Creola had given her something to sleep, too.

"I admit, I have other secrets," Faraday stated.

"Are you going to tell them to me?" she asked.

"Do you want me to tell you now?"

"No," Paris answered honestly. "I've had enough for one day. Actually, for a lifetime. But what about tomorrow or next week or this month? Sometime. Promise that you'll tell me when I ask."

"Paris, I'll tell you whatever you want whenever you want."

"Why?" she asked. "I don't want your secrets tonight, but I want to know why you help me and are so loyal?"

"Have you looked in the mirror?" he asked.

"Are you saying because I'm hot?" she joked.

He giggled. "No, Paris. I guess you're kind of okay to look at. Honestly, I'm helping you because you're good. You're true. You're someone I want as my friend. And if I'm going to tell my secrets to anyone, I think it should be you."

Paris pulled her covers tighter to her chest, feeling confused and happy and excited for the next day. She had parents who she had to get to know, who she wanted to know. Who she thought would be amazing and fun and probably teach her more than all the knowledge in the Great Library. She had a future with Happily Every After College that she couldn't wait to pursue. She had friends who she never wanted to let go of...ever. For Paris, that was more than enough.

"Okay, tell me your secrets later then."

"That is my promise." Faraday buried more into her sock drawer.

"Goodnight, Faraday." Paris yawned. "Thanks for your help today."

"Goodnight, Pare," the squirrel chirped. "Always and forever."

With that, the fairy godmother who was so much more than that fell asleep, happy and content for once, looking forward to all that she'd do to make the world better tomorrow and every day after that...like her parents.

SARAH'S AUTHOR NOTES
APRIL 20, 2021

Thank you so much for reading and all the support. I swear, on the hard days, you all really cheer me up and remind me why I do this. I'll go onto my Facebook group and you all are so nice about the books and even seem to think (with possible questionable judgement) that I'm sort of okay. I'm having that Sally Field moment. "You like me. You really, really like me." Anyway, thanks for liking the books. That's what counts. I portray myself as what I want you all to see. Make no mistake, in person, I'm usually a jerk. I wrote a couple of books about it. But I'm glad you all are nice to me. Thank you.

Now let's get down to business. There's something important to address. Mike and I have been working together for four years. We've crafted eight series together. For those counting, and you know that I am, that's currently sixty-three books. Why am I outlining all this? Is it because I'm about to get all sentimental?

Hell nah!

Sixty-three books later and Michael doesn't even know how to spell my name! My name is Sarah. With an h. Without that, it doesn't spell haras backwards. Thanks for really knowing the real me, Micheale. I'm sure you'll come up with some excuse about how autocorrect messed it up in the last author notes spelling my name Sara. Well, I've been typing my name for a mighty long time and autocorrect has never been like, no I think you meant to say Sara, not Sarah. Actually more often than not, my name gets corrected to Satan... Is that weird?

Don't worry though, I'm going to let this name business go, because I'm the bigger person, Mikke.

The things I do for you all, the reader... I got drooled on by a longhorn and a bison wiped its boogers on me. All for you!

Actually, that's not what happened entirely, although the booger part did. After a year and some change, I was finally able to return to Baton Rouge to see my family. My parents always plan adventures when we are reunited. One such adventure was a swamp tour, which I put into the Liv series when she meets the Sand Man. We've also done a harrowing trek through the Red Woods, where I was pretty certain we were going to fall off the side of a cliff because who needs guardrails on hairpin turn roads on top of mountains?! And then there was a weekend in Glacier National Park in Montana. In freaking January! That's where I learned a healthy appreciation for the fact that I don't have to shovel my driveway in LA. Those adventures also went into the books.

So when my parents asked if I wanted to go on a safari at dawn while I was visiting, I jumped at the offer, saying, "Oh, think of the fodder!" See, I really do all this for you, the reader. You're welcome.

My stepmom wanted to do the first tour of the morning because the animals would be waking up and more importantly hungry. Turns out they were freaking starving!

I'd just gotten back from Scotland and was waking up at three o'clock in the morning, so I wasn't worried about getting up for the early tour. Actually, my question was, what will I do from three in morning until the sun rises and all you lazy bums wake up and join me?

So we get on this jeep in the backwoods of Louisiana and drive out with a huge sack of food, plastic cups and wearing clean clothes. In hindsight, I didn't really need to shower that morning.

I'll sum up the trip this way: the giraffes were peaceful, the bison knew nothing about personal space, a gazelle stole my cup and then mocked me, and a few dozen longhorns crammed their heads into our jeep jostling for food (which will wake you up better than coffee).

I, of course, included my adventures in this book as part of the meeting with Bermuda Laurens, the author of Magical Creatures. Pretty much what I put in the book is what happened on my safari adventure. I love animals, so I'd definitely do it again, but next time I'd bring a blanket to wipe the bison's noses.

Okay, without further ado, I turn you over to the one, the only, Machel.

Much peace and love,
Tiny Ninja

MICHAEL'S AUTHOR NOTES
MAY 6, 2021

Thank you for not only reading this story but these author notes as well.

I would like to provide a gentle, caring rebuttal to my BFF collaborator and what she said in her author notes.

First, I'd like to point out the correct spelling of harass has two Ss at the end. So, if I follow the logic Sarah put into her author notes...

I should spell her name *Ssarah*.

I had faulty fingers one time, and now I must deal with Tiny Ninja® and all her wonderful sappiness and caring. I mean, Sarah obviously cares since she brought the mistake up with such concern and empathy, right? I prefer joking around to the understanding and...

BWAHAHAHAHAHA! Sorry, I couldn't keep a straight face on that one.

Here is another try at it.

Subconsciously, my fingers flubbed and provided her with a reason to climb up on a soapbox and get into my face about my old and failing fingers. Now, I admit it, Ms. Noffke. I'm getting old, arthritic, forgetful, and other ailments that come with being over fifty-something years old.

However, I will be the older person, one full of wisdom and peace to provide an example for Sarah to follow when she gets to my age.

Until then, I suggest you folks in California be careful of anyone driving a Prius.

If they park it all wrong, it might be Sarah. Allow her a few years to mellow before meeting her in person.

I think she's great in person, but I'm an author, and there is no telling what stories I tell myself about how the conversations went afterward.

<wink>

It's okay, Ms. Noffke. You shall attain inner peace as you grow older. I promise.

I know she reads these when the books come out. I'm guessing you wouldn't have expected me to mature to the point of being the kind, considerate elder statesman. Well, I'm trying it on for size.

I might decide the next time I didn't like it

Ad Aeternitatem,

Michael Anderle

** PS – Sarah told me she was going to give me @#%@#% on a ZOOM call. I failed to reply I would be like a limb bending in the wind.

How did I do?

ACKNOWLEDGMENTS

SARAH NOFFKE

I have so many people to thank who make this all possible. Firstly, thanks to Mike, who really pushes me to be a better writer, coming up with the best ideas, not just the really good ones. We work together pretty well, I'd say. I wonder what he'd say... Anyway, MA gave me the opportunity to write with LBMPN a few years ago and it's been life changing. He's very supportive and really cares. Thanks Bird Killer.

A huge thank you to the LBMPN team who work tirelessly so that I have less stress. Thanks to Steve and Kelly for making my life easier and being on top of everything. Thanks to Tracey and Lynne for fixing all my editing mistakes. A big thank you to the JIT team whose feedback at the 11th hour before publishing is invaluable. Thank you to my alpha readers Juergen and Martin. Thank you to everyone who makes getting the books to the reader possible. I really can't do this without you. And you make it so much more fun.

Thank you to my daughter, Lydia, who inspires my stories over and over again. She's my muse and we are always discussing story. She's an avid reader and listens to the Liv Beaufont series at night and reads the Sophia Beaufont books with me before bed. She also reads other authors, which I guess is okay. But my point is that she's supportive of me in so many ways. I need to stay immersed in this universe and remember all the details. There are 12 book in each series so there's a lot to remember. And Lydia loves my stories and then also supports me by listening and reading them so I can keep crafting. But also, she puts up with me when I go all psycho pants during a big crunch of a deadline. I will be the first to admit that I'm pretty intense a day or two before a book is due. And she always just smiles and says, "Mommy, you can do it."

Thank you to my family, the Scotsman and all my friends. You all are always so supportive of me and for that, I'm infinitely grateful. I really couldn't do this without the encouragement of those I love. On the really tough writing days, the Scotsman points out all the things that I don't see, like my dedication to the craft or how much readers are enjoying the books. I don't know what I did to have the most loving and thoughtful people in the world in my corner, but I'm going to do everything to keep them and hopefully keep making them proud.

And finally, thank you to you the reader. Without you I wouldn't be able to do what I love. Your support means so much to me and my family. Thank you from the bottom of my heart.

Love,
Tiny Ninja

BOOKS BY SARAH NOFFKE

Sarah Noffke writes YA and NA science fiction, fantasy, paranormal and urban fantasy. In addition to being an author, she is a mother, podcaster and professor. Noffke holds a Masters of Management and teaches college business/writing courses. Most of her students have no idea that she toils away her hours crafting fictional characters. www.sarahnoffke.com

Check out other work by Sarah author here.

Ghost Squadron:

Formation #1:
   Kill the bad guys. Save the Galaxy. All in a hard day's work.
   After ten years of wandering the outer rim of the galaxy, Eddie Teach is a man without a purpose. He was one of the toughest pilots in the Federation, but now he's just a regular guy, getting into bar fights and making a difference wherever he can. It's not the same as flying a ship and saving colonies, but it'll have to do.

That is, until General Lance Reynolds tracks Eddie down and offers him a job. There are bad people out there, plotting terrible things, killing innocent people, and destroying entire colonies. **Someone has to stop them.**

Eddie, along with the genetically-enhanced combat pilot Julianna Fregin and her trusty E.I. named Pip, must recruit a diverse team of specialists, both human and alien. They'll need to master their new Q-Ship, one of the most powerful strike ships ever constructed. And finally, they'll have to stop a faceless enemy so powerful, it threatens to destroy the entire Federation.

All in a day's work, right?

Experience this exciting military sci-fi saga and the latest addition to the expanded Kurtherian Gambit Universe. If you're a fan of Mass Effect, Firefly, or Star Wars, you'll love this riveting new space opera.

NOTE: If cursing is a problem, then this might not be for you.
Check out the entire series <u>here.</u>

The Precious Galaxy Series:

Corruption #1

A new evil lurks in the darkness.

After an explosion, the crew of a battlecruiser mysteriously disappears.

Bailey and Lewis, complete strangers, find themselves suddenly onboard the damaged ship. Lewis hasn't worked a case in years, not since the final one broke his spirit and his bank account. The last thing Bailey remembers is preparing to take down a fugitive on Onyx Station.

Mysteries are harder to solve when there's no evidence left behind.

Bailey and Lewis don't know how they got onboard *Ricky Bobby* or why. However, they quickly learn that whatever was responsible for the explosion and disappearance of the crew is still on the ship.

Monsters are real and what this one can do changes everything.

The new team bands together to discover what happened and how to fight the monster lurking in the bottom of the battlecruiser.

Will they find the missing crew? Or will the monster end them all?

The Soul Stone Mage Series:

House of Enchanted #1:

The Kingdom of Virgo has lived in peace for thousands of years...until now.

The humans from Terran have always been real assholes to the witches of Virgo. Now a silent war is brewing, and the timing couldn't be worse. Princess Azure will soon be crowned queen of the Kingdom of Virgo.

In the Dark Forest a powerful potion-maker has been murdered.

Charmsgood was the only wizard who could stop a deadly virus plaguing Virgo. He also knew about the devastation the people from Terran had done to the forest.

Azure must protect her people. Mend the Dark Forest. Create alliances with savage beasts. No biggie, right?

But on coronation day everything changes. Princess Azure isn't who she thought she was and that's a big freaking problem.

Welcome to The Revelations of Oriceran. Check out the entire series here.

The Lucidites Series:

Awoken, #1:

Around the world humans are hallucinating after sleepless nights.

In a sterile, underground institute the forecasters keep reporting the same events.

And in the backwoods of Texas, a sixteen-year-old girl is about to be caught up in a fierce, ethereal battle.

Meet Roya Stark. She drowns every night in her dreams, spends her hours reading classic literature to avoid her family's ridicule, and is prone to premonitions—which are becoming more frequent. And now her dreams are filled with strangers offering to reveal what she has always wanted to know: Who is she? That's the question that haunts her, and she's about to find out. But will Roya live to regret learning the truth?

Stunned, #2

Revived, #3

The Reverians Series:

Defects, #1:

In the happy, clean community of Austin Valley, everything appears to be perfect. Seventeen-year-old Em Fuller, however, fears something is askew. Em is one of the new generation of Dream Travelers. For some reason, the gods have not seen fit to gift all of them with their expected special abilities. Em is a Defect —one of the unfortunate Dream Travelers not gifted with a psychic power. Desperate to do whatever it takes to earn her gift, she endures painful daily injections along with commands from her overbearing, loveless father. One of the few bright spots in her life is the return of a friend she had thought dead—but with his return comes the knowledge of a shocking, unforgivable truth. The society Em thought was protecting her has actually been betraying her, but she has no idea how to break away from its authority without hurting everyone she loves.

Rebels, #2

Warriors, #3

Vagabond Circus Series:

Suspended, #1:

When a stranger joins the cast of Vagabond Circus—a circus that is run by Dream Travelers and features real magic—mysterious events start happening. The once orderly grounds of the circus become riddled with hidden threats. And the ringmaster realizes not only are his circus and its magic at risk, but also his very life.

Vagabond Circus caters to the skeptics. Without skeptics, it would close its doors. This is because Vagabond Circus runs for two reasons and only two reasons: first and foremost to provide the lost and lonely Dream Travelers a place to be illustrious. And secondly, to show the nonbelievers that there's still magic in the world. If they believe, then they care, and if they care, then they don't destroy. They stop the small abuse that day-by-day breaks down humanity's spirit. If Vagabond Circus makes one skeptic believe in magic, then they halt the cycle, just a little bit. They allow a little more love into this world. That's Dr. Dave Raydon's mission. And that's why this ringmaster recruits. That's why he directs. That's why he puts on a show that makes people question their beliefs. He wants the world to believe in magic once again.

Paralyzed, #2
Released, #3

Ren Series:

Ren: The Man Behind the Monster, #1:

Born with the power to control minds, hypnotize others, and read thoughts, Ren Lewis, is certain of one thing: God made a mistake. No one should be born with so much power. A monster awoke in him the same year he received his gifts. At ten years old.

A prepubescent boy with the ability to control others might merely abuse his powers, but Ren allowed it to corrupt him. And since he can have and do anything he wants, Ren should be happy. However, his journey teaches him that harboring so much power doesn't bring happiness, it steals it. Once this realization sets in, Ren makes up his mind to do the one thing that can bring his tortured soul some peace. He must kill the monster.

Note This book is NA and has strong language, violence and sexual references.

Ren: God's Little Monster, #2
Ren: The Monster Inside the Monster, #3
Ren: The Monster's Adventure, #3.5
Ren: The Monster's Death

Olento Research Series:

Alpha Wolf, #1:
Twelve men went missing.

Six months later they awake from drug-induced stupors to find themselves locked in a lab.

And on the night of a new moon, eleven of those men, possessed by new—and inhuman—powers, break out of their prison and race through the streets of Los Angeles until they disappear one by one into the night.

Olento Research wants its experiments back. Its CEO, Mika Lenna, will tear every city apart until he has his werewolves imprisoned once again. He didn't undertake a huge risk just to lose his would-be assassins.

However, the Lucidite Institute's main mission is to save the world from injustices. Now, it's Adelaide's job to find these mutated men and protect them and society, and fast. Already around the nation, wolflike men are being spotted. Attacks on innocent women are happening. And then, Adelaide realizes what her next step must be: She has to find the alpha wolf first. Only once she's located him can she stop whoever is behind this experiment to create wild beasts out of human beings.

CONNECT WITH THE AUTHORS

Connect with Sarah and sign up for her email list here:

http://www.sarahnoffke.com/connect/

Michael Anderle Social

Website: http://lmbpn.com

Email List: http://lmbpn.com/email/

Social Media:

https://www.facebook.com/LMBPNPublishing

https://twitter.com/MichaelAnderle

https://www.instagram.com/lmbpn_publishing/

https://www.bookbub.com/authors/michael-anderle